MW00533945

FLORENCE A. BLISS

This book is a work of fiction. Names, characters, places, and incidents either are products of the author's imagination or are used fictitiously. Any resemblance to actual events or locales or persons, living or dead, is entirely coincidental and not intended by the author.

TAKEN BY HIS SWORD
Swords of Chevalerie, Book 1

CITY OWL PRESS
www.cityowlpress.com

Cover Design by MiblArt. All stock photos licensed appropriately.

Edited by Jessica Shearer.

For information on subsidiary rights, please contact the publisher at info@cityowlpress.com.

Print Edition ISBN: 978-1-64898-460-0

Digital Edition ISBN: 978-1-64898-459-4

Printed in the United States of America

Dedicated to my mom.
Aggressively supportive in everything I do.
Love love love you.

Chapter One

The men of Provence loved everything about their swords. The brutal strength. The unyielding power. The length.

And no men were better with their swords than the sons of the Duke of Chevalerie.

CHEVALERIE, PROVENCE, FRANCE, 1654

Steel cracked hard above Philippe du Chevalerie's head as he caught the sharp of a blade with his own sword. He pushed the metal off with a zing and jabbed forward. His feet: *slow, quick, quick*. His opponent bent and countered, attacking again from above. Philippe caught the man's sword at the hilt, stepped in, parried up the shot, and yanked the weapon right out of his hands.

"Son of a *bitch*!" His cousin Laurent yelled as his blade clattered to the ground. "Good move."

Philippe grinned. "I told you to watch your lower right."

"One more?" Laurent asked.

They paused in the glistening sunlight, glazed in sweat, while onlookers whooped and cheered. The two had been training on the edge of the marketplace since late morning and had drawn a ring of spectators. Philippe nodded towards Laurent. They charged each other like battering rams.

The collision came loud and heavy, splitting through the buzz of the market. It was just the distraction Philippe needed. As third son of the Duke, he would be leaving in a few days to lead a mission north to figure out who was terrorizing and torching a series of villages. But, for now, he could ignore that responsibility, at least while he had a sword slashing at him. Laurent launched forward to deliver a strike to Philippe's flank which cut into his protective gear. Philippe absorbed the shock and countered with a fast jab of his sword. Laurent ducked and threw an uppercut, which caught Philippe off guard and clipped his chin. Philippe shook his head, pivoted back, and came around with the hilt of his sword to his cousin's temple, stopping just before he made contact.

"*Merde*!" Laurent threw his hands up in defeat. "You're too much today. I'm out."

"You got a few hits in," Philippe said, rubbing his chin. He smirked, and his cousin snorted at him. The townspeople swarmed them then, complimenting their form and offering treats they had picked up in the market.

"Oy, *Monsieur* Philippe," called a pretty maid working at a nearby stall. She held out a bright green apple. Philippe eyed the offer. A welcome diversion, he thought, but he would have liked... something different. Once long ago, he had tasted a peach. A perfect, ripe, delicious peach and nothing else had ever compared. But peaches were a rare find, so he walked to the maid, plucked the apple from her fingertips, tossed it in the air, and caught it with a clap in his hand. The maid demurred her eyes, but he didn't miss the smile on her lips. It was unfair, he thought, how easily it came, the devil growing inside him. He watched the maid and bit into the apple. Then he moved his thumb against the old scar at the bottom of his lip to collect the juice, and he grinned at her.

Just then, a rumbling went through the crowd. It started at the stone arch entryway at the bottom of the road and flashed through the market like lightning. Philippe followed the current of excitement and saw a troop coming toward where he stood. Four—five— six men on mount came into view, but nothing struck Philippe as odd. They didn't seem aggressive; the horses bore no marks of affiliation. Just regular mercenaries. But the people around him continued to gawk and stare. Voices popped. Fingers pointed. Women jumped on their suitors' backs to see above the crowd, while children scampered onto market stall poles to get a better view. By instinct, Philippe grabbed his sword.

He stood on his toes and scanned down the road, looking through the marketplace, past the spices in jars, over the olives marinating in the sun, past the cheeses, chickens, eggs, grapes, and buckets of tripe. He searched through the mercenaries and down their ranks, to the rider on the last horse of the party. And the spectacle made his sword strike full attention.

It was a woman in tight, dark breeches and a billowy cream-colored shirt cinched on the outside by a plain leather corset. A simple dark shawl covered her head and wrapped around her shoulders, leaving only her eyes exposed, which she kept fixed on the road ahead. It was not typical attire for a young woman, but that's not what made people stop and stare. There was danger in her. She brought with her some force, not just in her proud posture, but in the air around her, and it thickened in Philippe's throat. He was drawn in, fascinated, couldn't look away. An impulse told him to call out, to get her attention somehow, but he stood there unable to speak, frozen in the crowd.

Then suddenly, she turned to him. Philippe, startled by her attention, felt some quiet explosion go off in his brain. She stared into his eyes as she passed by, and he had the sensation that she would call out his name, to greet him like an old friend. But then she winked at him and turned away, continuing up the road toward Chevalerie Palace. Philippe stood there dumbfounded, shaken, confused. And as his thoughts and rationale began to piece themselves back together, they all screamed one thing:

Who in the hell was *that*?

He spent a moment standing with a half-eaten apple in his hand, staring down the road like a fool. Then the voices around him came back into focus. "'Tis the lady guide," someone whispered. "She's led many dangerous mercenary groups."

"I hear she has the strength of a man."

"I hear she has the strength of ten."

"*I* hear she sucks their strength out right through their willies!"

Now Philippe was running to meet this person before she slipped away.

Up the steps to the palace, around the back, he raced to the stables as he peeled off his protective equipment, leaving it in a trail. He skidded to a stop just before he came around the corner. He counted five horses outside and the men who matched, but the woman was not there.

"*Salut*," Philippe called. "What is your business at the palace today?"

They bowed their heads to him, and the man he had seen at the front of the party spoke. "Our companion has been summoned by the Duke, *Monsieur*. You must ask her for the details."

"And where is she?" Philippe asked, more anxiously than he intended.

"Already in the stables."

He nodded his thanks to the man, jogged up the stone path leading to the large stable doors, and pushed inside. Philippe called a sharp order, scattering the stablemen. And there he saw her, past rows of grazing horses, grooming her animal with her back to the entrance. Her thick, dark hair tumbled out from under her scarf in waves, meeting the waist of the pants she wore tight across her hips. He had never seen a woman wear men's clothes in such a way, and how the breeches hugged her backside was almost obscene.

He cleared his throat. She did not turn around.

"Excuse me," he said. "*Mademoiselle.*"

"May I help you?" she said, still not turning to him.

He approached her, taking in the sight of her knee-high riding boots, strong legs and that perfect backside he could almost feel in his hand. He came up next to her as she groomed her horse, his body going rigid. She still wore the trail cloth around her nose and mouth, so he could not see her face. "My Lady," he said. "I would like to know from where you came."

"No," she said without regard. Her voice was a song.

He took another step towards her as she rounded the horse's haunch.

"Well, then I would like to know your name."

She passed the brush over the horse's rump then looked back over her shoulder. "No," she said, her tone sparkling.

Another shiver went through his body. Those shimmering eyes seemed familiar, but without the rest of her face, he could not place her. She began to move around the horse again. He followed. "Then remove your scarf," he said. "I would like to see if the bottom half of your face is as pretty as the top."

"No," she replied, still inching away from him.

"*Jolie*, do you know who I am?" he said, taking slow steps in her pursuit.

"*Oui*, you are the son of the Duke."

"Then you are aware that when the son of a duke makes a formal request, you shall abide."

She stopped to stare him down with large, innocent eyes. "But, *Monsieur*, I was not aware that your request had been formal."

She turned away and continued grooming the horse. She was teasing him now. He liked this kind of foreplay, whatever it was, and he was sure it would end too soon. He took a more aggressive step toward her, invading her space. "I *formally* request that you take off your mask."

She threw down the brush and dusted her hands against her legs and, squaring her shoulders, looked up at him. She reached out to walk her fingers up his chest and stood on her tip toes to bring her lips right up to his ear. "No," she whispered.

He watched a moment, dumbfounded, not used to a woman so bold. Then he snatched her hand and held it tight to his chest. The beat of his own heart surprised him, just as his gesture seemed to surprise her. There was something in her eyes he couldn't grasp: a memory, a feeling fighting to come through. But he shook it off and grinned. "You are insubordinate," he said, voice low but playful. "Now remove that scarf or I shall do it for you."

She cocked her head, a smile back in her eyes. He breathed her in, as delicious as any peach he'd ever tasted. He reached up to pull the scarf away, thinking only of how sweet her lips would be.

All of a sudden, she struck both hands against his chest and pushed him back. It was like he took a cannonball to the chest. He sucked in a breath as her leg slipped between his and caught the back of his knee. She pulled forward and before he could think another thought, he was flat on his back, staring up at the ceiling. He shook focus back into his head and saw her standing at his feet with her hands on her hips.

"Who are you?" he asked, stupid from the fall.

She dropped to all fours and crawled across him like a lynx. He felt her breasts press against his torso while she drilled into his eyes with her stare. She settled above him then reached up to remove her scarf. That's when he saw, for the first time, the beauty beneath it. He knew this face from somewhere long ago, but his brain was too sluggish to make any connections. Her full, raspberry lips parted, and she leaned towards him. He thought for a second, she might kiss him. He arched in response, but she moved past his lips to his ear.

She whispered, her voice pure as dew, "I'm the one who gave you that scar." Then without another beat, she traced the old scar at the corner of his lip with the moist tip of her tongue.

He was out of his mind, not understanding if the woman on top of him was looking for a lover or just looking for a fight. Then, just outside the stable, he heard his mother's voice calling, "Alexandra? Where are you, *chère*?"

The woman popped up and dusted herself off, leaving nothing but cool air where her body had seconds ago been pressed against his. She jogged away and Philippe was left staring at the muzzle of her horse, who chewed a mouthful of straw and watched Philippe unsympathetically.

Regaining some control over his body, Philippe flipped over to watch her. Outside, he saw that she picked up speed and ran to his mother who embraced her. He could make out nothing beyond the happy chatter between the two women. It was Alex. Little Alex. His heart dropped into his stomach, as old, terrible feelings of guilt rushed to him. Alex and his mother linked arms and walked towards the palace.

He didn't know why she had come back or how long she would stay, but as he breathed in her luscious scent still clinging to his skin, Philippe knew, unequivocally, that he was in trouble.

Chapter Two

The palace doors burst open with a warm energy Alex hadn't felt in years. With Duchess Laure on her arm, Alex entered the sunlit grand foyer that she had torn through hundreds of times in her youth. The footmen bowed, while maids rushed to curtsy before her with wriggling excitement.

The greeting was unexpected and overwhelming for Alex, who had been living so far from high society. But it filled her heart to see the happy faces she had grown up with.

"We are all pleased to have you home," the Duchess said.

Alex ran her fingers across the fine carving of an armoire and breathed in the scents from her childhood: potted lavender, polished wood, warm bread. Just then another maid hurried into the room and upon seeing Alex, dumped her tray of biscuits.

"Oh, *mademoiselle* you are here!" she squealed as she hugged Alex around the neck, knocking Alex off balance. "It has been no fun here without you!"

The Duchess laughed while Cosette, the head maid, tutted at the girl who was still clinging to Alex. "All right then, have your hug and clean this up," Cosette said. The girl huffed and dipped down to clear the mess from the floor.

Alex stifled a laugh, knowing just what it felt like to be scolded by Cosette. In the years Alex had spent as a ward to the Duchess and living under this roof, Alex's mischievous nature had not escaped Cosette's firm hand. Especially when it came to Alex training with her sword in this very foyer.

Cosette turned to Alex. "It is very good to have you home, love." She squeezed Alex's hand warmly. "I haven't seen you since, well... Since..." Cosette faltered.

A hot burst of shame hit Alex's gut. She had hoped that she had stayed away long enough, but it seemed that what she had done had not been forgotten. Alex folded her shawl over her arm and looked at Cosette. "I am very happy to see you *Madame* Cosette," she said. "I promise not to cause any trouble while I am here." Then she grinned, a playful child again. "I know how you hated it when I would steal chocolates."

"You may have all the chocolates you can fit in your cheeks," Cosette said. "It is these silly maids I worry will stuff you to bursting." She pointed behind her to the giggling girls trying their hardest to do their duties.

"Come, *chère*," said the Duchess. She guided Alex to the parlor while the staff whisked in and laid the tea setting out.

Cossette chirped orders until everything had been placed, fluffed, and situated. "Out, out," she said, clapping the staff out of the room.

"My goodness, Alex," said the Duchess. She rested herself on the couch. "It's been so long."

"Six years," Alex said. *Almost to the day*, she thought.

"You were just sixteen," the Duchess said, reaching forward to prepare the teacups. "Far too young to be on your own." She tsked and shook her head.

Alex looked down at her hands, feeling guilt stir within her. She knew she had caused the kind woman to worry by running away without a plan, in a storm of anger and shame. In hindsight, Alex now understood that she had been too young to leave, and entirely too young to start working as a guide, no matter how good she turned out to be at it. But she hadn't been able to stop herself. If Alex could go back and do things differently, she would. If she had been smarter—stronger—maybe she wouldn't have caused the humiliation and disgrace to her former guardians that prompted her to leave in the first place. Maybe a lot of things would have been... different.

When she left Chevalerie six years ago, Alex swore to never return —she didn't *deserve* to return. Then, from the hand of an innkeeper in a town Alex frequented, she received a letter from her former home. It had stated simply that they needed her and the skills she had honed on the road. For just a second, her shame forgotten, a chance to redeem herself became all that mattered, and she got back to Chevalerie just as soon as she could. Now, here she sat while the Duchess poured her a cup of tea.

"Are you happy to be here once more?" the Duchess asked, tinkling a spoon in her own cup.

"I am just happy to be at your service," Alex said.

"Well, you will talk with my husband about that matter," The Duchess responded, looking cross. "You know how *I* feel about your situation. I think you've punished yourself long enough."

"I am not punishing myself," Alex said, uncertain if she was even telling the truth, but at the same time hoping to convince the Duchess that she was.

The Duchess put her hand on Alex's knee and asked the question Alex knew had been coming. "Have you seen Philippe yet?"

At this, Alex tried not to roll her eyes too hard. She knew she might see Philippe while she was here, but when she'd ridden into town today, he was the first person with whom she made eye contact. He was not the coddled boy, fresh from a peaceful tour that she had fallen in love with years ago. His brown hair, lightened by the sun and grown out from the tight cut he'd once worn, was swept back imperfectly from his face. He seemed thicker and rougher and far more rugged than she remembered. He was a man now, she realized with a bit of a shudder, a war-hardened man.

His eyes were the same, though. Those warm, searching eyes were exactly the same.

She'd felt a flush go through her when she saw him. She no longer had feelings for him. That had been nothing more than a childhood infatuation, but she hadn't expected to be so insanely attracted to him again, either. In her mind he was a careless boy, but standing there in the market was someone different. He was strong, experienced, and bold to stare at her the way he did as she had ridden into the city. She had refused to let it shake her.

Instead, she'd winked at him and had planned to continue to the castle without any further interaction.

Then, suddenly, he was there, next to her in the stables. And some other woman came out of her, born of too many fantasies of what could happen if she came across him on new footing. She was proud, confident, and sexy. Yes, very sexy. She had licked the scar right on his face. What had she been thinking? She would laugh at the absurdity of it if she wasn't sitting with the Duchess and holding a hot cup of tea.

Without warning, there came a commotion from the hallway. Philippe walked by the parlor doors and did a double take when he saw Alex and Duchess Laure sitting together. He looked flustered, a mess.

"So, she is staying at the palace, then?" he asked.

"Yes, *mon ange,* for now," replied the Duchess.

He started to say something and stopped. Then started again and stopped. Then turned his head and walked away.

"What is wrong with him?" Duchess Laure asked.

"He had already come to meet me in the stables, *Madame*. And excuse my language but," Alex said, looking down to hide a grin. "I do believe I knocked him on his ass."

"Oh," said the Duchess, nonplussed. She waved her hand dismissively. "I'm sure he deserved it."

Chapter Three

For many years, the people of Provence rejoiced under the leadership of Duke Guillaume du Chevalerie and his wife, the beautiful Duchess Laure. A generation ago, the region had been in turmoil. The French, fiercely independent and mistrustful of power, had rebelled against a greedy duke. Guillaume led that rebellion, overthrowing the corrupt régime. The King himself, recognizing Guillaume's potential, appointed him as the new duke, and in this position, Guillaume had proven to be a potent commander, a champion of his people, and an invaluable asset to his country. Not only that, but he'd also bred three strong sons, each of whom had made the country proud in battle. Guillaume had at his ready everything he needed to protect his land.

Now, a crisis was unraveling in the North.

Someone was attacking villages. At first, isolated to a small corner of northern Provence, it seemed to be common robberies between village rivals. The attacks had grown in force and number. Reports indicated a rogue group, not large, but still dangerous. They raided for gold, slaughtered livestock, and burnt farms to the ground. These attacks were strange: small in scale and scattered. Experience told Guillaume that a larger insurrection was building. He had seen small groups grow to hurricane force—his own rebel group had built itself up in the thick forest to the West—but, for the moment, he didn't know what this group wanted or where to find them, so he couldn't tie a noose around their necks.

He wanted to end it before the movement had a chance to grow, to attack with the full strength of his army, but the damn rogues proved impossible to find. After every raid, they retreated and disappeared. He suspected they hid in the serpentine caves of the North; a place where rats would hide but no decent man would enter. Guillaume struggled with how to defend his people. He could charge forward with the trained and fearsome soldiers of Chevalerie; however, this was inefficient and would cause panic. No, he needed a more careful and organized approach. A subtle investigation, a trail to throw them off, an unexpected ambush. Guillaume trusted his intuition and was glad to have one of his sons at hand for the mission. Philippe, his youngest, was a little impulsive, but capable of leading a group to corner and crush these agitators. Philippe couldn't go without some help, though. The northern territory was treacherous and uncharted. Guillaume knew of just one guide who could claim knowledge of these parts.

And his wife wanted to kill him for hiring her.

"*Monsieur* Perreault?" Alex called into the empty training arena at the back of the Duke's palace, hoping to find the palace master-at-arms who had once been her teacher. She crossed the floor where she'd attended swordsmanship class as a girl and called his name again to no answer. Outside, the sun was setting, sending the last darts of sunlight through the high-slatted ceiling. Her boots crunched across the dirt as Alex came to the end of the floor and entered the small equipment room she used to sneak downstairs to, to train late at night. Lighting the oil lamp in the dim room, she was delighted to find the old training dummy she had favored among the stacks of feather mattresses and racks of protective gear. She squared her shoulders and raised her sword. With a fast attack she left a new mark on the block of wood.

She whirled around and cracked it again. But then she paused. She closed her eyes to listen. She breathed in. The silence of the room had changed. The air had changed. She wasn't alone anymore. And she knew it wasn't *Monsieur* Perreault who had found her.

She turned to face the entrance of the room. There he stood, leaning against the archway, that smug, half smile having returned to his face.

It was eerily similar to another scene from their past. Alex held her sword out, signaling to him not to come any closer.

"I have come from the tavern," Philippe said. "Where the whole town speaks of the lady guide." He unsheathed his blade. "If the stories I hear are true," he continued, raising his own sword to meet hers, "then you have become quite the formidable opponent." He circled her, their swords crossed in the air, keeping them apart.

She was careful with her words. She didn't want to show too much pleasure in the encounter, but she couldn't deny her enjoyment at the chance to best the man who had sent her running years ago. "I have always been a formidable opponent," she said. "I'm just a little taller than I was the last time we fought."

He continued moving her around. He swung low with his sword, and she batted it away. "You have changed a great deal since I saw you last," he said, his eyes on her body. "But I bet you still fight dirty."

Alex smiled to herself at his teasing. Maybe now, as an adult, she could enjoy the turmoil he stirred inside her. She knew his intentions, and those young, innocent feelings no longer had a hold on her. She had encountered too many cruel men on the road, and she had learned from Philippe himself of a man's true nature: uncaring and insincere. Still, she watched him, unable to deny the way he made her quiver inside.

Philippe stopped in front of her. He placed his sword on the ground and held up his hands. His fighting stance disappeared, and he took a step closer. She backed away still holding her sword out at him. He gently pushed her sword aside and reached forward to take her hand.

She let him, unsure of what he was doing.

He took a breath and then spoke, his eyes searching hers. "When I saw you this morning, I reacted to you as a man does to... an intriguing woman. I did not realize who you were. Then it occurred to me," he paused, "that I never apologized for what I did."

Alex did not want to talk about such things. Those were not happy memories. She would never let him know that they still hurt her heart. "You're forgiven," she replied, hoping to end the line of conversation.

He stared at her a moment longer. "Are you sure?"

She looked down. It was still hard to look at him, even after all these years. Then she forced herself to meet his eyes again and nod.

Thankfully, he didn't linger, and he reached down for his sword. "Now," he said as he rose, his sly grin back. "Would you care to show me what you've learned on the road?"

She felt heat flush over her at the thought of sparring with him once more. It was a dangerous game she was inviting but also too good to pass up. She squared her shoulders and narrowed her eyes. "You are no longer the only master here," she said, her confidence returning. "And I don't wish to hurt you, *Monsieur*."

"I have heard that from you before." He touched the scar on his lip and looked at her, accusation in his eyes.

"I very much meant to hurt you that time," she purred.

"Ha!" he called, seconds before cracking his sword against hers.

The battle between them came hard and fast. He drove her across the room, not giving her a chance to adjust to his strength. She came back just as aggressively, accepting his blows then dominating him, pressing him back across the floor.

He had the strength; she had the speed. He again took control and fought her into a corner. She jumped onto the mattresses and leapt from one stack to the next. He was at her heels, but she darted over the clutter like a dragonfly and landed on a solid trunk. She swung her blade from above. He caught it with a clang and pushed her back. She almost lost her balance but steadied herself against the nearby wall.

She sucked in a breath. Was the room this hot, or was it her? Did he feel it too, she wondered? He gave no sign of discomfort—his jaw was set in battle, his muscles strong with skill, his sword as dangerous as ever, and that damn humor still in his eyes. Why did he insist on looking at her like that? She wanted to smack the expression off his face. He moved again to take her over. She responded by placing her foot on his chest and shoving him away. He stumbled back, and it gained her a few inches of dirt to land on.

As soon as her boots hit the floor, he was on top of her again. She whirled around and whacked his arm. He grunted and whipped her across the thigh in response. She winced, absorbing the shock of his sword. They rallied again across the floor, dodging the dummy that stood in the middle. The humor in his eyes was changing into something else. He was enjoying this far too much, and it unnerved her. Then, feeling the heat growing inside, she began to understand. His moves became jagged and blunt, just as the precision of her own attacks was dulling. Blood rushed through her body, and she felt faint as she struggled to keep him from getting closer. She slashed at him again, this time across his trunk, hoping he would retaliate. Pain would wake her up.

He took the blow and came towards her with even more force. She struck him again; he came closer still. He was fighting now just to eliminate space, she realized. For a second, she wondered what he would do to her if he caught her, and she sucked in a sharp breath at the thought. No, she couldn't let it happen. She struck him again. And again. He did little more than back her across the room. And she was proving powerless to stop him.

Then with one quick move, he jumped forward and cracked the bottom of her hand. She yelped as pain spasmed her fingers into releasing her sword. It popped into the air, and he snatched it with his free hand. Then he threw both swords to the ground with a noisy clang. He took two heavy steps towards her, his thick, powerful body muting her movements. She backed away until the wall stopped her, crushing her against it.

"I want to kiss you," he said.

Alex felt the words come out before she could stop them. "So, kiss me," she replied.

In less than a second, his lips were on hers, his hands in her hair. Desire was a thick musk that poured out of him, and she couldn't deny that it thrilled her. He wasted no time and his lips parted hers. She felt the warm invasion of his tongue. Having never kissed a man this deeply, she followed his lead, and matched his movements with her own.

He was kissing her with more than just his lips. He used his whole body to squeeze the reason out of her. His hands began moving down her sides. They stopped at her hips, where she felt his fingers dig into her. Then he lifted her and pressed the hard length in his pants against the one spot on her body that could make her fall apart. The pleasure of contact shot through her, and she had to break their kiss as a ragged gasp escaped her lips.

Her own desire was a revelation, but somewhere, swimming in the back of her mind, was a tender kiss from long ago: their first kiss, her only kiss. She had spent many nights idly imagining encounters between them, in which something more grew from that simple kiss, but this was well beyond what she was prepared to handle.

Philippe recaptured her lips and moved against her as he held her nailed to the wall. Her body was blooming, but she knew it wasn't right. It was too intense. It was too fast. She would have to stop this, but it felt like a crime to do so.

He was the one to break away. "Shall we try to make it to another room?" he asked. His eyelids were heavy and his tone pure syrup. He nipped at her lips as he waited for her answer.

"What do you mean?" she asked, her mind not working.

"Or we could be scandalous and drop here to the floor."

"For what?" she asked with an edge to her voice, reason coming back to her.

"To make love, darling," he said, still moving in rhythm against her. "Please don't make me beg. But I will if that's what you like."

She held her hand out against his chest. "I do not intend to make love to you," she spat out.

"And why not?" he asked, trying to kiss her again. "Your reputation as a lover precedes you."

She shoved him. "You lie," she said.

Now it was his turn to stare at her. "*Mademoiselle...*" he started, releasing his hold on her body. "Alex," he said. "I'm sorry if this is not what you wanted. But it is widely known that you have taken many lovers. I don't see why you would still hate me so—"

"Those are rumors," she interrupted.

"But–"

"They are rumors," she said again. At least now she understood this sudden attention. He didn't think of her as anything special. He just thought she'd be an easy lay.

"Oh no," he said. He dropped his gaze and backed away from her.

A laugh bubbled out of her. "You clearly haven't changed much."

He didn't look up. Instead, he rubbed his forehead with his index finger and thumb. "Alex," he said. "I don't know what to say."

"Don't worry about it," she said. She picked up her sword. "And thank you for the apology, *Monsieur*." She curtseyed low to the ground before leaving him in the training room, alone with the dummy.

Chapter Four

Philippe felt terrible. He had never insulted a woman like he kept doing with Alex. And the problem was, he really liked Alex; he always had. *Et mon dieu* had she become a beauty, like nothing he'd ever seen. The women he knew were simple, less complicated. Alex had an intensity to her that always drew him in. Unfortunately, it also made him act like a perfect idiot.

He stood in the equipment room, staring at the wall where moments before he'd held her captive. How had he read the situation so wrong? It wasn't like him. He ground his feet into the dirt then picked up his sword, took a few breaths, and walked blankly into the young night. The cool air felt good against his agitated skin. He smelled the scented, budding lavender as he found his way to a wooden bench at the entrance to the gardens. Up ahead was the stone palace. Warm lights glowed inside as snatches of conversation floated out the open windows. Down below, the town was nestled in the valley with the great arena far at the other end. He watched as smoke from evening fires streamed from the chimneys to meet the winking stars, the families settling in for the night.

Had he really been so out of line? Earlier that day, and after the initial shock of seeing her, he'd gone to the tavern, where he heard tales of the lady guide and how she took lovers like a man. Of course, he knew it had to have been exaggerated, as the stories of drunken men always are, but their words had convinced him she was no dewy maid. He'd been torn. The idea of sleeping with a woman who had no inhibitions was incredibly alluring and made Philippe want to sprout wings and fly back to find her. But there was something else, raw and almost painful, that had been triggered inside of him by their stories. The thought of her beneath some rutting beast of a man clenched his stomach, and he had to shake his head to get rid of the image. Was he feeling protective? The charming girl she had been lived in his memories. He knew the caliber of man she would find on the road. Who among them could equal a woman such as her?

After hearing their tales, his own desire had won, and he'd gone to find her. Philippe understood what it meant to be lonely and far from home, when finding comfort in another person is the only thing that can keep you sane. He didn't mean to hold any past liaison against her. When he found her in the equipment room, where he'd known she would be, she was every bit as bold and tempting as they had said. So why had she turned him away? At one point, they had shared a special friendship. If their swordplay was any indication of what could happen in the bedroom, why in the world would she say no? Of course, maybe she was still just angry. His apology had been flimsy. He could admit he was too eager to have her forgiveness to give it the proper weight. Maybe he had to pay in blood before she'd let him get closer. But he wanted to get closer. Everything about her drove him mad. Her eyes, her lips, her words, the fact that she seemed to hate him so. It all made him burn. When he had held her pinned to the wall and had been overcome with the intimate scent of her desire, he could think of no better way to finally bring them together.

However, if she was in fact still pure, he had just insulted her beyond belief. This possibility picked him up off the bench and took him down the stone walkway towards the palace's guest quarters. He usually had no trouble interpreting a woman's intent, but Alex, wrapped in pants and guarded with a sword, was a damn enigma, and he couldn't trust his judgment. He approached the low stone building at the back end of the palace. The voices of several men rang out of the courtyard. Philippe came around the corner and saw the men with whom Alex had traveled that morning.

He approached them, calling out, "Bonsoir, *Messieurs.*" He spoke to the older man, the one who had told him where to find Alex that morning at the stables. "*Monsieur*," Philippe said. "May I talk with you a moment?"

"Of course, my lord."

"Do you mind if we walk?"

The man nodded and rose to standing. As they walked away from the others, Philippe noticed a slight limp in the old man's step and battle scars covering his arms. Despite these signs of having fought many battles, the man still had a steady and calm demeanor, which made Philippe feel he could trust him.

"Please tell me your name," Philippe replied.

"I am Jacque Demore from Genoa. My family is in Menton now, not so far from here, *Monsieur*."

"Call me Philippe, good sir."

They walked for a moment, down the path towards the main yard. To their right, grass sparkled in the early evening mist, and to their left, several tall trees overhung the path. Jacque took his steps carefully, his limp slowing them only just.

Philippe continued, "How did you come to know your mistress, may I ask?"

"*Mademoiselle* Alex? I met her in La Rochette." Jacque answered. "I have this old injury that has kept me from finding much work," he patted his right hip. "People don't always trust a man with a handicap. But I can offer a sword and a knowledge of the country." He paused a moment to avoid a dip in the gravel. "*Mademoiselle* hired me to help with a large party of gentlemen traveling down to the coast. I was grateful for the opportunity. She's hired me and several of the others on many a job since."

"Would you say you know her well?" Philippe asked.

"As someone I have traveled and worked with, yes," he replied.

Philippe held his words for a moment. "I must ask you a delicate question," he continued.

"Please do so."

They came upon a bench beside the path. Jacque took a seat and Philippe leaned against a tree across from him. "There is a chance that I have offended *Mademoiselle* Alexandra," he began.

"That's a shame." Jacque watched Philippe, waiting for Philippe to continue.

"I had heard in the tavern this afternoon the great, and possibly embellished, stories of her... lovemaking." Philippe paused. "I assumed they were true."

Jacque snorted a laugh, then pulled a snuff box from his pocket. He put a wad of tobacco in his lip. "Would you like some?" he asked Philippe, holding the box out.

Philippe shook his head no.

Jacque returned the box to his pocket and continued. "*Monsieur—*" He corrected himself. "Philippe. Whatever you have heard was untrue."

"You don't know what I heard."

"Do you think a woman who invited that kind of attention could survive very long on her own?" he said, shutting the idea down as absurd. "I've never seen her involved with a man. In fact," he paused, spitting a mouthful of brown liquid into the grass, "I have seen her fight for her chastity. I dare say it has made her skills far sharper than mine."

Philippe was quiet for a moment. "I am an ass," he said finally.

"Perhaps you are," Jacque nodded. "But who of us isn't when it comes to a pretty face?"

The following evening, the Duke and Duchess sat with Philippe in the Duke's study, discussing the upcoming mission. Duchess Laure watched the two men go back and forth, marking towns that had been struck and trying to discern some meaning from the seeming chaos on the maps spread before them. The politics were important, but she, at the moment, was more concerned with her son, and if this mission he was being sent on would be safe. Just that morning, reports arrived that an entire farm had been burnt to the ground in the Peillon area, leaving another family without a home. Her husband was furious, which meant he was all the more eager to send the party into the unknown.

The primary contact for Philippe would be the Marquis du Ponce, an old comrade of the Duke and someone who held a tight rein on the northern reaches. However, the Marquis did not have the skilled fighters to go after the rebels or any idea what had prompted the violence. Her husband suspected it had something to do with the river that cut just above Ponce. It was one of the final territories of Provence and vulnerable to anyone who came in from the Alps. People from the north or even other Frenchmen could be the culprits. Perhaps some robber baron wanted to take control of the river to charge unsanctioned tolls to merchants but could not do so because the Marquis was so close. Whatever it was, her husband was determined to stop it.

The Duke sat at the head of the dark, heavy table in his high-backed chair where he had planned many missions, with Philippe to his right and the Duchess to his left. Laure looked over the map and saw the uncharted area they planned to explore, feeling a sense of dread come over her.

"I've sent scouts here, here, and here." The Duke pointed to three different towns. "They have not seen any shadow of unknown travelers." He dropped his finger to a section of the map that showed very little detail. "They're here. I'm sure of it."

"Father," Philippe said, "I know the foothills well, but I've spent the majority of my tours in the East. I can't lead a troop with any kind of certainty through this region."

"That is why we have hired a guide to accompany the group."

"What guide knows these caves?" he asked. He paused for a moment then looked to Laure. "No," he said.

"It was your father's idea," she replied, shaking her head.

"What should I do?" said the Duke, his voice insistent. "Put my men in jeopardy because the guide who knows this area best happens to be a woman?" He looked at his wife. "You started this when you let her take up the sword."

"Well that was just child's play. How was I supposed to know she would run off like she did? This is..." she trailed off. "This is dangerous."

"It will be difficult, yes," said the Duke. "But it doesn't seem like this is a very large rebel group at the moment. The men going with Philippe are all well-trained. It is unlikely she will be caught up in the fight."

"I will watch out for her, Mother," said Philippe looking back down to the map.

She eyed him. "I know you will," she said. "But you must protect the men. And yourself. This may prove to be an unnecessary burden."

Just then came a knock at the door.

"*Entre*," said the Duke.

The door opened and Alex closed it behind her as soft as a blush. "My Lord, My Lady." She nodded her head.

"Come dear, sit with me," said Laure. The girl approached the long table and sat, looking from the Duchess to the Duke.

"Tell me, Alex," said the Duke. "What do you make of this map? Do you know this area well?" He pointed to the circled section they had just been over.

Alex looked over the parchment. She ran her fingers over the markings. "Here," she said. "There are a great number of caverns in this region that aren't marked on any map I've seen. Even this is muddled and unclear. This valley exists, but the map has it covering far more area." She leaned forward and pointed to a section that was covered by trees. "Where this shows the valley leading into forest is incorrect. This is the beginning of the caves. The rock juts out of the ground and before the trees realized they weren't growing on land, they rooted themselves into the stone. It can be very deceiving if you hedge the area, but once you get into it, you can begin to understand the secrets." She leaned back and addressed the Duke. "If your marauders wish to hide, this would not be a bad choice."

"You have traveled this area?" asked the Duke.

"Indeed," she replied. "I've used it as a shortcut into the Mercantour Valley."

"Is it very treacherous?" asked Laure.

"It is not easy. It's dark and muddy. I wouldn't take a group of dandies through there, but the well-traveled Cliffs *du Soliel* towards the south are far more perilous."

The Duke addressed Alex, his countenance softening as he spoke solemnly to her. "We always marveled at your ability to hold whole maps in your head when we would take you on hunts as a child. It's no surprise you have built a reputation of your skills as a guide." He put his hand over hers. "I wouldn't put you in danger for this mission if we didn't need you. Are you prepared to take this burden on?" He watched Alex carefully.

"*Oui Monsieur*, I am happy to assist in any way I can." She smiled. "Besides, I believe I shall enjoy traveling with you once more."

"Oh no," the Duke responded, "'tis not me leading this one. I have been away from home too long." He leaned back into the cushion of his chair. "No," he continued. "You shall travel under the lead of Philippe."

Alex blinked a few times as the smile fell right off her face. "Right," she said with a quick nod to her head. She looked back down to the map and traced the lines with her finger.

The Duke continued, his tone commanding again as he addressed Philippe. "I should like you to be off in the next day or two."

"There is much to prepare," Philippe replied. "I haven't even brought all the men together yet. Not all have traveled that far north. They must be briefed on the conditions."

"And also," interjected Duchess Laure, "It would be a shame if they had to miss the tournament. Many of them are competing this year. Surely, the mission can wait until the day after."

"That is five days hence?" asked the Duke.

"I could have everything organized by then," Philippe said. "I should like a few opportunities to review the plan with everyone."

Laure noticed that Alex spoke no more, nor had she looked up from the map. The men continued to discuss the task while the girl was silent. Laure also noticed that Philippe's eyes kept darting back to Alex as he spoke to the Duke and then away again. Well, she thought, it seemed they hated each other again. If those two could just cool their heels, Laure was sure they could be good companions. She said a quick prayer for the safety of the journey. She hoped her husband was not underestimating the trouble they would encounter. If nothing else, it would be an interesting adventure, she thought, as she let a worried sigh escape her lips.

Chapter Five

The Chevalerie sword fighting tournament blazed through the town at the end of every summer. What had begun as a regional display of skills and power, had grown into a massive competition in which rivalries were settled, alliances strengthened, and entire wars were avoided. It wasn't just entertainment; it was one of the most important political events of the year.

All put together by the Duke and Duchess.

Around the Chevalerie city walls, contenders, merchants, and spectators camped for days before the event, painting the valley into a tapestry of multicolored tents that displayed the colors of families and cities from hundreds of miles away. The camps butted right up to the base of the city walls, topped with its own blue and gold flags and banners. South of the valley, set high on a hill, was the ducal palace presiding over the town. To the far north was the massive circular arena where the event was held, which had stood since the Romans had settled the city a thousand years before.

The morning of the competition, Alex denied passage with the Duke and Duchess in favor of travelling the streets herself and experiencing the festivity. As she wandered towards the arena, she was fascinated by the exhilaration flowing through the streets. The marketplace was more chaotic than she had ever seen it. The churches were overflowing with last-minute prayers for victory, while gamblers spewed odds at everyone passing by. By mid-morning and just before the games were to begin, Alex arrived at the base of the arena, where the fervor was at its peak. People wove around each other, clogging the walkways. Meat roasted on spits, singing rained down from balconies, children squealed and tumbled through the crowds. The air was heavy with sweat and excitement.

On the steps of the arena, a juggler whooped and tossed knives, trying to steal the crowd's attention from a troubadour orating a story of the great warriors who had battled in the arena. To the left, two women used liquid dyes to paint a man's chest with Chevalerie's city colors. In the shadows were lovers, tangled up together, not at all hidden. Caught off guard, Alex watched for a moment until a toothless old lady knocked into her and thrust a bite-sized piece of honeyed bread into her hand and then demanded a coin. Alex dug for her coin purse before entering the stone arches that would lead her to the Duke's private entrance. As she entered the arena, she nibbled on the sweet bread, enjoying it so much she licked every drop of honey from her fingers.

The stairwell funneled the commoners towards the unnumbered seats below and the lords and ladies to the ticketed seats above. The stone of the stairwell was cool against the warm morning and Alex ran her hand along the walls, anchoring herself, as other spectators jostled her along. She remembered the last time she had entered this arena. Then, she had climbed down, below the penny seats, into the bowels of the arena that boiled with the fever of those who came for glory. She'd been filled with a hatred then that, to this day, left her scarred. But now, she climbed and climbed until she reached the grand entrance, the one reserved for dignitaries, royals, and special guests of the Duke and Duchess.

She greeted the guards and was allowed through the final archway that led to the private seats. The Duke and the Duchess were seated along with other town officials. Philippe was there too, at the far end, but she didn't look at him. The Duke and Duchess rose, and Philippe stepped up behind them to welcome her.

"Did you enjoy the fairgrounds, *mademoiselle*," said the Duke, greeting her with a kiss on the hand.

"Yes, of course," said Alex with a small smile. Such formal greetings always made her feel silly. She took her seat next to the Duchess, purposely sitting far from Philippe "But, I believe the excitement has gotten the best of some of your citizens."

"Ah, let them enjoy," the Duke said. "It is these freedoms I must protect." He turned to Alex. "I hate to bring up the mission while we are here for the enjoyment of the games, but you must understand my race with time. If the attacks from the North reach here, the cogs of this city will halt. We connect the East and the West. Look at these people." He cast his hand out towards the arena. "The diversity. I dare say all of France could fall if this city is compromised." He nodded his head in encouragement. "You must guide this journey well, young lady."

"I will do my very best, My Lord," Alex replied. While she dreaded the very idea of this journey, now that she knew Philippe was leading it, she pasted a confident smile on her face. She did not want to let the Duke down, as he had always been so good to her.

She trusted the Duke and his instincts. She knew that he had been very careful and deliberate in his selection of men to go north. Ten soldiers had been hired, and they had met together as a group over the last few days. Many of the men had fought beside Philippe in skirmishes with the barbarians throughout the mountain ranges. They were a mix of pikemen and musketeers from both the King's and the Duke's army, all battle-scarred and looking for action. There was nineteen-year-old Claude who she remembered from her swordsmanship classes; he could barely lift his sword as a child. He didn't look much stronger now but was said to be quite accurate with a bow and arrow. The oldest of the group was Henri the mapmaker, in his forties, who was known to have a nasty dependence on whores and gambling but was otherwise reliable and always in need of work. Philippe's cousin Laurent would be his second in command, a man Alex had met several times growing up. Two brothers, Bernard and Luc, had a set of matching lazy eyes and were known in Chevalerie to take to the bottle. Young Sébastien looked up hard to Philippe, and Maurice seemed sneaky but otherwise jovial and entertaining. Alex was the sole mercenary.

Then there was Philippe, their leader, she thought with a sickening twirl to her stomach. She had wondered how well Philippe could manage the group of men, him being younger than many of them, and far more privileged. Part of her hoped he would prove ineffective and get overrun by his recruits, but after mere minutes of meeting as a group, she could feel the strength of his leadership and the respect he garnered. He had undeniable authority and spoke with knowledge and confidence. The guide in her was relieved. The woman in her was pissed.

After that kiss they had shared in the training room, she had decided to erase him from her consciousness. It was a shame because their brief contact had caused a waterfall of emotions inside of her. But, once again, he managed to make her feel stupid and weak like no one else ever had. The worst thing was, it was all her fault. She had invited the attention the moment she'd entered town, when she had winked at him... and then straddled and licked him in the stables. She wanted to beat her own ass over her shameful behavior.

Horns blew from the arena floor and a shock of excitement rattled the stands. Alex bit her lip in enthusiasm as she watched the line of guards parade onto the stadium floor. From the side, she could feel Philippe staring at her, or at least she thought she could. But she kept her eyes trained ahead. Down below, the guards positioned themselves into tight military lines. On command, they raised their pikes and dropped to one knee. Cheers from the stands exploded to the heavens. Then *Monsieur* Perrault walked to the center of the ring and stood before the soldiers. He raised his hand to hush the crowd. A young boy knelt and presented him with a great scroll and a velvet bag which held the names of the contenders. Excitement smoldered in the air.

"A little different than last time you were here?" The Duchess whispered to Alex with a smile.

"Very much," Alex nodded with a laugh.

The Duchess squeezed Alex's knee, and Alex watched as the games commenced.

"On this day, thirty-three years ago..." began *Monsieur* Perrault.

Chapter Six

That evening, the ballroom was gloriously decorated for the champions' ball. Everything glittered with polish and sheen. Golden pillars lined the room, and deep blue satin drapes outlined the latticed windows. Chandeliers hanging from the high ceiling glowed with hundreds of twinkling candles and illuminated the family crest at the head of the hall. The palace staff circulated among the twirling guests with glasses of fine liqueurs. The Duchess had spared no expense in celebrating the honorable swordsmen that had made Chevalerie proud.

The Duke and Duchess sat towards the head of the room, presiding over the illustrious event. Everyone was in a jolly mood after the competition. A new champion had been crowned and no great upsets had happened like many years ago. Though they had each fared well, none of the men traveling with Philippe had won the title. The title was taken by a brick wall of a man from the East, who looked as though he had descended from Mount Olympus. Feeling especially frustrated, Philippe decided that he would participate and take the title himself the next year. Too long had it gone to someone outside of the region.

He sat near his parents, his thumb rubbing the scar on his lip. In line with his sour mood, he had no interest in the party that night. He was too preoccupied with the journey tomorrow and the one thing he had to do that night before they could proceed.

The people danced before Philippe and his parents as a popular waltz began.

"Come, my boy," he exclaimed, slapping Philippe on his back. "'Tis your last night in town. There are many beautiful women. Enjoy yourself."

Philippe grumbled and waved him off. "I have not the right mind for women tonight, father."

"You need to relax," said his father. "You need your wits tomorrow, but tonight you should get any restless energy out."

That's when *she* entered the room. Philippe saw her instantly, entering far towards the back. She wore a simple cream-colored gown that had a deep ruby brooch at her breast. Her hair was pinned back from her face, but still tumbled down her back. Her dress was far simpler than the other women in the room, but instead of making her get lost in the crowd, she stood out as being all the more elegant. Philippe watched, mesmerized, as she moved towards the front of the room, where she bowed before his parents, and continued to ignore him. She had ignored him completely since the night he'd kissed her. He made a point of watching her whenever he could, but she never turned to his eyes. Not even once. It was driving him insane. During preparation meetings when he would speak to his troops she would look down, or away, or at a map, anywhere in the room but at him. What could he do? He couldn't get her to even *look* at him. She didn't disobey him in any regard, she just wouldn't give him her eyes. And oh, how he felt it. It was the one type of contact that had always connected them beyond words and social protocol, whether fighting, teasing, or in the moments when there was more. The funny thing was, he'd never even thought it significant, until it was gone.

Tonight, he would address it. Before they left on this journey, he had to address it, if for nothing more than the success of the mission. He couldn't have her avoiding him in any way, and it had nothing to do with his own guilt or his attraction. They had to be comfortable working together, for the mission. That was it and nothing more, he told himself again and again.

He continued to watch her. She dipped through the crowd as several men turned and took her in. He saw her decline a dance with a heartbreaking smile, and he felt his blood pulse in his veins as each new set of eyes landed on her. Finally, she worked her way to a small corner near the balcony doors, where she sat down, placing her hands in her lap.

When she stopped, he stood.

"Where are you going?" asked his mother.

"I shall return," he said over his shoulder as he made his way across the same path she had taken. Philippe made less of a stir than Alex had on the dance floor, but it still took him a moment to get through the crowd. When he approached her, she kept her eyes averted.

"I need to talk with you," he said.

"The trip is all set. There is no pressing need," she said.

"I should like to talk to you in private," he said again.

She stood up, preparing to walk away. He blocked her.

"Don't worry, *Monsieur*," she said, adjusting the lace around her waist. "I shall cause you no grief on the road," she replied, her eyes cast down. "I will be supportive as your guide." She began to move around him.

"I still need to speak with you," he said, blocking her path.

"I have no interest in talking."

He reached forward and grabbed her arm. "Sorry to do it this way, but you are as stubborn as an ox. I shall not begin this journey with you until you hear me out."

Holding onto her arm, he moved her to the balcony doors and pulled her outside. He released her and for the first time since he had kissed her, she looked directly at him, but this time with an anger in her eyes that could have stopped the crusades. It shot an arrow straight through him.

"Whatever you wish to tell me, I don't wish to hear it," she spat.

He took a step towards her, but she backed away. He took another step and she backed away again. Exasperated, he struck like a snake and grabbed her hand. She tried to jerk it away, but he held on.

They stood staring at each other for a moment, Alex glowering and Philippe feeling a heady rush at seeing that fury in her eyes again. He took a deep breath and lowered himself to a bow.

He touched his forehead to the back of her hand. After a moment, he spoke. "I wish to apologize for the wrongs I have done unto you." He paused. "All of them."

"You've apologized to me already."

"Not really," he said. He raised his head and looked up at her. "You never deserved any of that treatment, and I am sorry."

She glared at him and then turned towards the sky, starlight falling across her face. Then she sighed and brought her eyes to meet his. She nodded but said nothing more.

"I'm not asking for forgiveness at this moment," he continued. "I do hope to have it one day. But for now, I promise you will see a different side of me on this journey. I won't make you uncomfortable." He paused. "I would like us to become friends again."

"It would make everything much easier," she sighed.

"We must be able to work together."

She nodded. "Okay," she conceded.

Philippe stood up and smiled at her. "Come now. Enjoy the rest of your evening. That is all I wished to say." He held his arm out back towards the party.

Across the great hall, the Duke and the Duchess sat in rapt attention watching the door to the balcony as Alex and Philippe reentered the ballroom. Upon returning, Alex went in one direction and Philippe the other. But this time, Philippe wore a small, private smile as he worked his way back through the crowd.

"Have I made a mistake in putting them together for this task, *Bleu*?" asked Guillaume.

"I'm done trying to protect Alex from him. They are adults. They have to figure it out for themselves," replied Laure.

"Protect Alex? Look at that fool," he said. "Smiling like a dope. I hope he can keep his head on straight. This is important business they set out for in the morning."

"You have chosen your soldiers well, *mon amour*. Don't worry about it now. 'Tis up to Lady Fate to decide what happens on their journey. Let's just hope *she* protects them."

Philippe approached them. "Goodnight Mother, Father. I will retire now. We must be up before the sun." Then, with the same quiet grin, he left the great hall.

Guillaume breathed heavily. "That's the first time he's left a ball alone."

"It's about time," said Laure.

Chapter Seven

SIX YEARS EARLIER

A young Alexandra De Foix wanted to be the best swordsman in all of France.

Tomorrow would be the first step. She would compete in the sword fighting competition, the first female ever to compete. Her age dictated she would fight with the juniors; her skill promised to win her a championship. It was a huge honor to be included. She wanted to make her benefactors proud and, truth be told, knock a few of the boys out flat.

Late the night before the competition, sweat burned into her eyes and her wild dark hair snapped like a whip behind her as she ran through every move she knew. *Coup de Jarnac, coup de main, coup de grace.* She was in the equipment room, where she practiced during the day with the rest of the boys in her class. But now, she was alone. She lunged forward and caught an imaginary opponent on the knee. She dodged a slice to her belly and swiveled around to land an uppercut to the jaw of another. She extended her sword again, preparing to launch a plunging cut to the neck of her next opponent, but before she could find her balance, she hit a hollow in the dirt. Her feet flipped into the air, her sword spun off to the side, and she landed hard on her back, the sharp release of breath ripping through her with cat's claws.

She stared up at the ceiling, blinking in a daze. But her senses came back with crushing clarity when she heard a sudden burst of laughter from the entryway.

"Alex," he called. "You must not do *that* at the competition."

"*Monsieur*?" she choked out the words, scrambling up just enough to drop into a bow. "What are you doing here?"

"Get up," he said, still teasing. "I came to practice for tomorrow. I'm glad I won't have to do so alone."

Alex grabbed her sword and stood tall, though she wanted to run screaming in the other direction. No one ever came down here late at night when she practiced in her boy clothes. Of all people to show up... As he came towards her, the edges of her vision rippled and blurred until the walls, the racks, the floor fell away, and there was only him. He was tall, confident, and carved from stone; his light brown hair, cut short and clean, the unrestrained strength humming just beneath his clothes. She knew his face by heart—every angle, every expression— but his eyes made her suffer the most, casting spells on her with every glance. At nineteen years old, he was already an accomplished soldier and a battlefield over which girls much older and more sophisticated than her fought.

Philippe.

She did not want to be in love with him.

She was, however, stupidly in love with him.

"Were you watching me?" she stammered.

"Yes." He said, his dark eyes glowing gold in the light from the oil lamps. "You're better than when you're in class."

She blushed. "They won't fight me if I win every time."

He smiled. "Let's see if you are ready for tomorrow."

She hesitated. "But... we are alone."

"Afraid I'll hurt you?" He raised his eyebrows and unsheathed his own brilliant, powerful blade.

She lifted her sword, feeling very unsure of her skills when they were to be measured against his. Philippe, home to compete in the master's portion of tomorrow's competition, often came to the class to help the students practice. She'd sparred with Philippe before, many times. But never alone. Never without rules. She suddenly became aware of why it was inappropriate for a young man and a young woman to be alone together.

He lunged forward and whacked her sword. The strike came hard and splintered her balance. He struck again. She blocked him. Barely.

"Fight back," he said. He throttled her harder, sending her back a few steps. "Don't make it easy for me."

She swallowed hard and struck at his flank. He smacked her away like a gnat. She was better than this, but looking into his eyes was difficult, and she knew she was outclassed, outmatched, wildly unprepared for such an experienced partner. Desperate, she lunged forward. He dropped down, dodging the attack. Then, with no time for her to stabilize, he swung his blade around to swat her.

Right across her bottom.

Alex froze at the sting and looked at him with her mouth open in shock.

He raised his eyebrows. "Mad yet?" he asked.

All at once, her skills rushed back into her rattled bones. She launched herself at him, cracking her sword against his. The onslaught came unexpectedly, causing his confident smirk to retreat. She pushed him back with delight running through her. He was not an easy target, but she would not be dominated without a fight.

Alex had learned that boys fought with a teeth-bearing savagery that she didn't have. They ignored the rules which she had memorized. It made men dangerous. She knew this was what kept them alive in battles and what fueled their arrogance outside of the ring. She wanted it, whatever they had, but her gentle nature was behind every parry and every cut. She worried that this thing men had was decidedly male, and she would never unlock the unrelenting power she saw in them. Instead, she relied on her wits. Most of the time, it was all she needed to outmatch her young opponents. And though Philippe was as sleek and smooth of a fighter as they came, she was going to gamble that he didn't know about the soft patch of dirt that had flattened her moments before.

His moves were powerful and fast, and she could not manipulate him with ease. They cracked blades like lightning. Her muscles burned, but she refused to give up her sword. She'd realized she could move him by applying just the right amount of pressure. Too much and he would take over. Too little and she'd lose all control. She leaned to the side and he came after her. She arched back to bait him, and he thrust his blade towards her. She guarded and countered, moving them both steadily to the target. They were getting close, but with excruciating slowness, and she didn't know how long she could hold out. She swallowed hard, panting, her heart breaking out of her chest.

Then, like an earthquake shattering a mountain peak, his left foot caught the weak spot in the dirt, and he stumbled. His stance weakened for just a second. She wasted no time, cracked him hard on the knee, and knocked him to the ground. She swung her sword and held it right to his neck, her exhausted muscles spasming as she did.

Breathing hard, he broke her gaze to look to the floor where he had fallen. Then his eyes came back to her. "I do believe you cheated," he breathed, an amused expression on his face.

"I have no idea what you mean," she teased, the point of her weapon at his throat.

He threw his sword to the ground, conceding her win. He laughed, unrestrained, then grabbed her blade and pushed her back. "Come on, little fox," he said, calling her by the nickname he had given her years before. "Let's go down and cool off by the river."

She looked at him, not sure if she should. But how could she say no to those beautiful, gold-ringed eyes?

Alex had come to live at the Duke's manor when she was nine years old. Her father had died in a hunting accident and her mother never recovered. Even when young, Alex saw that her mother was a weak woman, unable to move forward, determined to wither. Alex vowed never to be like that. When her mother passed, swallowed by drink and desperation, Duchess Laure—a childhood friend of Alex's mother—swooped in to give Alex a home.

Alex remembered two particular feelings on the day she arrived at the palace. A sensation of relief when she saw the Duchess's gentle face. She knew this woman would care for her with the certainty of childhood instinct. Then there was another indescribable feeling when she saw the Duchess's twelve-year-old son, Philippe, sword fighting with other boys. It started in the top of her belly and spread until her fingers and toes tingled. Was he handsome? Was it his talent with the sword? Alex didn't know. What she did know was that she wanted to chase him. She put down her satchel and without a second thought, she shot after him like an arrow.

She remembered hearing the Duchess laugh as she ran after the terrified boy, and she knew that meant it was okay.

Now, as they approached the river on the eastern grounds of the palace, she wished she could stop chasing him. Though he had always been kind to her, it was clear to her, even young, that Philippe was interested in things Alex couldn't give him. As she grew up and he came and went from the palace, learning to campaign alongside his father and brothers, the distance between them increased. She decided she would never compete for his attention, despite her feelings. Instead, she funneled her emotions into her sword, and that's where they stayed.

The bank of the river smelled rich with greenery, and the bright full moon lit the path turning everything silvery gray. Alex followed Philippe to the river's edge. He sat down in the cool moss and loosened the collar around his neck. "Come now," he said. "I have left my sword behind. I won't attack you."

Alex hesitated a moment, then dropped her sword and sat next to him. She wished the confidence she felt in a spar could help her here. She didn't know how to act, what to say. She cursed herself for not paying attention to her lessons in decorum. She took a deep breath—his manly scent doing nothing to calm her—and tried to fake it.

"I wouldn't have worn such clothes if I knew I'd see anyone," she said.

"It will be our secret," he said. He shifted his weight, and his leg was pressed against hers.

She looked to the place they touched. Surely, it was by accident. He couldn't know what the contact did to her.

"Philippe?" she started, speaking, saying anything to distract herself. "May I ask you something?"

He looked at her. "Of course," he said after a moment.

His eyes were different from when they practiced—softer, warmer. She looked away but continued. "It is something I have wondered for a long time. There is no one better to ask than you—"

"Ask me, *chérie*," he pressed.

Alex swallowed to calm herself. "How do I take a man," she asked, looking back to him, "once he has put me down?"

Philippe stared at her and blinked wide eyes. "Um, what?"

"I'm not very good at grappling." She shrugged. "You know, if I lose my sword during a spar and get wrestled to the ground. I don't have the strength to fight them off. Do you have any advice?"

Philippe gave his head a quick shake and coughed. Then turned to her and spoke sternly. "Well, my advice would be to try and avoid being caught under the wrong man at all costs." Then he winked. "In terms of grappling, of course," he said with a roguish smile.

A hot fever of a blush came over her. "I didn't mean—"

"Tell me," he said, still grinning. "Why are you so taken with sword fighting?"

"Why?" she echoed. Did he not remember giving her her first sword? Or how he had let her win when they played as children? She couldn't say such things. But there was another truth, and she felt a proud smile creep onto her lips as she said it. "I'm good at it," came her reply.

He laughed again. "You are indeed." He rested back on his elbows. "You're different from other girls," he said, working his eyes across her face.

"No kidding," she said. She tugged at her pants.

"That's not what I mean," he said, his voice soft.

She turned to him sharply and saw a shade to his expression she had never seen before. It was raw and indulgent and caused her to shiver in response. What had happened? What had changed? Something spiraling deep inside her told her that he was no longer looking at her like a girl. This was a man responding to a woman.

"Alex," he said. His voice had gone gravelly.

"Yes?" she replied, the words rushing from her lips.

"Has anyone given you your first kiss?"

"My first kiss?" she laughed. "The boys are all scared of me."

He reached forward to tuck a strand of hair behind her ear. "I'm not," he said, hesitating a moment, before he let his next words spill into the night. "Would you mind if it were me?"

The world came to a sudden standstill, sure that she was dreaming. Taking a shaky breath, Alex whispered with her eyes cast down, "I wouldn't mind."

"Then lie back, little fox," he said, his eyes sparkling, "So I may find your lips."

She leaned into the soft moss. *It can't be. It can't be.* Her mind spun the words over and over as he placed one hand on the ground beside her. He hovered above her, a hair's breadth away. She looked into his eyes and felt everything else slipping away. The water rippling beside them was gone. The moon above them was gone. Her breath slowed; her lips tingled. And there was only Philippe.

He dropped his head, enough to make contact. His lips teased hers apart. Then he moved closer, giving Alex her first taste of intimacy. He stroked his hand through her hair, and took another delicate drink from her lips, lingering long enough to change Alex's entire world. But before pressing his body closer, like she thought he would, he stopped and pulled back.

He looked down into her eyes, brushing his thumb against her cheek. "Come now," he said. "You must sleep if you plan to win."

She wanted more, she wanted everything, but she would take it as a promise of what was to come. He smiled, then he rose and held his hand out. She took it, and they began the walk home.

The moonlight brought them to the back doors of the palace. As they approached, Philippe leaned in to give her a quick kiss on the cheek.

"Go in, *belle*," he said, smiling. "I shall leave you here."

She nodded and grinned, drunk on the magic of the beautiful life that had just been sworn to her.

She realized, walking up the steps in a daze, that she had always been fascinated to learn what it took to become a man. But at that moment, and for the first time in her life, Alex wanted to know what it meant to be a woman. Whatever it meant, giving up her sword, becoming a proper lady, she didn't care. She would become whatever he wanted her to be if it meant being his woman.

Odd, she thought briefly, that he didn't come inside and go up to his own room.

The next morning, Alex stood in the preparation area next to the arena where the games were being held. The town was alight with energy and the little practice cove set up for the juniors was filled with the sounds of clanging swords and boys shouting. Alex stood alone, unfocused and dreamy. What better feeling was there than to be in love? Doves in her heart! Harps strumming above her!

Then she heard a voice that could destroy her on even the best of days.

It was Emily, beautiful Emily in a lavender silk gown, with her bouncy blond hair, pouty pink lips and ice blue eyes. She glided up to Alex with an expression Alex knew meant trouble. Emily came from a well-known and well-connected family in Chevalerie. She was a few years older, and everything Alex wasn't: graceful, stylish, elegant. Vindictive and cruel. Though Alex could knock down boys twice her size, Emily fought with weapons Alex didn't understand, often teasing and confusing Alex to tears.

Alex *hated* Emily.

This time, though, Alex knew something Emily didn't, and a newfound confidence wrapped her in knight's armor.

"Not now, please," Alex said, trying out a haughty air. "I haven't the time."

"Don't talk to me like we are equal, are you thick?" Emily tugged Alex's hair.

Startled, Alex lost the grip on her sword. It clattered to the ground. "Don't touch me," she stammered. Oh, she could not wait to see Emily's reaction when Philippe declared his intentions.

Emily grabbed the sleeve of Alex's dress, pulling her close. "Stay away from Philippe," she whispered in Alex's ear. "He is mine," Emily growled.

Alex pushed out of Emily's grip and backed up. She hadn't wanted to say anything yet, but Emily was making things quite impossible. Really, it was her only choice. She couldn't deny it would feel very good to put Emily in her place for once. "I don't wish to inform you this way," she began with newfound sophistication. "Philippe shall declare his intentions for me soon. Perhaps even tonight at the champions' ball." The words made her feel prouder than she ever had in her life.

"Oh, you poor, silly girl." Emily laughed mirthfully with her hands up to her lips. "Do you think you deserve a man like him?"

"But," Alex hesitated. "It's true."

"He told me he practiced with you last night," Emily said. Then she lowered her voice and leaned in. "Then he warmed my bed."

Alex stared at her, not quite understanding. "What do you mean—"

Emily crossed her arms. "Think hard," she said, a smirk at her lips.

It couldn't be true. Surely Philippe wouldn't have kissed her if he didn't plan to pursue her formally. But the more Alex thought about it, the more Emily's words rang true. Philippe hadn't made any promises or said he had intentions for her. He hadn't lingered with her, stealing more kisses in the moonlight. He hadn't even pretended to go to his own room in the palace after they said goodnight. Alex blinked. Her gushing happiness drained into the dirt below, leaving her stinging and parched.

"Emily," came a commanding voice behind them. It was Philippe. He'd come around the fence and stood just a few steps away.

Emily turned to him. "There you are, My Lord," she said in a sugary tone. She curtseyed low to the ground then rushed to take him by the arm. "Philippe, Alexandra seems to think that you have intentions for her." Then she asked, "Is that true, *Monsieur*?"

The bewilderment on his face said enough. Alex looked away, the horror of her delusion becoming real.

Then Emily called to the boys around them. "Look! Look at her, everyone. This stupid girl thinks she has won the heart of the Duke's son." Her laugh came like a cackle.

"*Emily*," Philippe hissed. "Stop it."

But Emily wasn't done. Her audience grew, the boys leaning against the fence or on the hilts of their swords, happy for the entertainment. "How have you won his heart, dear?" Emily continued. "With the drooping ribbons in your hair?"

Her words started a cascade of jeers, the boys taking the chance to throw out the taunts they couldn't get away with during class.

"If I were Duke, you'd be in the stocks!"

"Leave the swords for the men!"

"Try the hilt and you won't need a man!"

"*Arrêtez*!" Philippe commanded, silencing the boys, save a few coughs and chuckles.

"You're right, Philippe," Emily simpered. "Let us leave this child to play with her toys." She moved towards Alex once more and whispered through her teeth, "Stay away from him, dirty girl, or I shall cut the waves from your hair and feed them to the chickens."

That's what it took. Something exploded inside Alex, angry and primal. Before she could think, she had cut the distance to Emily, seized her by the throat, and slammed her against the fence behind them. Alex didn't know if it was this latest stunt or the years of humiliation at Emily's hand, but something had changed inside her. Her fear was gone. There was only instinct.

Emily tried to scream, but no sound came. Alex snarled at her, "So have your lord. But if you ever touch me or threaten me again, I will gut you like a hog."

Without warning, Alex felt a strong arm around her middle. Philippe pulled her back and Emily crumpled, gasping to the ground. Alex fought against his grasp.

"Alex!" he cried. "You must stop!"

She threw an elbow and broke his hold. She whirled around. His eyes were disbelieving and frantic, but she was no longer affected by his face. She hated him and everything about him. How could he be so disgusting? To share a kiss with her and then find another's *bed*.

"Alex," he said. "I'm so sorry I have given you the wrong idea—"

"No," she said, backing away. She didn't want his words. Then she picked up her sword and ran, away from him, away from Emily, away from her foolish thoughts forever.

It wasn't anger that drove her to do what she did next. It wasn't heartbreak or sadness. It was the cutting shame that she'd been so willing to change herself for a stupid, inconsiderate man. The feeling was hot and profound and poisonous in her veins.

And the only way she could make it better was by making it much, much worse.

Horns blew as the final preparations on the arena floor commenced. The excited rumble could be heard well across the valley. People in the stands stomped and waved blue and yellow scarves in crazed anticipation of what was to come.

Philippe sat beside his mother and father in their seats at the head of the arena. Below them, porters raked the dirt on the stadium floor while the juniors lined up for their competition. He strained his eyes to see if Alex was with the boys, but the group was shielded by an overhang, and he couldn't find her among them. After he'd dragged her off that buffoon Emily that morning, he hadn't seen her again. It all happened so fast; he hadn't even defended Alex. Now, he didn't know if she would compete. He'd ruined the day for her, he was sure. He'd ruined a lot of things.

He felt like an ass. A complete ass.

A line of guards marched out onto the arena floor and positioned themselves in formation. Philippe sat with his head resting on his hand, unable to summon the desire to clap. The last thing he had meant to do was hurt her. The kiss they'd shared had been so innocent. He just thought it would bookmark a special moment between them. Alex couldn't have thought that it meant more; she hadn't even come of age yet, and he was quite young himself to enter into an official courtship. Plus, he'd shown restraint for once. Didn't she appreciate the fact that he had been so respectful? Did she know what that meant? He really hadn't meant to do anything wrong...

But the truth was, Alex had captivated him. And he did something bad because of it. He'd realized on the riverbank that night that she was becoming a woman, her sighs and blushes causing a ribbon of desire to run through him that he didn't want to ignore. He wanted to taste her—her sweetness, her irreverence, her hunger—before another man claimed her, and it felt even better than he had expected, even though he knew it was wrong the whole time it was happening.

Why, *why* did he go to Emily, he thought, dropping his head into his hands. He'd seen the way Alex had looked at him, with stars in her eyes. He'd realized immediately that he couldn't let it stand. His freedom to come and go, to campaign, and to explore the world would be taken away if he entered a courtship. He hadn't thought, just acted. Going to Emily was a simple way to ensure he wouldn't encourage anything more with Alex. He hadn't thought further than that, hadn't thought about how Alex would react.

He was an ass. He shook his head and rubbed his forehead. An absolute ass.

The guards completed their display below and filed off the floor. *Monsieur* Perreault stepped into the arena to address the cheering crowd. He opened the large scroll and commanded his voice above the curtain of noise. "On this day twenty-seven years ago, the Duke of Chevalerie established the first tournament for the skills of sword fighting in this very arena. It began as a contest to find the most talented and brave fighters, who would help protect the borders of our city. Today it awards us the most accomplished swordfighters in our land and beyond, who shall one day lead us in battle against our foes, and the foes of France."

Applause erupted as people showed both enthusiasm for the games and allegiance to their Duke. *Monsieur* Perreault basked in the attention before using his hand to shush the spectators once more.

"The rules are simple," he boomed. "The first two opponents are chosen at random. The winner of the match will choose the next contender, and so on. The judges will present awards for skill, dexterity, and endurance. The overall point bearer will be named the grand champion." He paused and flourished his hand. "Under the watch of the Duke and Duchess of Chevalerie and God in Heaven, the tournament shall commence!"

The excitement came like an avalanche, a roar rumbling through the stadium. After a laugh and a shrug at the frenzy, *Monsieur* Perreault continued. "We shall begin with the junior competition, to be followed by our masters. Awards for both groups will be presented at the end. May I have the bag with the names of the junior challengers, please?"

A young boy ran onto the grounds with a velvet bag. Philippe's heart seized, hoping Alex had come to compete. She could be the junior grand champion; he knew it. She was crafty and skilled, especially compared to the boys in her class. Plus, he knew just how much she wanted to prove herself.

Monsieur Perreault plucked a name from the bag. "Éric Ansel!" he cried. The fans applauded as the young fighter walked out to the center. *Monsieur* Perreault preened his garments and cleared his throat before taking the next name. By his chortling laugh Philippe knew whose name it was. "Alexandra de Foix to the ring!" he called.

Philippe ground his knuckles into the seat, pleading with the fates for her to emerge. He did not want to be responsible for her missing this honor. All he had wanted to take were her lips, but he feared he had taken so much more.

Alex popped out of the group of boys and came onto the arena floor. She would be fighting, he realized, his heart growing light again. He hadn't ruined everything after all. He let out a long sigh of relief, thanking the heavens for the reprieve.

Monsieur Perreault said a few words to the competitors then backed away. The two squared off and faced each other. The crowd hushed, awaiting his command.

"*En garde,*" he called.

The fighters touched swords and held their positions.

"*Prêt,*" he said.

The stadium stilled in anticipation.

Monsieur Perreault paused before continuing. "*Allez!*" he called and scurried back across the dirt.

The audience settled for the fight, but once the start was called, Alex dropped down, spun around and knocked the boy right off his feet. She held her sword to his neck before he'd even had a chance to move.

She'd won.

The spectators were on their feet screaming both praise for the skill and admonishments at the insolence. Alex hadn't scored many points, but she'd come out fighting, that was sure. Philippe shook his head and grinned.

"Oh dear," said the Duchess, stifling a laugh. "Poor Éric."

Monsieur Perreault tried to settle the audience once again, taking a moment to realize that he was on again, but the people were rabid with excitement. He approached Alex to determine who her next opponent would be.

But something was wrong; Alex and *Monsieur* seemed to be arguing. *Monsieur* Perreault shook his head, getting more and more agitated and violent with his gestures, while she stood back with her arms folded. People in the stands around Philippe began questioning what was happening. The murmur rippled through the crowd. Finally, *Monsieur* Perreault walked to the judges' table, his face set in consternation. There, the judges listened to him and then looked at Alex standing defiantly, alone in the middle of the ring.

"What is going on?" his mother asked. "Her move was legal. What are they doing?"

Monsieur Perreault stretched a large scroll across the judge's table. Philippe guessed it was the official rules, but he couldn't imagine what they'd be looking for.

After several long moments, in which the crowd had begun chanting their impatience, *Monsieur* Perreault came back out beside Alex. "Alexandra de Foix will be challenging..." He trailed off and cleared his throat. "Alexandra de Foix will be challenging his Lordship, *Monsieur* Philippe du Chevalerie."

The spectators went into an uproar. Philippe sat stunned in his seat. What the hell was happening? This couldn't be right.

Monsieur Perreault continued, "We have checked the official documentation. Though there is no precedent for a junior challenging a master, there is, apparently," he looked back to Alex, "no rule against it. Lord Philippe," he cleared his throat again, "to the arena floor please. Or," he said, "You will forfeit the championship."

The Duchess turned to Philippe, her dark-blue eyes flashing red with fury. "What did you do?" she asked through clenched teeth.

Philippe couldn't speak, let alone answer. He stood up, dazed. He didn't want to fight Alex, yet if he refused, he would be shamed for declining the battle. He moved through the stands, with the buzzing of confused whispers trailing him. He hopped the fence that ringed the dirt and walked across the ring, though he felt unaware of what his limbs were doing.

Monsieur Perreault looked stricken as Philippe approached them. Philippe stood before Alex, her eyes black with hate.

"Don't do this," Philippe pleaded with her. "Don't be stupid."

"I wish to fight you one more time."

"You will lose. You know that."

"I will hurt you first."

Monsieur Perreault stood to the side. Reluctantly, Philippe took his stance. She looked different; it was more than the loathing shining back at him. He was an enemy to her, he realized. And this was going to be a real fight.

They raised their weapons. The gamekeeper called the start.

Philippe braced himself for the move she had used on Éric, but her sword came from the top this time, knocking him off balance and scoring the first touch of the battle. He spun around and caught her weapon mid-air before she could strike him again.

"I cannot go easy on you," he shouted between clangs of their swords.

"Don't." She spit the word through her teeth, attacking him with an upward thrust. He avoided it but missed his chance to counter as she had already repositioned herself for her next move.

She fought like a fiend, coming at him again and again. They made short work of the ground, tracing trails through the dirt. Philippe fought back, but she drained his strength.

She snapped around and caught him across the arm, causing him to wince. He realized that he would need to finish this to avoid as much humiliation as possible. With two aggressive steps towards her, he took command of the fight and put her on the defensive. He drove her back until she was at the edge of the ring. She stepped onto a bench against the wall, putting them eye to eye.

"You can't win, Alex," he shouted.

"Like hell," she shouted back, just making a blow to his chest.

He whipped her arm with his blade, but she held fast to her sword. He would have to wrestle it out of her hand. He moved in closer, stifling her range with his body. With his left hand, he grabbed her wrist and held her sword to the rail behind her, his own sword ready to deliver the winning move.

"You are outmatched," he said. "Drop your sword before I must hurt you."

She bore into his eyes, refusing his command.

With one last move, he twisted her arm back over the fence. She let out a yelp of pain, and he heard the sound he'd been waiting for: the clang of her sword as it hit the ground.

It was over. He avoided her eyes, the eyes of *Monsieur* Perreault, and everyone in the audience. It was a terrible win. He regretted every moment and knew he would feel the sting of this for a long time. He loosened his hold on her, wanting to get off the floor and away from it all as soon as possible.

But Alex wasn't done. In the split second of release, she reared back and slammed her head against him with the force of a stallion. Stars exploded like a cannon blast in his vision, and his mouth overflowed with blood. He heard the crowd gasp. He stumbled back and caught fat drops of crimson in his hands. She stood before him, her face smeared with his blood. He brought a hand up to his mouth and felt the meaty split along the bottom of his lip.

Rivulets of blood weaved through his fingers before coloring the ground. His head swam and he felt himself drop to one knee.

It was quiet as she picked up her sword, nodded her defeat towards *Monsieur* Perreault and walked off the floor.

He saw only her empty footprints in the dirt before his eyes went completely dark.

Chapter Eight

CHEVALERIE, PROVENCE, FRANCE 1654

No sooner had the sun crested the horizon the morning after the competition than Philippe's troops took their first steps past the city limits. They would be traveling to a small town northwest of Chevalerie that day, which they could reach by sunset at a comfortable pace. They had a zigzag trail planned to get up to the town of Ponce, which would be their home base while they canvassed the caves. Though their objective of finding these men was not secret, and establishing a presence was the goal, the suspicion that the rebels hid in the caves would only be shared with high officials.

Alex stroked her horse's side as they moved ahead. The sun was thawing the nip of night by then. She peeled her scarf off and let it drape over her lap. This was quite an impressive envoy. There were the primary soldiers, the mapmaker, and several camp porters charged with tending to the horses, making camp on nights in the field, running messages, and making sleeping arrangements before the rest of the group entered towns. And of course, it was led by Philippe, a respected noble. Usually, her groups were much smaller, dirtier, rougher. This was first class all the way.

She watched up ahead, past brothers Bernard and Luc, beyond young

Claude, over Laurent, to where Philippe led his horse down the trail. He was a proud leader. Alex wondered why he chose to go on this mission. As the son of a duke, he could have it much easier. He'd done his duty for the King and could live the life of a gentleman for the rest of his days, never wanting for anything. Perhaps he had political aspirations of his own and looked to make himself known. His father's title would pass to his eldest brother, Michel, so if Philippe wanted a title, he would have to earn it himself from the King of France. But she had never known him to have great political desires. Did he do it out of duty to his family and country? She guessed he was too selfish to do anything without recompense. He was arrogant and spoiled. The kindness of his parents and their success as leaders would be enough to carry him through his life, so why did he work harder than he had to?

Her horse shook his head, and she patted his mane. Philippe wouldn't need to consult her during the day's ride. This was a well-known and well-traveled path, so she hung back in the procession. She had agreed to be amicable with him for the needs of the journey; however, there was no need to press that promise at the moment. He had apologized to her the night before, which she hadn't expected, but what did she ever expect from him? He seemed sincere, and the gesture soothed her animosity. Truthfully, she knew she should have apologized to him too, right then, for her actions years ago. But even after all this time, she just couldn't let the hurt go.

The trail was becoming less manicured as they approached the trees at the forest's edge. Shaggy bushes tossed limbs into the road like dirty laundry. The leaves high above them were tinted with gold and fluttered in the breeze. She watched Philippe up ahead as he held the reins and guided his horse down the path. It was too bad, she thought, as attraction simmered inside her. If only they hadn't met until they were older, and she had indeed grown into a lady equal to his station rather than the trail rat she had become. Despite his careless actions with her, she didn't think he was a bad person. Privileged, cocky, yes, but not *bad*. She stared at his sturdy back and she saw the muscles flexing as he reined his horse. He was confident as the lead. And strong. She liked how he had played with her when they fought, how he teased her blade with his own. In an instant she was back in the training room, imagining his face and that predatory look as he pursued her. *No.* She stopped the memory from coming through.

It was something she had refused to think about in the days since it had happened. Because it hadn't meant anything, because it still had the power to undo her. It wasn't her he wanted, she reminded herself. She wasn't special, she could have been any woman that he watched with those seductive eyes. But hadn't it seemed like she was the only woman in the world to him? She felt him push her against the wall as the memory struggled to break free. What did it matter if she played a little with the sensual moments between them, like a cat with a ball of string? Up ahead, he signaled for the group to slow as they entered deeper into the forest, and she caught a glimpse of his face, his brow furrowed in thought. She liked the way his eyes had felt on her. The thought rolled a tremble up her spine. The memory of their fight, the heat and desire between them, sat in her consciousness, waiting to be sprung. All she had to do was say yes and open up that memory like a gift. What would it harm?

She was losing the fight. She decided to give herself one minute to feel all the lust and longing she could handle. Then she would seal it up again. Her eyelids fluttered as she watched him up ahead, her lips parted and she was back in the training room, yes, with his mouth and heavy weight against her. Her body reacted as she remembered the feeling of him pressing into her. What would have happened if she'd let him continue? If he'd opened her shirt and she felt his warm touch on her exposed skin. If they had indeed dropped to the ground as he had suggested and, yes, she'd let him explore her body? Would he have been gentle with her, or, she swallowed, not gentle at all? Warmth rushed through her and for a soft, sultry second, she held the feeling close to her heart.

Then, as if she had called his name, Philippe turned his head and caught her staring at him. Startled, she coughed and pretended to wave a fly away, which knocked her shawl off her lap. She snapped down to grab it and almost fell off her saddle. Flustered, she looked back at Philippe. He watched her strangely for a moment, and she was sure he knew everything. Then he threw her a slow smile and turned back towards the trail.

Alex blinked and sat rigidly in her saddle.

Well, fuck, she thought.

Chapter Nine

They traveled through the morning, stopping by a bubbling little stream that cut through a lazy green meadow filled with yellow poppies for a well-deserved lunch of jams, cheese, and bread. The men ate as though it had been days since their last meal, the warm ride that morning having already begun to tire them out. Philippe paced as he crammed a hunk of bread in his mouth, unable to settle in. Though there was little risk of confrontation in this area, he remained hyper-vigilant and alert so his company could relax. He ran through his list of tasks in his mind. Men, horses, maps, supplies. The scouts had already been sent ahead to prepare accommodations, and the porters were busy tidying their path. He checked everything once and then again.

He refused to be overwhelmed by this unclear and complex mission. He didn't have much information to go on, and he already felt the needling fingers of frustration piercing his patience. He wanted to start assembling the clues as soon as possible. So once the men began licking crumbs from their fingers, he hustled them up to leave. He fed his horse a handful of sweet grass and retied the pack to the saddle. He scanned the men and did another mental survey of everyone's condition. Maurice's horse would need a new shoe soon; Daniel's water sack had torn; Bernard had clearly hit his flask pretty hard but seemed the better for it. Once satisfied that everything was accounted for, Philippe prepared to saddle up himself. Before he did, he keyed into a conversation between his mapmaker and his guide.

They were about to enter the sun-soaked Bright Hills, which had several possible trailways for them to use. Alex was recommending going straight through some of the ravines. It would be faster and shield them from the day's high heat, at least for part of the journey. The streams would also be running, which would be nice for the horses. The mapmaker, Henri, however, disagreed.

"It will be too much water. We should go over the top," he insisted.

"That path is far more strenuous," countered Alex. "And we'll be exposed to the sun with very little shade."

"If you are wrong," he sneered, "we shall be wading our horses through an angry river rather than a stream."

"I'm not wrong, good sir. There have been no storms to disturb the flow of water."

Philippe mounted his horse and trotted over to them. "We are ready to leave. What is the problem?"

"My Lord," said Henri. "Your guide here wishes to travel through a blocked path to gain a little shade. 'Tis not safe. We must go over the hill rather than through it or risk the danger of unrestrained water against our horses."

"Ah, Henri," Alex teased. "I think you are more worried about getting your fancy boots wet than your horse."

"My boots?" Henri blustered. "These cost more than a penny, young lady!"

"Okay, okay," said Philippe. He turned his head. "Alex?"

"We face no issue traveling the path I have suggested. It is safe. The call is yours, *Monsieur*," she replied, looking at him with deference.

Philippe looked from Henri to Alex, weighing both of their arguments. In the end, he had sworn to treat her no different than any other guide he had worked with. "It is simple," he said. "We go where our guide guides us." He grinned at Henri. "If she is wrong, we can hold it over her head the rest of the journey." Philippe then turned and called for the men to start.

He gave it no more thought and left the two of them to sort it out. But the small smile she had tried to hide wasn't lost on him.

Chapter Ten

Their destination for the night was Peillon, a timeworn village set right on the edge of a cliff in the *Cote d'Azur* with a spectacular view of the valley and the little chimney-topped farmhouses that inhabited it. Alex had stayed in Pellion several times during her trips up and down the region and she knew it well. It had stone walkways with an elaborate network of steep streets and uneven stairs. Grey green olive trees decorated its small gardens, and a modest church stood at the center with a pearlescent red mosaic fountain before it. The town itself had been untouched by the rebel group, but the patchwork farms in the valley below had not been so lucky. These were the closest attacks to Chevalerie to date.

As the party traveled the valley, Alex could see Peillon up ahead, jutting out into the late afternoon sunlight. But the farmland they were crossing was steeped in a smoky haze that stung her nose and caught in her throat. As they continued through the heavy air, they came upon the remains of the latest attack. They would investigate the farm in the morning, but the party still slowed as they passed. Alex remembered the farm. Once a cheery place with olive trees lining the drive, it was now a black skeleton that still singed the air. Even the animals had not yet returned to investigate the area, shrouding the valley in an eerie silence which was broken only by the tinkling of sheep's bells, reaching their ears from far off herds.

A short while later, after having come through the valley, they reached Peillon and arrived at the inn. Alex settled her horse and entered the stonework building, to find Philippe already negotiating with the innkeeper.

"I just need the beds in the barracks and the one private room, *monsieur*," said Philippe.

"I tell you, I do not allow prostitution in this establishment," the wiry haired innkeeper blustered.

"She is our guide. I assure you..." Philippe started.

"I mean the girls can do what they want in the tavern next door," the innkeeper continued. "That's none of my business."

"The private room is not for prostitution," Philippe said to the man. Philippe rubbed his forehead, looking frustrated.

"In fact, I quite enjoy the little redhead myself," the innkeeper said as if Philippe had not even spoken. The man held a finger up. "But not in these rooms."

Philippe put the money on the counter and reached across the desk to grab the key. He pushed the key into the innkeeper's hands. He nodded towards Alex. "Her," he said.

The innkeeper bustled over to her. "Come, girl. No male visitors. There are several spots available outside the tavern for that. But not in here."

Alex looked back at Philippe. He shrugged and turned to join the rest of their party.

She knew this inn and this innkeeper. She'd battled with him before. Whenever in towns, she always *tried* to get herself a private room, but they were usually double the price and innkeepers were suspicious of single female travelers. Instead, she would often eat, pay to wash, and then camp outside. But traveling with this party, she had standing she wasn't used to. So she kept her mouth shut, nodded three more times to promise she wouldn't bring any men back to the inn, and let herself be left alone in a lovely little room. With access to a private balcony!

For a moment, Alex forgot the disturbing scene they had passed in the valley. She rushed across the room and threw open the balcony doors. She leaned over the edge as far as she could to see the valley they had crossed. The sunset blazed the smoky fields in gold and blended the sky from the bright blue above her to fiery orange on the horizon. She breathed in the clean air, thinner and sweeter this high up, as the wind pulled the curtains out to flutter around her. In all her time on the road, she'd never had a view like this all to herself. It was so much more than she needed, and her first instinct was to give it away, or share it, or... something. She didn't know why Philippe had gone out of his way to allow her this extravagance.

But she couldn't deny, it sure felt great.

A little while later, after taking the chance to wash and luxuriate in her beautiful room, Alex entered the dining hall of the tavern. By then, the men were well into their drink, and the opportunistic women from town were well into the men. Bernard and Luc led the pack, smashing their cups together before every drink. Sébastien, far more interested in the women than the alcohol, had a light-haired doll on his lap, who was busy giving him chances to look down her bosom. The newly married Auguste shook his head at a dame and took a hard drink from his mug while another pretty woman with thick powder on her face picked several coins from Maurice's belt. Before Alex could decide if she should tell him, Maurice stole them right back while the woman gave a flirty grin over her shoulder to someone else.

The barmaid brought Alex some stew and crusty bread with a plate of olive oil. Alex's stomach growled as she tore at the bread. The only one missing from the hall, she noticed, was Philippe. She imagined the other private room in the inn had gone to him. Was he already there with some woman who had charmed him? That bastard, she thought, her mood changing. She picked up her fork and stabbed at a chunk of meat in the stew.

It wasn't long, however, before he arrived. He was dressed in the same clothes he wore on the trail and still looked haggard from the road, haphazard hair pushed to the side. He scanned his men and when he saw her, he smiled. He shared a quick exchange with Laurent. Then he sat at the far end of the table for his meal... and stared right at her.

Alex felt like an animal caught. She looked away and then back again, but he was still watching her. A flame of panic went over her. What was this all about? Did he want her to see him choose a girl for himself? So she would be sure he was no longer interested? Maybe seeing him kiss another like he had kissed her—hard, but at the same time soft—would take away its magic.

She fluttered inside, thinking about the kiss. She grabbed her cup to take a gulp of water but missed her mouth and splashed it down her shirt. She looked up, and he was still watching. *Dammit.* If every night was going to be like this, she would go eat in the stables with the horses. She focused on her bowl, determined to finish her meal and get out of there before she saw Philippe with his hand up some maid's skirt. But every time she looked, he was still alone, just watching her. No hands in any maids that she could see.

By the time she was taking the last spoonful of her meal, the men had begun disappearing with their dates. Auguste fell off his seat in a drunken stupor to a raucous round of laughter. Alex took the commotion as her own cue to stand up and stretch, ready to head back to her room. But once she did, she saw Philippe, across the hall, do just the same. She dropped a coin on the table, and he did the same. She wrapped her shawl around her; he adjusted his coat. Then as she turned and made her way to the exit, she felt him do so as well. In the cool night, they crossed the short alley that led to the inn, watching each other. The doors to the inn were propped open and Alex went inside. For a fleeting second, she wondered if he planned to follow her to her room and a cascade of *yes*es and *no*s went through her. But when she turned to go down the hall leading towards her room, Philippe remained at the archway to the barracks.

"Goodnight, Alex," he called. Then he smiled and winked at her and disappeared into the darkness of the room.

She stood there a moment, wondering what had just happened. Then she shook her head. It had to all be a coincidence.

Chapter Eleven

The next day, they stood at the blackened farm they had passed on their way in. The sun just over the horizon, many of the men were hanging back by their horses, the activities from the night before still keeping their eyes droopy. A high-ranking lord was at Philippe's side, explaining what was known about the attack. Alex kicked through the rubble as they talked.

"The owner of the farm said he saw three men on foot," the man said. He had a high brow and thick, swept back white hair. He was proud, but there was a layer of nervousness just below the surface. "But it was dark, and he could tell no more."

"Three men could hardly burn a farm of this scale that fast," Philippe countered, bending to pick through the rubble. "There had to have been more." He trailed off. "No one had any ill will against the family?"

"Not that we know of."

"Did the family survive the attack?" Alex asked.

The lord turned to her. "Yes, *Mademoiselle*." He nodded. "They are safe. Destitute, but safe."

Alex strode away as the men talked, kicking a trail across the path. She pushed a fallen beam over with her foot, looking for any hint as to who these men were. She walked around the back of what had been the main house, tracing the tarry bones of a wooden fence until she came across a well with stones greased and blackened by the smoke. Alex swept some debris aside and her eyes darted over the earth she had uncovered. There, cooked into the dirt, were a series of footprints. She kicked back more of the rubble, unearthing the story of the night. She tallied the prints then let out a high-pitched whistle, calling the men.

"There were eight of them," she explained when Philippe and the lord were in range. She nodded towards the trail leading away. "The three the owner saw came out last. The rest were already back here with the horses."

Philippe came closer to inspect the trail. "That seems more likely." He squatted down and touched the earth. "Eight men. Eight horses. That means they have money." He sifted the dirt between his fingers, lost in thought. "Why would they attack a farmer?" he mused before standing up.

The question lingered as they finished their investigation. They left shortly thereafter. Their next stop, Lantosque, would be a day and a half journey through easy, albeit rocky, country. The road was well-known since many merchants and mercenaries traveled this strip of towns up the countryside. Heavily wooded mountains stood far to the west, bordering Provence, while the river grew wide in this region, spilling a thousand tributaries into the lowlands and making the terrain lush and cool, a treat for the horses. As they rode, the men traded theories about their targets. Privileged French youths out to make trouble; Puritan zealots frustrated with slackening morals after the war; revolutionaries who thought they would make better nobles than the current ones—it was still too soon to tell.

As night approached, they stopped to camp in a small clearing filled with blue chicory flowers and surrounded by elms. The men threw out their bedrolls while the camp porter tended to the food and drink. Alex took a few steps away to wash up in a nearby stream. She scanned the area and began pulling young saplings down into knots. She'd become proficient at setting traps over the years and had a method of positioning a set of noisy whip-traps to alert her if anyone tried to sneak up on her in the night. She bent another young branch to secure it and plucked a leaf of wild mint from a bush. She put it in her mouth and chewed as she worked. If tripped, the snares wouldn't do much more than wake her up, but they had saved her butt a few times and always helped to make her feel a little safer.

Once she felt good about doing what she could to secure the area, she reentered the camp. She was surprised to see that the camp looked as though it had been set up hours ago. The horses were tied off and nibbling at thick stalks of grass, the fire was blazing with a cauldron of soup steaming over it, and the men were sitting around the fire or on their nearby bedrolls. Alex was impressed. Soon the porter whistled for dinner, and she grabbed a bowl. Then she sat on a nearby log and watched her travel companions as she ate, her feet stretched out in front of her.

Alex had traveled with many different parties of men before, but she'd felt a quick camaraderie with this group that she wasn't used to. Maybe because she didn't have to do the usual convincing that she was capable or remind anyone that she had a sword to protect herself from any advances. Maybe it was simply that they were a friendly group who kept her entertained. Either way, she was growing to care for these scruffy rascals with whom she traveled, she thought, while she spied Henri across the camp as he accidentally dipped his long beard into his soup.

As the rest settled down with their food, Bernard and Luc began singing a song about a bawdy lady who was missing a leg— "She'll wrap one leg around you. With the other, confound you! That's the way of the lioness whore..."

"It's '*Lyonnaise*' whore," Maurice hollered at them, laughing. He rose to take another helping from the cauldron over the fire. "She's from *Lyon*. She's not a three-legged lion, you idiots."

Claude looked up from his bowl. "I've been singing it wrong my whole life."

Maurice sat next to Claude and slapped him on the back. "Stick with me, kid. I know all kinds of dirty songs I can teach you. Correctly." He laughed again, and together, the men started the song from the top.

Philippe seemed to be paying little attention to the rest of the group and was instead busy checking supplies and preparing for the next days' journey. Alex let her eyes and attention follow him and wondered again what he hoped to gain from this mission. Despite his competency as their leader so far, she feared the spoiled boy would come out again. Part of her was afraid to put too much trust in him. She feared their mission would fail if Philippe couldn't handle the responsibility. She watched him at the center of camp as he took a bowl of soup for himself. Then he looked her way. She worried for a moment he would spend the whole night staring at her again, but this time, he came across the camp to sit right next to her. Alex tensed at the sudden closeness.

"How is your horse holding up?" he asked as he sat.

"Very well," she answered, eyeing him. She was still unsure if she could relax around him, but if he were to continue to offer peace, she would continue to accept. "He is used to these trails."

"We will need to look at the maps tomorrow evening to plan out which route we will take north of Aliette."

"I have been consulting with Henri. He has more knowledge of the area than I gave him credit," Alex said. "We believe we have a good plan for getting there safely."

"Do you have everything you need?" he asked. "Are you comfortable traveling with us?"

"I am used to much worse," she admitted with a small smile. Since he seemed intent on conversing with her, she decided to just ask the question on her mind. "*Excusez-moi, Monsieur,* but I would request that you clear something up for me," she said, glancing toward him.

"Of course," he replied.

"I understand why these men choose to participate in this mission," she said, nodding out towards the camp. "They are very loyal to your father, and he is paying them well. But you have a title in your home. You could be sitting in a bathtub full of cherries with willing maids tending your every desire."

He leaned towards her with a smirk, throwing a gentle shoulder at her side, "How do you think I spent my summer?"

She turned sharply to him.

Philippe laughed and looked at her incredulously. "Do you really think so little of me?"

She felt herself blush, embarrassed he had gotten her with his teasing. "No. I just," she stammered. "I wondered why..."

"I am privileged, I know," he said, turning serious. "But it is my duty." He shifted his weight. "And there are few men I would trust to protect our people in my stead."

Alex looked down at her hands. It would be so much easier if she could just hate him.

Philippe took a few bites of his soup. Alex sat in silence, not knowing what to say. But then he spoke.

"Do you remember the competition? Years ago?" he prodded.

"*The* competition?" she choked, surprised at the turn in conversation. "The one I was in?"

He nodded. "You know I lost, right? *After* I came to," he said. "Didn't even make it through my second fight." He shook his head with a chuckle. Then he glanced towards her, his eyes a little more serious. "You shook me up pretty bad."

A rush of guilt and regret ran through her as she looked at him. There was a lot she could say, that she *should* say. But in the end, all she could get out was, "Good." A grin now touched her lips as she realized, somehow, they had lightened the past. Just a bit.

He laughed, a loud, sudden sound. "Alright, alright, fair enough," he said, his laughter settling into a soft smile.

She couldn't be sure, but she thought she saw a flash of affection shine across his face, but she chose to ignore it. It would do her no good to start thinking those thoughts again, especially just as they were beginning to get along. Alex rose and dusted off her pants. "Now, if it does not offend, My Lord, I should like to take my leave to rest."

"It does not offend, but if you don't start calling me Philippe, I could still have you sentenced for insubordination."

She smiled to herself, feeling warmth and contentment from his attention. "Philippe," she conceded. She owed him that much. "*Bonne Nuit.*"

With that she walked to her bedroll, checked her supplies and weapons, and tied one last branch near her position. She noticed Philippe giving her a perplexed look as she did. She then laid down and folded her arms across her chest. She squeezed her eyes shut, trying to bring on sleep, but more importantly, trying to banish the thoughts of the man who she had left sitting on that log, not more than ten feet away, as the rest of the men continued to sing about the lady from Lyon around her.

Chapter Twelve

Over the next week, they traveled northward, back and forth, in what seemed to be the pattern of the marauders. Philippe was pushing them at a quick clip now, and for the last two nights, he moved them through the towns just long enough to investigate, then marched them well into the night before allowing everyone to settle down to camp. He was impatient. Ponce was their final destination and only a two-day hard ride from Chevalerie, but their journey was lengthened by the need to visit each victimized town on the way up there. He was finding that there was no great difference, however, or any good clues anywhere they stopped. The story had been the same in each town: farms had been attacked just outside town walls, destroying an innocent family's livelihood in the process. Hoofprints and tracks indicated they were the same attackers, though witnesses always reported seeing fewer than there actually were. It seemed as though whoever was doing this was trying to make it look like they had fewer resources than they did.

Loss of property was not the only way the towns were affected. He saw it in their eyes, though they tried to put on a brave face when he questioned them. The lords, magistrates, and other town leaders were fearful. They couldn't protect their people from these unknown attackers, and they had not yet gotten relief from the Duke. Provence was a region of honored and independent lords, each fiercely protective of their territory, and though they worked well together under the Duke, very few would admit distress. The charred frames of former homes at the edges of their towns spoke loudly: the region was under attack. No one knew who would be struck next.

In the last town they visited, a little hub that caught the traffic between Lyon, Geneva, and Chevalerie, the scene had been the most jarring. This farmhouse was still smoldering, having just been attacked the night before. The townsmen had been fast with water. They saved the barn and the back of the main house, but the family was missing their youngest son. It was Laurent who had found him. Philippe's party had entered a smoke-soaked bedroom, and as Laurent kicked the bed in disgust, the blackened body of a child tumbled onto the floor. Philippe heard the men gag behind him, his own stomach heaving with revulsion.

Helplessness and rage pulsed through him as he had to inform the huddled family that the child had not escaped. He bowed his head, knowing this was his fault. The family would never be whole again because he was too slow to unravel the puzzle. It consumed him. He was used to fighting men he could identify and overthrow either with his own sword or with the army behind him. This game of chase in which he was engaged was almost too much, and it was all he could do to hold back and move thoughtfully through the countryside. He wanted to charge, to attack. But he restrained himself, lest he cause the rebels to disperse prematurely. Gathering intelligence was for his oldest brother or his father. Philippe was a man of action and wanted his victory before anyone else was harmed.

There was a bright spot in this mission for Philippe, despite his frustration. That funny little creature was still at the back of his procession, quiet and reserved, setting traps wherever they stopped. His distance seemed to be what she wanted, and it was the only way he could think to make amends for his embarrassing behavior in Chevalerie. From afar, though, he couldn't deny that she made him smile. Every so often he'd catch her eye and think for a moment that she'd softened towards him, and he'd feel elation well up in his chest. But then she would turn away, uninterested, leaving him unsettled and confused. Why did he respond so foolishly towards her? He wanted her to like him; that was true. He wanted to prove that he was not such a bad guy. He sensed that it would take time, but even that upset him. What if they completed this mission, and she went on disliking him? Philippe lived a life of assuredness and absolutes. There were too many unanswered questions in his brain at the moment. Simply put, he was going nuts.

He had ridden his horse away from his men, through a low woodland area filled with waxy jasmine shrubs and violet harebells hanging from their stalks. He needed to clear his mind of any thoughts of the little fox and rethink his plan. He hadn't thought they would get so far with no hard evidence. He didn't know from where the rebels originated. He didn't know from whom they took orders. All he knew was that their numbers were small, and their hearts seemed cold.

His mind was going in circles. What had they missed? Someone had to have seen something beyond shadowy figures in the night. These were men, not spirits, escaping through the trees. In the distance, he spotted a small farmhouse with a curl of smoke rising out of the chimney. It was far out of town, and though it would be an easy target, Philippe guessed it might have been spared just because it would not have been noticed. Still, something in his gut told him to knock on the door and see if the owner had anything interesting to tell him.

Chapter Thirteen

The party had been moving at a steady pace through a shaded area and into the late morning sun. Their next destination, a small town in a stretch of flatlands, was still a half day away, and Alex was passing the time by daydreaming about a good meal and a comfortable bed. The mood of the party had changed from adventuresome to dreary. The men were disheartened by the lack of progress and the grisly scenes they had discovered, not to mention the aggressive pace of their leader. It seemed that the initial comforts of their travel party were already wearing thin, and everyone's hopes for a quick and easy payday had been dashed. The men needed to drink. And they needed women.

Staying in town that night would be a welcome rest for them all, including Alex. She'd come to expect a room all to herself when they were at an inn, and she was eager to eat something hot in the tavern. Then she thought that tonight might be the night Philippe would take a woman, and it soured her fantasizing. She knew it was coming, but still, after several nights in different taverns, he always went to bed alone. He'd hang around just until she went to her room each night. She hadn't figured out his intentions, but sooner or later, the tolls of the mission would push him into bed with someone. Despite her resolve not to be affected by it, she knew it was going to upset her when it happened.

At the moment, the group was stretched out over a long road. She did not see Philippe at the front, but he often left the procession to scout. The warm sun made her feel lazy, and she let her body sway to the steps of her horse. Suddenly, the *thump-thump-thump* of horse gallop brought her around. Philippe was cutting across the valley, coming right at her. She adjusted her posture, waiting to be addressed.

"Alex," he called, his face set in thought. He pulled the reins of his horse and slowed to her pace. "Do you know the *Sable Noir* Forest through here?"

"Yes," she replied, unsure of why he was asking, but she could see he was intent on some new suspicion.

"I'd like you to take me through it."

"What do you aim to find?"

"I visited that farmhouse a mile back and the proprietor said there was smoke from a campfire at the center of it not two days ago. I should like to see if there is anything left."

"The forest is impossibly thick. We can't go in altogether like this. In fact, it is much easier on foot."

"I only intend that you and I go. I just want to find that campsite. You're the guide. Guide me."

"Indeed," she replied, focusing on the mission and calling upon the knowledge she had of the area. "It is cut by a narrow river. If they had a camp, it's probably along the banks."

They made quick preparations. It was barely noon, but they would have to hurry if they were to follow this tangent and still make it to town before nightfall. The forest was small but very dense with uneven terrain. It was roughly a mile into the heart of it, but it would not be easy going. The rest of the group continued on schedule to the town with Laurent at the lead while Alex and Philippe departed.

Philippe led her back through the valley and to the edge of the forest, where trees suddenly knitted themselves together like a blanket. There, they tied their horses off by a creek with plenty of young grass to occupy the steeds and took what they needed in their rucksacks.

"Are you ready, *Monsieur*?" Alex asked, gesturing to the dense forest before them. "This will not be so clean as we have traveled thusly."

"Are you saying I don't know how to get dirty, *Mademoiselle*?"

She teased. "I am saying you are a lord, My Lord."

Philippe waved her off with a chuckle and entered the wrap of trees.

They walked in silence, adjusting to the thickness of the woods. There had been a great wildfire in this region twenty years before. It wiped out much of the verdure, but the fertile land sprang forth five trees where there had been only one before. It created a netting of saplings and young pliable branches amongst the massive dead trunks, whose black flesh fed a myriad of new plants; themselves becoming pillars of green life that supported a vast canopy above them. The scrub on the ground was just as thick and tangled. Their boots crunched as they climbed over fallen stumps and flowering shrubs. Alex stayed at the lead, pausing occasionally to adjust their path. If she brought them true West, they should reach the water quickly. Then they could follow the river until they found the camp.

"I feel very conflicted at the moment," said Philippe as they stepped over a steep rock formation.

"Why is that?" she asked over her shoulder.

"I am watching you carry that heavy pack. If you were a normal woman, I would ask to carry it for you. But I think you will perhaps hit me again if I suggest you aren't capable."

Alex gave a quick laugh. "So do you dare ask me to take my pack or not?"

"*Aye*, unfortunately my training as a gentleman supersedes my desire not to have you split my lip again." He put on his most debonair voice. "May I carry that pack for you, *Mademoiselle*?"

Alex slung the bundle off her shoulder and tossed it at him. "I won't turn down the offer. Not from a gentleman," she said, amused by his display. She unsheathed her blade to cut a wider path to make the going a little easier on them. "You're funny, Philippe," she observed after a moment.

"I'm actually quite charming," he said. "Not that you really ever got to see that side of me."

"Oh, I have seen it," she said with a smirk. She glanced back at him over her shoulder, enjoying the conversation.

"I believe," he continued. "If you were a man, we would have been great friends."

"We used to be friends. When I first arrived in Chevalerie," she pointed out. "I wasn't a man then."

"No." He laughed. "You weren't." He paused, then his words softened. "What do you say, Alex? Have I earned your forgiveness?"

She wedged her boot between two rocks in order to get up a ledge and looked back at him. He was smiling at her, but then his face changed, and she caught a glimpse of how badly he wanted to be forgiven. Seeing for a second that he wanted something she could give him, she was seized with a desperate desire to give him anything he could ask for. But she also knew how easy it was for him to divert his attention away from her, and it stung more than a little that what she had to offer would never be enough. Still, there was no reason not to grant him her forgiveness at this point. He'd treated her well on this journey. And every day she spent near him, she grew to like and respect him more. "Alright, I forgive you," she said. She hoisted herself over the rocky ledge and glanced back at him.

She saw him smile as he looked down to navigate the rocks.

She continued forward. She could have dropped it. Part of her wished to pretend that she had no fault. But she didn't deserve to take his apology and tuck it away without bearing her own burden. "Philippe?"

"Yeah?" he replied, coming up over the rocks. He rubbed his hands together and stood before her, waiting for her to continue.

Why was it still so hard to look at him? "I'm sorry," she said once she could meet his eyes. "For challenging you like I did. I shouldn't have put everything on display like that. In front of everyone." She whacked at a branch with her sword. "It wasn't fair."

He watched her for a long moment. She couldn't read his expression. Alex began to worry that he was going to unleash all the bad things he ever must have thought about her, after she humiliated him and his family. But when he finally responded, all he said was, "Thanks, Alex."

She nodded and turned back onto the path. She cut at a low-hanging shrub and attempted to be playful once more. "So if you like," she said over her shoulder. "You may call me friend again."

"Okay. Friends," she heard him repeat, with a laugh, once she had turned away.

They continued in silence from that point. Alex cut the path and Philippe followed close behind her. They communicated effectively with just their bodies, and she began anticipating the easiest paths for him to follow. As they came upon the river, the knots of trees slackened, relieving the need for such choreographed movement. "There," she said, pointing to a pocket of brush that had been squashed into the water. "They traveled along here." She bent down to the stream to dip her hands in. She brought cool water to her face. "How long ago did you say the farmer saw the fire?"

"Early yesterday morning."

"Should be easy to find from here."

She led them across the river and up a tributary that fed into the main pour. Alex focused on the story told by the terrain. They'd crossed the water here. They stopped and shared a drink there. They were big. And clumsy. Not the svelte fighters of the south. They didn't think anyone would look for them this deep in the woods.

They continued for another half mile, when she spotted what they had set out to find. "Look," she said, pointing to a small clearing with a firepit at the center. She felt a prickle of adrenaline run up her back. Philippe moved in front of her as they crept in. Upon coming closer, she realized that the campsite was not abandoned. Supplies were still laid out and ready for use. Philippe held his arm out to keep her back. When he was satisfied that it was unoccupied, he waved her over. "They could return at any moment," he said to her, holding his finger up to his lips.

Warning bells went off in her head. Alex was aware that the situation could become very dangerous very quickly and she took every step with care as she skirted the camp. Finding information on these foes was critical, but there were more of them than she and Philippe could handle. Philippe was less cautious, using his boot to kick over a rucksack and nudge through its contents. She noted that he probably never had to move with much caution, whereas for Alex, caution was what kept her alive. If she were alone, she would have gotten far away from here. But she wouldn't impede Philippe's search, so she countered her fear with her practicality. She looked around for a sapling and worked it into a quick knot, enough to give someone trouble if he came too close. Then she wrapped another and another.

As she worked, she spied the hilt of a pistol tucked into someone's bag. She stepped towards the pack and pulled it from its cover. As she did, she spilled a box of black powder into the dirt. She hadn't seen many pistols.

They were usually confined to military operations. The ones she had seen were owned by noblemen. She held the pistol in her hands, perplexed.

Philippe came over to her. "What did you find?"

"They're carrying pistols," she said.

"That makes no sense." He bent to run his fingers through the blackened dirt. "Why would they be pillaging for trifles if they can afford pistols?"

A sudden string of voices coming from the trees at the other side of the camp clipped their speculating. Philippe grabbed Alex by the arm to pull her back away from the clearing. In a panic, she realized she still held the pistol and tossed it back towards the bag from where she had plucked it. Philippe moved fast and she was barely able to get her footing before they went over a tangle of branches and down a slope. He looked around and indicated that she duck into the small cavity created between the two fallen trees. Her instinct was to run. There was a ravine not far away, but she didn't know how many men were coming or how skilled they were at tracking. Besides, the look on Philippe's face meant he was not to be questioned, so she crouched down and reclined into the recess. Philippe slid next to her. They were side by side, angled towards each other, with just enough room to be concealed. Philippe situated a fallen branch to hide them.

There were six, seven, *eight* men, she heard, rasping in a dialect of the north. She didn't understand everything they said, but among their grunts and shouts was the tail end of a conversation about Philippe's party, who they had been observing move from town to town. As the men rattled on, she hoped the disturbances she and Philippe had made in the camp would go unnoticed, but shortly thereafter, someone balked. His pistol had been tossed into the dirt and he was busy accusing the others of trying to steal it. Then another shouted that his things had been disturbed too, and suddenly there was silence. Alex looked up to Philippe as he clenched his jaw. "Just don't move," he mouthed.

She heard the zing of metal blades coming out of sheathes as boots skidded down the slope behind them. Alex smelled the dust from the dirt as they came closer. She squeezed her eyes shut, preparing herself to fight. Once, when she was new to this life, she had been chased by a group of men and she ended up hiding under the floorboards of a well house. They'd given up and left the area not long after, but it was three days before Alex could bring herself to leave. The fear of being captured had paralyzed her. And that same fear had the potential to come back to her anytime she found herself outnumbered. She could take two, maybe three, but not more, surely not more than that. She breathed through her nose, trying to calm herself, as she ran through moves and techniques she could use to protect herself. She never dared to think about what could happen to a woman on her own like she was, but in these moments, when she was immobilized, it was hard not to think of what could become of her. Despite her best efforts, she felt her body begin to shake.

She realized, this time, she wasn't alone as she felt his arms wrap around her. She closed her eyes and rested her head against his shoulder, taking the moment to snatch this small chance at comfort. She would hate for him to think of her as weak or scared. Part of her was embarrassed and would have pushed him off, but his gesture was kind. And in that moment, she needed the relief. Her tremors began to subside.

Outside the men crushed through the brush and dirt around them. She heard them move out and then near the hovel where they hid. Philippe's hand went to his sword as they waited to be uncovered. Alex braced herself to attack.

Suddenly, a loud crack rang through the forest, snapping Alex to alertness. She and Philippe looked at each other, wide-eyed. Her snare!

She heard as the men scrambled back toward their camp. "We have to move. Now," whispered Philippe as the rebels behind them shouted confused accusations at each other.

"There's a ravine. Due East." Alex said. "Ten minutes and some luck."

He nodded, his eyes intent and focused on her. "I'll follow you."

They slipped out from the hiding spot. With Alex in the lead, they moved forward, darting between areas of cover. The shouts and clangs rang out behind them as the rebels spread out looking for the intruders. For a moment Alex felt their pursuit, but by their sounds and noises she could tell they had no focus or direction. She and Philippe kept moving until they finally came to the ravine. Philippe skidded to the edge and lowered himself down to the first ledge. He held out his hand to Alex and she scooted down alongside him. They continued the twenty feet of descent and then rested, out of breath.

"Do you hear them?" Alex whispered, still cautious.

"Not anymore," he responded.

"They didn't seem all that bright."

"They're not revolutionaries," he said. "They're mercenaries."

"How do you know?"

"They speak an uneducated dialect. They're poor, yet they have expensive weapons. Someone hired them."

"You think someone hired them to attack the villages?" she asked.

"Yep," Philippe said, his eyes fixed towards the north. "Now we have to figure out who."

After another hour of quiet and careful movement, they circled back and found their horses. It was nearly dusk by then and with great relief they greeted and mounted the beasts, their weary bodies eager to be carried for a while. They trotted through the sparse trees that lead to the valley and hit a full gallop once they reached the flat earth. Alex was wiped out, and she still felt the effects of the adrenaline ticking through her body. She watched him as he rode in front of her. Always determined, always moving forward. She envied him having that kind of direction. She appreciated the compassion he had shown her. Maybe he wouldn't be such a bad friend to have after all, she thought, as she urged her horse forward.

Chapter Fourteen

The following morning, as the crew prepared for the day's journey, a message from the Duke came from Chevalerie. Riders had traveled day and night to reach them. The poor boy who arrived with the parchment early in the morning, the last in the rally, collapsed off his horse once he handed the message to Philippe. It seemed another two farms and a mill had been torched near Aliette, a town they had not yet reached. The Duke was furious that these men were still at large. He wanted to know Philippe's progress. Had they identified their target? Had they any leads at all?

The letter spurred Philippe into action. He should have been up there by now. From the day they set foot out of Chevalerie, he should have charged up the countryside with hell's fury and chased the criminals into their rat holes. These latest attacks could have been prevented. Why did he go against his instinct?

He knew the answer. The plan had been laid out with his father before they had left, and he knew there was reason for it. Their indirect path was partly to give the rebels a sense of security that their hideout was unknown. Then they could more easily be trapped. If Philippe's objectives were discovered too soon, they would scatter, and he did not want to get into a chase across the open countryside. Still, he thought he had room to alter the course and told the men to prepare for a hard ride. They had planned to take a few days to get to the town of Aliette, stopping at several villages before moving into the cooler Alps region. Still, it seemed that the longer they traveled, the more danger the towns were in, and he would waste no more time getting to what seemed to be the epicenter of the attacks.

As they came into the *Canyon de Cuivre,* the gateway to what was considered the northern region of the Duke's territory, his company seemed to be in a better mood, despite the aggressive pace. The night before at the inn had raised their spirits, and the promise that they were getting closer to their target had perked them up as well. Philippe led the party through the canyon, shrubbed with bushy holly oaks, his mind all over the place. Finding that campsite the day before had been very informative. He wished he had brought someone else with him when he and Alex had gone into the *Sable Noir* Forest. Had he confronted the men with another sword, perhaps he would have taken a prisoner or two. But he just couldn't risk it with Alex at his side.

Alex.

Instead, he had pushed her into the hollow between two tangled trees and prayed that they wouldn't be discovered. He knew she was a competent swordsman, but there were too many of them. It had been foolhardy to enter the forest as he had. He never expected to come upon anyone; truthfully, he was using it as an excuse to get a little time alone with her. He had needed her to find the campsite, surely. But, also, he wanted her attention and the chance to be teased by her again. If nothing else, at least he'd won back her friendship. He laughed to himself remembering that unexpected sting when she called him a friend as they had moved through the woods. He'd never had a friend like her before.

He galloped at the head of the convoy. They had to move fast in order to reach Aliette by nightfall. He checked back over his shoulder. Laurent was good, his soldiers were strong. Alex and a few other camp maintainers kept pace in the back. He turned towards another slope bordered by trees and narrowed his eyes as the wind came up.

Thinking back to the forest, he knew that if it had been any other moment, he would have enjoyed being pressed against her. But there had been danger outside. He didn't know if he could fight at her side. Against her of course; he delighted in pushing her around and being pushed back, but he worried he would be all too distracted if she fought beside him. When he battled, though he had an awareness of his surroundings, the moment his sword was locked with an enemy had to be solitary. One man; one opponent.

Then, just before her trap had saved them, he had felt her shivering next to him. He realized that Alex was scared. All at once, he would have taken on an army for her. Instead, he did the only thing that made any sense in the moment, and he pulled her close. Then he felt her exhale against his shoulder, and he wondered why she would put herself through all this. Philippe knew that if he were ever captured by anyone other than the worst of barbarians, his father's title would protect him. But Alex? He shuddered to think about it. He vowed in that moment to never let it happen.

The sun traveled across the sky while the convoy made their trail. The trees began to thin as they came out of the canyon and hit an incline. The smooth dirt turned rockier, and the horses took their steps more carefully, slowing the convoy. Philippe decided to let the men take their lunch. They crammed bread and what cheese they had left into their mouths. Henri had been doing a fine job of charting their progress, considering much of this area was undocumented. Alex advised him to turn east to avoid the rockier part of the mountains, claiming they could cut across a valley, but they still would have a hard half-day ride left. As they sat in the sun, Philippe began composing a letter to his father. He didn't have anything substantial to say, though, so he put his writing utensils away as quickly as he'd gotten them out. He was antsy to go but wanted his men rested. He let them stretch out and close their eyes a moment longer before pushing them to mount up and continue the journey.

They arrived in Aliette several hours later, weary and hungry, just as the sun dipped below the mountains. The town was tucked amongst the emerald pines that collected snow in the winter and near a thrashing stream that never was thirsty for the cold mountain water. Off to the East, on the great jutting mountains that historically protected the borders of Provence from invasion, snow caps had already formed. But Aliette itself would enjoy a few more weeks of nice weather before the first storms began. The inn was near the town entrance. The building was squat but spacious with a domed roof and a large fire pit at the center of the great hall. The rooms held three to four, and the men were happy to have the space and the beds. As always, Philippe made sure Alex had a room to herself. He would have liked to share a room with her one night, but he scolded himself for the thought.

The men settled and gathered in the tavern. There was a particular fervor in the air that night. Tomorrow they would ride to Ponce, which would serve as their base as they explored the caves, and the real challenges would begin. But tonight, they had nothing to do but enjoy themselves. Once Philippe had his meal, he chose his seat with a line of sight to Alex. She seemed fine; his men were situated with girls and drink. For the moment, everything was calm. He suddenly felt a finger run down his neck. He turned to see a dark-haired woman soliciting his attention with a raised eyebrow and politely declined.

When he looked back to Alex, she was gone. *What the hell?* He scanned the room but couldn't find her. He looked down at his half-eaten meal, and realized his peaceful evening was over. He jumped up and was out the exit in a snap, still pulling his jacket on as he stumbled through the door. He peered down the dark street, looking both ways until he saw her figure at the far end of the road, just before she disappeared around the corner. He was relieved to see her but irritated she had snuck away. Where was she going? And *why* was she going alone?

The moon was a glowing pearl against a clear black sky. But even with the light, Alex was hard to track. Quiet as a moth, she almost disappeared in the night. He crouched and moved behind her, ducking into doorways and alleys every time she paused. For a moment, he thought to call out and simply ask what she was doing, but he didn't want to give her a chance to hide her motive. There had been too many challenges on this trip: his inability to target the attackers, his confusing feelings for her. He needed to accomplish something, and he wanted one of her secrets. So, he hunted.

Ahead, Alex slipped through the iron town gates and waded through a patch of tall grass before reaching the tree cover. She turned back once again to scan the path behind her. Philippe squatted behind a bale of hay. When he looked up, she had disappeared into the forest. He cursed himself as he ran the rest of the distance to the trees.

Once in the forest, he tracked her steps and followed her fox-like noises. He stayed silent, stayed low. His muscles burned. He breathed through his nose, wanting her scent. He wondered if she was trying to run away, but surely, she wouldn't go without supplies. Was she looking for clues? For danger? He didn't want to think of her running into a group of bandits on her own. Then another terrible thought entered his head. Perhaps she was meeting someone. Maybe she had a lover who lived out here. He felt his chest catch fire with jealousy, thinking about what made this man so special. He racked his brain for any backwoods gossip of men living alone deep in the forest in these parts. But there was nothing he could remember.

They toiled over an incline and were now coming down a slope. His muscles twitched with agitation. He knew his energy could give him away, ruining his chance to see what she was up to. Just then, he stepped on a foul branch. She turned and he thought for sure she had seen him. But after a moment of strained silence, she continued forward. He let his breath escape his lungs.

Off in the distance he heard the sounds of running water. It wasn't rushing, not a river or a stream. It was a gurgle, a bubble, like a kettle being poured. His brain worked on this as he continued to navigate the terrain. Then, all at once, it hit him. The hot springs. Alex was headed to the secluded hot springs of Aliette.

Up ahead, she finally stopped. Philippe could see the pools, silver and steamy against the light of the moon. Alex turned and peered into the woods, but he was too well hidden in the brush. Then, without hesitation, she dropped her shawl and her sword belt and began unlacing the corset that held her shirt against her body. He froze, realizing he could stay there and drink her image, and no one would ever know. His body reacted immediately; his heart jumped into his throat. He watched, mesmerized as she loosened the laces, imagining what lay just beneath the fabric.

Then, he tore his eyes away with tremendous effort and a will he didn't know he had. He couldn't do it; he couldn't watch her unaware. But turning around and leaving her alone wasn't the answer either. It was dangerous to be out this far, all by herself. What if she encountered a camp, or a rebel, or fell and twisted her ankle? He couldn't leave her. No, he really only had one choice.

He'd have to join her.

Without any more consideration, he flung himself through the brush. "What are you doing here?" he demanded with faux shock and outrage.

Alex jumped and grabbed her sword, but looking at him, realization flooded her face. "What are *you* doing here?"

"I asked you first," he said. He walked to the bank and stood across from her. He was elated to have succeeded in tracking her all the way out here. Now, having come this far, having caught her all alone, he felt his sinful side begging to be let out.

Alex had her sword out towards him. "Stay back," she warned.

"I'm not going to throw you in," he said, grinning. "You can release your blade."

She watched him as if she did not trust his image. "You followed me," she said, glaring. Then she dropped her sword to her side.

The large trees had receded near the edge of the water. Rock took the place of dirt. Smooth stones that had bathed in the springs for centuries housed the steaming pools, while larger rocks created divisions and cascades within them. Philippe folded his arms. "These are the Springs of Aliette. You can't think you are the only one who knows of their existence," he teased. He sat down on a boulder behind him and put his hands on his knees, waiting for her reply.

"No, of course not," she admitted, clearly flustered. "But I *am* one of the few people who knows how to find them."

"I am the son of the Duke," he said, enjoying the chance to taunt her. "Don't imply you know my territory so much better than me."

"Okay then," she said, pushing her hair back out of her face. "You found these springs all on your own. And arrived at the same moment as me."

"Strange," he said, still grinning.

"So what do you suppose we do?" She folded her arms in front of her, signaling that she wasn't quite ready to play like he was.

"What do you mean?" he asked innocently.

"We can't go in together," she balked, disbelief in her expression.

"Why not?" he countered. Then he reached down and began unlacing his boot.

"No. No. Nope." She put her hand out to halt his actions. "Do not take that off."

"Do you now claim to own the springs, *Mademoiselle*?" He pulled his boot off and tossed it to the side.

"You're right," she said, sarcasm clinging to her tone. "You are the lord, and you know everything and own everything. I shall leave." She dropped her sword into its sheath and began fastening it around her waist.

"Wait a second," he said. "There is no reason two *friends* can't go in the springs at the same time." He paused, looking at her with a raised eyebrow. "We are friends, right?"

"Yeah," she said dismissively, not looking up. She secured her belt and relaced the undone part of her corset.

"Then what is the problem?" he pressed, hoping to push her over the edge.

She rolled her eyes at him and cinched her waist.

"Stop," he said. He couldn't help laughing at her rush. "Hear me out. It is a beautiful evening. We both—independently—had this idea to go to the springs. We *are* friends, as you stated the other day, so why should one of us miss out on this lovely adventure for the pleasure of the other?" He stopped to gauge her reaction. She had stalled, holding the edges of the laces. She didn't look convinced. If he could just push it a little further... "Unless, of course," he began, "you fear you won't be able to control yourself when I strip down to my underclothes." He let that sizzle in the air.

She started in without hesitation. "I won't be able to control myself? Really? That's what you think?" She squared her shoulders and put her hands on her hips.

"I can't see any other reason," he said with a shrug. "If we are friends and nothing more, then there shouldn't be any problem."

She scoffed. "Alright then, *friend*," she said. She tipped her chin up to him. "You first."

He hadn't really expected that to work, but he wasn't going to wait for her to change her mind. He made quick work of his other boot, stockings, and the rest of the trappings he wore around him. Her arms were folded in front of her now, and she wore a half-amused, half-scornful look. She watched him with the pride of a king, daring him to become shy at this game.

But he had nothing to be shy about. He knew the effect his body had on women, and better yet, he knew how to exploit it. She was the one who had never played this game before, and he felt a shiver go across his skin at the idea of having her as a willing student once again. He reached back and yanked his shirt over his head, careful to expose each muscle as he let it drop from his arms. Her expression remained constant, and she stared at him without flinching, but her lips parted, and her breath quickened. He didn't want to push her too far. But he *did* want to push her.

He moved his hands to his pants and undid the clasp. He stared smugly at her, enjoying the slow breakdown of her façade. He was in control now. He looked at his hands deliberately, attempting to draw her eyes further down. It worked. And he saw she was now appraising the most intimate part of him. He moved his breeches down until he wore just the fitted fabric of his undergarment. He tossed his pants across the rocks. When he looked at her again, she was staring back with stormy eyes. Then, with nerve that belied her sex, she ran her eyes down his bare body and up again. He stood before her, feeling his power over her, not wanting to stop teasing her. He put both thumbs behind the tie of the last material that covered him and began to push it down...

"Wait," she croaked, her voice broken and weak. She cleared her throat and held up her hand. "That's plenty."

He laughed and removed his thumbs, holding his hands up in surrender. She was right. He'd already crossed the line he had promised he wouldn't, but he felt drugged watching her in the steamy clearing. Why had he been trying so hard to mask his attraction? He could hardly remember. He could only think that the second part of this game was still to come. He folded his solid arms across his chest, proud and tall. "Well then," he said. "It's your turn, *amie*." His voice rumbled with the challenge.

Alex cleared her throat, took a deep breath and blew it out like a kiss. She unlatched her sword belt and placed it on the rocky ledge behind her. She followed the same pattern he had shown her, taking a moment to undo her boots and remove her stockings. She did it all while watching him. Those big, innocent eyes were wide and filled with moonlight. His breath caught as he suddenly realized he was standing in only an undergarment with nothing to hide him if he couldn't control his body's reaction to her form. He reminded himself that he wasn't thirteen and the mere sight of a woman wasn't enough to make him crumble. But then she unlaced the corset that held her shirt close to her body, and the fabric billowed around her in waves. He felt the urge to reach under it and discover the feel of her against his hands. Before he could linger on the thought, she pulled the shirt over her head, leaving only the thin, clinging chemise to cover her, and then there wasn't a single, rational thought in his head.

His control, where had it gone? He felt his whole body change. A throbbing beat out of his chest and radiated through his limbs. His own breath quickened. His muscles tensed and the smile he'd worn a second ago dropped from his face. His arms fell to his sides, and his hands pulsed open and closed with each breath, searching in vain for a phantom connection to her. He was no longer a lord. He was nothing more than a dumb beast.

She seemed to sense this change in him, and now it seemed to be her turn to tease him. She bit her lip through a smile and drew a finger down between her breasts, letting her head fall back and mouth fall open as she did. She undid the tie of her pants as she looked at him with those dark eyes, now not so innocent. She knew what she was doing. She had known all along, he thought, feeling foolish but absolutely aroused at the same time. Her hands slipped over her hips, past undergarments similar to his but far more revealing, exposing her bare legs to him inch by devilish inch. Her smile was sweet—*no*, he thought, *inviting*—and in that instant, he knew that she had won. She had won the game and he couldn't even remember how it began. Standing there, in the last shred of fabric that kept him from knowing her fully, she was a melody that made him ache. Her body was strong but also remarkably delicate as the stars shimmered above her. He would have done anything to explore her soft skin with his fingertips, his lips, his tongue.

He stood rooted to the ground, unable to look away, unable to speak. The truth was, she had wrecked him. He had no power, he had no control, only a deep well of desire. Alex held her posture, more coquettish and playful than he had ever seen her before. Then she turned and glided over to the water.

She slid into the pool, and he watched her curves disappear into the water. Then she turned back, looking at him from over her shoulder, her hair just touching the lip of water, her form outlined blue in the starlight. "What are you waiting for, *camarade*?" she teased.

He tried to speak but couldn't. No words came to his lips and even if he had a thought, he didn't think his tongue could get it out. So instead, he took a few steps towards her in a daze. His feet were heavy and his balance was off. When he stepped into the water he misjudged the depth, tripped, and with a great splash, he tumbled into the pool.

When he came back up, he shook the hair and water out of his face and heard something that shot a spark of happiness through him.

Alex was laughing.

The music of her laugh brought him back to his body, and he smiled at her. He flushed in the hot water, unsure if it was his want causing it to bubble with heat. But perhaps the warmth came from her voice or the flood of relief that broke inside him once he realized he'd given her a reason to smile. He looked down at the water, momentarily overwhelmed by the wish that he hadn't behaved so badly in the past. His eyes couldn't stay idle for long, though. The trails of her hair reached out into the water, and he found himself following them back to her body. The chemise did little in the way of modesty, and he saw the swell of her breast just hidden by her long hair. She dipped herself deeper into the pool and then rose again, the water slick and glistening against her skin. Despite his best intentions, he was enthralled and couldn't help moving towards her.

"I should have liked to have this pool to myself," she said with a purr, a smile still on her lips. "It seems too small for two."

Her teasing allowed him to find his words again. "When in truth it is far too big," he drawled, his voice deep in his throat. He pursued her, moving closer as she inched back around the edge of the spring. He had tried so hard to manage his desire for her. He had promised to keep things professional during this trip; God knew how many times his attraction for this woman had turned so terribly wrong, but it was so deep-seated in him by now that he could no longer fight it.

Alex stretched her arms out in front of her. "You stay back," she said, that smile still in her eyes.

"I shall try," he said. "But you have left your sword on the bank, so you have no means by which to protect yourself."

"Well, *Monsieur*," she purred again, "I am much better at grappling than I used to be."

He groaned and fell back into the water, the words having knocked him clean over. "Now you are just teasing me," he said when he emerged.

"I am sorry," she said coyly, "but I don't know what you mean."

"You are not so naïve that you don't know what you are saying." She smiled at that and continued slipping through the warm water. He was helpless to resist the pull and he continued his slow pursuit of her. "In fact," he continued. "You are far too alluring to be so innocent."

Her eyes opened wide as his comment put a blush in her cheeks. She looked down and drew a circle in the water. "You still don't believe my innocence?" She asked, looking back at him, her eyes glimmering with playfulness once more.

"I do. But I don't understand it." He paused. "May I ask you a question?" he said.

"Aye," she replied.

"There is something I wonder about you."

"Aye," she repeated.

"You shun the traditions of womanhood, but why have you not shunned..." he hesitated. "All of them?"

She looked at him quietly. "You mean to ask why I have not taken a lover?"

"Well, you have taken on the life of a man. But none of the fun."

"Ah," she said, tucking her chin down to her chest and looking up at him blithely. "It is very fun to take a man down with my sword."

He moved around her, still searching for a way to get closer. "Answer my question," he pressed.

"I will," she said, his boldness seeming to shake her. "But then you will answer one for me?"

"I agree," he said and took the liberty to run his eyes over her body once more.

She dipped again into the water, a slick stream licking her skin and changing the pattern of her hair across her breasts. "Well, *My Lord*," she began. She was sarcastic at first, but then her face changed. She looked away, and when she looked back to him, her eyes were full of inexperience, and it was the first time he had seen this face on her since she was young. It roused intense feelings inside of him.

"Philippe," she corrected herself, using a smile to hide her nerves and giving him the rare gift of his name. "I don't trust myself," she said. She lowered her gaze. "I am weak. I fear I would get attached. To someone who isn't as attached to me." She brought her hands up to follow the ripples in the water. "And besides, it could never be what I hope for."

"What do you hope for?"

"I don't know," she murmured. "To feel special, I suppose."

He said nothing for a moment, her words having struck him deeply. He wanted to take her in his arms, to hold her body close in the hot water, but he feared she would run like a wild animal if he tried. Instead, he spoke softly, earnestly. "Alex." He made sure to look deep into her eyes and hold her gaze. He wanted her to know he was sincere. "You are special. Don't you know?"

She broke his eye contact. "I am strange," she said with a smile before letting it fade from her lips as she spoke her next words. "It is not the same thing."

He watched her, still pressing closer, unable to stop. "A man would be lucky to have you," he said.

She laughed away his words. "You are being kind," she replied. "But now it is my turn to ask a question."

Why didn't she believe him, he wondered. Did he not seem sincere? He wanted to press further but instead acquiesced, still afraid of pushing her too far. "Alright," he said finally.

With his assent, her brashness returned. "Why," she began with a teasing smile, "do you wait for me to go to bed each night in the towns? Do you fear I will run off with your horse?"

He stared at her for a long moment. "I thought it was obvious," he said, looking into her eyes as bright as the stars. "I want you to see that I go to bed alone."

She had come to the end of the pool by then, and they both stopped moving. The air around them was swollen and thick with moisture. Her hair glistened, her skin shimmered. Philippe watched her chest rise and her lips come apart. He ached with want. It hurt how badly he wanted to touch her. But his desire was far beyond physical. He wanted to kiss her, to wrap her legs around his waist, to be inside her, but more so he wanted to confess he felt things for her that he couldn't describe. He didn't know what was happening between them. He only knew he didn't want it to end.

When he could fight it no longer, he moved to make some kind of contact. He edged closer to her, desperate to touch her. She was cornered now and couldn't back away any further.

As if by reflex, her hand shot out, and she pressed the tips of her fingers against his chest to stop him. They looked at each other for a long moment, and he felt his breathing deep and heavy. His heart thumped arrhythmically in his chest.

"Stay there," she said, her voice soft but persistent, like the mist on the water.

He didn't move closer, but nor did he back away. Instead, he grabbed her hand and pulled it tight against his chest, against his pounding heart. "Alex," he whispered. He wanted to say everything he felt but could think of no words that would be right. Instead, he brought her hand up and touched her fingers to his lips. "I shall do anything you ask of me."

The water grew too warm, and soon, they decided it was time to leave. They dressed quickly, enough words having already been said. It was a pleasant walk, though the moisture on their skin and cool evening air urged them not to linger. Some great wall had been broken, and there was an ease between them that hadn't existed in a very long time.

As they approached the town and slipped through the streets once again, they spoke for the first time of their childhood, of the days when Alex chased Philippe through the gardens of Chevalerie. Soon they were on the doorstep of the inn, and it was time to end the night. The next day would take them to their final destination and require their wits to be intact. They passed through the tavern, unnoticed by the men loudly engaged one way or another and stood before the hallway that led one way to Philippe's room and the other way to Alex's. Philippe faced her.

"Well, goodnight," he said. Suddenly, he leaned in and gave her a quick kiss on the cheek before she could protest. Then he turned and disappeared into his room.

Alex stood in the hall alone, looking after him, her hand to the spot where he had kissed her. Her body was still damp and her clothes were heavy with moisture, but her heart was light. She smiled a private smile, still stroking her cheek. She turned to her room, her heart content. For the first time in many years, she could not think of one thing wrong with that man.

Chapter Fifteen

They set out to Ponce before the sun was up. The ride was furious as Philippe wanted to get there with daylight enough to see the positions of the outlying farms that had been attacked. They traveled a well-established road, everyone at the ready in case they came across the rebels. But Alex was sure they were in hiding now. The rebels wouldn't be so carefully covert just to force a confrontation on the road now.

When they arrived in Ponce, with the sun just starting to move back down towards the horizon, Alex was struck by how quaint the town was. She'd spent little time in Ponce, her travels always leading her around or quickly through the town, but it had a picturesque charm to it. Like Aliette, it was built for hard winters, but lavender and white poppies hung in pots on every shop window making even these unpredictable days seem cheerful. It was a larger town than most and it served as a trade post with many of the northern cities. Ponce was headed by a Marquis who had fought beside the Duke many years ago. Together, the Marquis in the North and the Duke in the South typically kept tight control of the region.

The group traveled through the smooth-stoned streets, a happy bit of comfort for the horses no doubt, and past an ornate clock tower at the center of the city. It was at least twenty feet high and made of a vivid blue-grey granite typical to the region. As they approached, the clock struck the hour, filling the air with chiming bells.

The square was bustling with trade and several merchants offered Alex their wares as the party passed. Trade seemed good, but Alex noticed several empty stalls and some of the permanent shops had their windows boarded up. The main part of the town had indeed been protected from the rogue rebel attacks, probably at the vigilance of the Marquis and his guards, but the farms had proven vulnerable and the effects were seeping through the town walls. In fact, it was likely the rebels traded here and used the very city as their base.

Coming upon the tavern at the far end of the square, the men had a moment to rest and tend their horses, but as there was still daylight, they had work to do. Maurice and Daniel stayed near to help arrange lodging. Auguste and Sébastien went with Philippe to meet with town officials and tour the victimized farms, while Laurent took the brothers, Luc and Bernard, to speak with the captain of the guards. Henri was tasked with drawing up corrections to the maps for areas they had passed. The rest of the party were sent to replenish supplies. Alex alone hung back, having not been given a task, with nothing much to do.

At first, she was irritated that she had not been given a duty, but her moment would come the following day when they entered the caves. The plan was to map and track the series of caves at the base of *Mont Verte*. With any luck, they could isolate these men before they knew their hiding spot was compromised. If Philippe's crew wasn't lucky, they would have to flush the men out and hunt them. From what Alex knew, there were three entry points to the cave system. None were far and they each could be reached in less than half a day coming directly from Ponce. On the inside though, the trails split out like an ant hill, going in a myriad of directions. How quickly they cornered the rebels and how easily they were taken down would be based on how successfully they navigated the complex system of caves.

But that was tomorrow. For now, she headed to the tavern and dug in her bag for her old, tattered copy of *Discours des Armes* that the Duchess had given her many years ago. She settled into a quiet corner and flipped through the familiar pages.

The tavern was a timbered building with high ceilings. There was one large fire pit at the center and two smaller ones at the edges of the room, but only the central one was burning. There were four heavy plank tables lined up two by two, and smaller tables against stone seating at the walls. The room itself was large and rectangular, with several open windows that allowed in plenty of light and a fresh breeze. Alex was tucked away with her knees up to her chest and her face in her book. There were few people in the tavern at this time, as the dinner hour was not yet upon them, but she could smell the beginnings of the stew for the night wafting out of the kitchen. The maid brought her a mug of cider and left her with a funny look. Alex was aware that she stuck out more during the day, but she shrugged it off.

Soon, she became engaged in a section about complicated swordplay between one rapier and two poleaxes to the point that she completely missed the figure standing before her. But her concentration was broken when she heard a voice she hadn't heard in years.

"Look who it is," a feminine voice trilled.

Alex looked up into the amused eyes of none other than Emily. Her childhood nemesis, Emily.

She was as beautiful as ever, but with a new maturity about her. Her hair was pulled back and she wore an elegant wine-colored gown, the cut suggesting her *Madame* status. Her blue eyes were just as crystal, her lips just as pouty as they had always been. She had grown but remained quite a vision to behold.

"Emily." Alex tried to hide her surprise, causally putting her book down and standing to offer a proper greeting. She instantly felt a fool in her breeches in front of such a splendid creature. For a moment, the two stared at each other, Alex unsure of how to act. Then, most unexpectedly, Emily broke into a huge smile and took Alex in a warm hug.

Alex, surprised by the embrace, patted Emily's back awkwardly. Emily broke the hug and stood back, still gripping Alex's arms. "Look at you," she said, looking Alex up and down with an approving gaze. "Simply amazing. I never would have guessed that you'd actually pursue a life on the road."

"I did," said Alex, a surprised smile on her lips. "What are you doing here, Emily?"

"I'm in the tavern to investigate who has come to my town. I am here in Ponce because the Marquis du Ponce took me as his bride," she said with her head high. "After you left Chevalerie. He came to find a wife and after one look, he would have no woman but me." She beamed, obviously very proud of her station. "He is a good man. I am very lucky."

"I'm happy to hear that," said Alex.

"And you're here with the Duke's men," said Emily in astonishment. "To investigate these raids."

"I am," said Alex.

"It's just amazing," said Emily. "Whoever heard of a woman like you? It must be incredibly interesting."

Alex was careful with her words, not quite sure of Emily's intentions, though her eyes did seem sincere. "It is interesting, to say the least," she replied.

"Would you come back and have tea with me?" said Emily. "I would love to hear of your journey, and I am always happy to hear news from home. I love it here, but I do miss the excitement of Chevalerie. And we never, ever have such interesting things here as a female guide! I just can't even imagine! Do say yes!" She gripped Alex's hand.

Seeing the friendliness on her face, Alex's old feelings of resentment towards this woman seemed silly. They were adults now and on very different footing. Plus, the thought of having a *female* friend was a luxury Alex was happy to experience. For a second, Alex did think to tread lightly, it was Emily after all, but then a childlike excitement gripped her. Alex smiled at the Lady Marquise before her. "I would like that," she said.

Emily had a carriage waiting outside to take them back to her home. Emily asked a hundred questions on the way through town. Alex did her best to answer them, though she wasn't extensively knowledgeable on all the gossip of Chevalerie, but the talk was light and pleasant. Of all the questions, Emily didn't mention Philippe once, which was for the best because Alex wouldn't have known what to say given all their history plus the new, fragile friendship Alex had just begun rebuilding with Philippe.

As they approached the manor, Alex looked on with wide eyes. It was a full-on palace, not just a manor. Every bit as majestic as the Duke's home, it was even more austere and opulent. It sat at the top of a hill, with ornate gates surrounding the manicured property. As they approached, Alex could see the well-tended gardens that led across the grounds.

The gates opened onto a fountain that consisted of staggered pools pouring from one into the next and ran the entire length of the drive leading up to the main entrance. On either side of the fountain were thousands of lavender and white poppies, in carefully delineated rows. Alex poked her head out the carriage window as they passed to see happy fish swimming through the waters and bees bumbling over the petals.

"My goodness, Emily," Alex gasped as she took in the elegant beauty of the grounds. "This is just beautiful."

"*Chère*, you should have seen this place when I got here. In desperate need of a woman's touch."

Within moments, they reached the grand front door of the mansion which opened wide to receive them. Attendants bustled around, ready for any whim of their Lady Marquise. A friendly-looking footman took Alex's hand and helped her out of the carriage with a bow, and she was passed on to the next set of hands which took her jacket.

Emily led Alex through the main hall— which was decorated with tapestries and paintings of the countryside—while giving maids and footmen orders and responding to their questions. High-reaching windows allowed light into the room. More flowers decorated every finely carved armoire they passed.

Their tour ended in the sitting room. A pair of maids opened the doors and a flurry of attendants rushed in, opening windows, fluffing pillows and lighting a fire in the fireplace. Alex stood still, trying to stay out of everyone's way. Emily glided past a round, gilded walnut table and beckoned Alex over. Alex dodged a few more maids and joined the patroness by the fire. Everyone was so welcoming; she had to admit the staff worked hard, but they seemed quite happy. Then before the activity settled, a young maid curtseyed and said tea would be out soon.

"Goodness," said Alex, as the parade of butlers and maids exited the room. "I didn't expect to find such luxury."

"This is just where we receive our guests. The real luxury will be found in the more formal areas," said Emily. "My husband owns the inn, the logging facilities, and several other businesses in town. He does not believe in letting his title do his work for him." She paused to examine the wood on an end table before calling a maid in to polish it. "He is a contemporary of the Duke you know," she said, turning back to Alex.

Alex nodded and ran her hand over the lavender cushions, unsure of what to say next, but Emily continued.

"I must confess," she began. "I heard news of this company coming to Ponce with a woman as its guide. I wondered if it was you."

"It was me," smiled Alex with a shrug, still unsure if Emily was teasing or truly being friendly.

"Alexandra," started Emily. "I have hoped for many years that I would have a chance to meet you again." She sighed, letting her hands relax on her lap. "I have always felt very bad about how I treated you when we were young. I had a mouth on me then, and I can only blame it on how much I desired to be the center of attention."

"Oh," said Alex, "I'm the one who attacked you, Emily. I should be the one to apologize."

"You did surprise me that time," said Emily. She laughed and shook her head. "I'll admit I deserved it." She reached to the table to straighten the teacups so that each handle angled in the same direction. "Everyone thought you were so extraordinary. I was very jealous of the attention you received."

"You were jealous of me?" croaked Alex, her hand shooting up to her chest. "Oh my goodness, you set the standard in the region. I always wondered how you could be such a star."

"That's nice of you to say," said Emily as she tilted her head and smiled. "I always thought you hated me so."

"I did hate you," Alex replied. "A lot." They looked at each other for a moment and at once broke into laughter.

With lightness still in her voice, Emily reached forward and took Alex's hand. "I should like to start over with you. As women. Not as children." She paused. "Just please leave your sword in its place."

"I believe that is fair," Alex conceded with a nod.

Just then, the doors opened. A man in his late fifties entered the room. His light-colored hair showed edges of gray, but didn't discount his virility. He was dressed in finery befitting the lovely manor and would be handsome by any estimation. He strode over to the couch and kissed Emily on the cheek.

"What is this I hear that my wife has a friend from Chevalerie to visit?" he said in a commanding voice.

"Hello darling," said Emily. "Alexandra, this is my husband, the Marquis du Ponce."

Alex rose to standing and curtseyed before the man, feeling awkward in her outfit. "*Monsieur*," she said.

"So you are the legendary female guide?" he asked as he took her hand. "Please sit, don't let me interrupt your reunion."

"I don't know about legendary," said Alex, sitting back down. "But I am the guide, yes."

"Do well, young lady," he said. "I am tired of these raids. They are affecting my business, and my beautiful wife here expects the finer things." He looked down at Emily, and she beamed back at him.

A maid entered through the servants' entrance with a tray of tea. She laid it on the low table before them and set out gleaming porcelain cups. She poured the tea and arranged a tray of delicate, flaky biscuits. The smell was glorious, and Alex's stomach rumbled.

"I leave you to your tea then," said the Marquis. "*Ma choupette*, I am meeting with the Duke's son. I shall see you for supper."

"Very well, *mon amour*."

"It was good to meet you, Alexandra, the lady guide," he said, turning to Alex. "Until next time."

Alex said farewell, then took her cup of tea. The mention of Philippe in the presence of Emily brought up immediate feelings of jealousy and inadequacy in her. Seeing the exquisite woman before her, she was once again reminded that nothing she could ever do could make her the kind of woman Philippe would truly consider.

After a moment, as if she had read Alex's mind, Emily spoke again.

"I don't mean to pry," she said, with a slow smile working across her face. "But now that we have put the ugliness behind us...I must ask you about Philippe." She stopped to select a biscuit with a strawberry jam center. "Anything there?" she asked lightly.

"Oh no," said Alex. "No, no, no."

"Come now, Alexandra," said Emily. "You are a beautiful woman, and he, I'm certain, is still a very handsome man. How exactly is that possible?"

"We are friends. That's all." Alex smiled, looking down at her cup.

"Men and women cannot be friends," she said, raising a finger. She looked at Alex and knitted her brows, "But I suppose in your situation that is fair." She eyed Alex for a moment. "May I offer some advice?"

Alex nodded.

"I do know Philippe well." She cleared her throat delicately. "Or I did at one time."

"I know," said Alex.

"He is a good man," she continued. "Maybe a little misguided, when it comes to women."

Alex nodded again.

Emily continued with a caring smile. "Take whatever you want from him." Then she reached across and placed her hand on Alex's knee. "Just be cautious, because once a man gets what he wants, *we* are the ones left with the broken hearts."

Alex spent the remainder of the delightful day chatting with Emily and shirking any duties that may have come up. Tomorrow she would be a guide, but today was about sitting by the fire with a very unlikely friend. Shortly after they had finished their tea, a nursemaid brought in Emily's two adorable sons of nine months and two years old. Alex fell in love with the little towheaded angels, who played at their feet. She couldn't have imagined a more pleasant afternoon. Emily had found a kingdom for herself, and despite their differences, it was a wonderful feeling to talk with another woman at length for Alex—she who spent so much time in the company of the gruffest of men. Emily, of all people. Who would have thought?

At half past five, the large door to the sitting room opened up. Several official-looking men who wore the Ponce crest on their chests entered, followed by Philippe and Laurent. The men brought chaos, swords clanging and boots trailing mud. They were clearly not aware anyone sat on the deep sofa by the fire. Alex noticed as Emily snapped her fingers and pointed for a maid to begin cleaning up the mess. The maid responded and scuttled over to the door with her broom.

The men spread out and Philippe approached the fire. He seemed very distracted to Alex. As he came closer, though, he noticed her peeking over the back of the sofa. His face softened for just a moment before he had a chance to acknowledge the entirety of the scene before him.

His double take was so sharp Alex was sure his neck would be sore the next day. He stared, his mouth gaping, at the two women tucked into the cushions. For just a moment the charismatic, perfectly charmed son of the Duke, had not a word to say. Alex hid a smile.

Emily was the one to speak first. She rose to her feet and held out her hand, a mirthful grin on her face. "On behalf of my husband, the Marquis du Ponce, I would like to welcome you to our town." She curtseyed before him. "I hope our accommodations are suitable for your stay, *Monsieur*."

Philippe came around to face her. He took her hand and kissed it as he bowed. He glanced towards Alex.

Alex remained seated, watching him crawl out of his skin. "Philippe," she teased. "You'll never guess who I ran into."

Emily lowered her hand. Philippe swallowed and composed himself before regarding her. "It is very good to see you, *Madame*. I did not realize it was Chevalerie's own Emily who married the Marquis."

Emily sat back down on the couch beside Alex. "It's true, *Monsieur*. I believe I have shocked both of you today. But you see, your scout had informed us days ago that you would arrive, and once I heard that a female guide traveled with the Duke's son, I was sure it was the two of you."

Alex continued, "We've been having a wonderful chat for the greater part of the afternoon."

"Oh," said Philippe, looking uncertainly from one woman's eyes to the next. "That's nice."

Emily rose once again, "Actually, I do need to go help prepare for supper. As mistress of a place like this, I cannot hide out for too long. Has my husband extended an invitation to dine with us tonight, *Monsieur*?"

"Yes, *Madame*, and I have accepted."

"Wonderful. And Alexandra, I would be honored if you joined us as well."

"After the tea, Emily, I would be a fool to say no."

"Splendid! We will have time for both business and pleasure this evening," she nodded, the excitement under her refined façade was evident. "Alexandra I will have a footman take you to the inn so you may dress for dinner." She hesitated a moment then held her head with resolve. "And you are more than welcome to wear your pants to dine. If it so suits you." She nodded. "But," she continued, "I do have some beautiful dresses I would be more than happy to offer you for the evening."

Alex grinned. "Perhaps it will feel nice to be out of these clothes for a change."

A flash of relief washed over the Lady Marquise. "Delightful!" she chirped. "I will have my head maid come retrieve you to see the gowns." And then, with another tsk to a maid who was slow at changing candlesticks, Emily was back to her duties. She directed a footman to show the men to the Marquis' study and scooted another maid to hurry and clear the tea setting. Then with the last rush of attendants to take care of things to her standards, Philippe and Alex were left alone.

Philippe sat down across from Alex, in the same spot Emily had been seconds ago. Alex was trying very hard not to laugh at the fluster in his cheeks, but she supposed she would have looked the same way if she had stumbled upon the two of them instead.

"So," began Alex, "What news do you bring from town?"

Philippe looked at her daftly. "You know who that was, right?"

"Yes, of course. Don't be silly. She seems to be quite comfortable here." She rested her hands on her knees. "I am happy for her."

Philippe eyed her. "What did the two of you talk about?"

"Chevalerie. I told her some stories from the road." She paused. "You."

"Me?" he asked. "What did she say?"

The footman entered to collect Alex then, and she rose to standing.

"Only things I already knew, *Monsieur*," Alex smirked at Philippe and curtseyed for the second time that day, the elegant surroundings infecting her.

Chapter Sixteen

The dining room displayed all the finery Ponce had to offer. Dark wood floors connected to a white wainscot that bordered the room. The upper walls were colored with a hint of lavender and carved back at intervals to hold imposing marble busts of the great men of Ponce. A large fireplace sat at the far end of the room with violet vases atop it, while two thick white pillars rose at either side of the entrance and connected to intricately carved crown molding. The high *trompe-l'œil* ceiling created the illusion of ascension while the crystal chandelier anchored it firmly at the center of the room. The cherry wood table, large enough for eight but set for four, sat below the chandelier and gleamed with polish. Philippe was shown his seat next to the Marquis who stood at the head of the table. Emily took her spot across from the Marquis and Alex sat before Philippe. The silver place settings twinkled in the candlelight, and the centerpiece boasted a bouquet of the same sweet-smelling poppies that could be found in the gardens. It was all very elegant and fine, Philippe thought, but it was Alex who took his breath away.

This was only the second time he had seen her, as an adult, in woman's clothes, and it was a lovely shock. Her gown was a dark emerald green with black lace accents and a straight neckline. Though it was cut in the style of the day, with an angled corset leading into a paneled skirt, Alex had rejected the volume that was popular in dresses, creating a more form-fitting silhouette. Her hair was pulled back and her bangs swept to the side. It highlighted her high cheekbones and bright eyes. When she smiled at her hosts, Philippe had to restrain himself from leaping across the table to taste her plump raspberry lips.

The Marquis leaned back as a maid placed a napkin across his lap. "I'm sorry, Philippe," he said. "I had hoped this to be more of a working dinner, but my wife insisted on something different."

"We don't get to entertain too often," said Emily. In contrast to Alex, Emily's indigo gown was so billowy, it puffed up around her in her seat.

"I'm very happy for the invitation," said Philippe.

"Has your family been in Ponce long, Marquis?" Alex asked.

"We emigrated from Savoy when I was very young," he said as another maid served croquettes. He held up his fork daintily, looking at the little balls. "We did not have much," he said. "But it is only since I married the Marquise that I fight to get food onto my fork," he said, stabbing at his plate.

"It's a wonderful time for you to be here," said Emily, ignoring her husband's complaint. "We are preparing to celebrate the Marquis' birthday. It will be the grandest event we have had all year." She turned to Alex. "Do say you'll join us. You must. I have already spread the word that the lady guide will be there and the chance to meet you has invigorated the town."

Alex hesitated. "As long as we are not engaged with our objectives," she said.

"Oh, you'll be done with that nonsense by then. Darling," she turned to the Marquis. "You promised we would have the ball as planned."

"Yes, *ma poupette*. I will do everything in my power to be sure the ball is not interrupted," he replied, still angling his fork. "It is my birthday," he said with a smile, "but I believe it is more important to my wife than it is to me."

Satisfied, Emily turned to Philippe. "And you too must come. I will not miss the opportunity to have the son of the Duke at the ball. When else will we have the chance?" She fluttered her hands as she spoke.

"I wouldn't miss it," he said.

The maid served bread and soon another brought a fragrant tomato bisque. Emily chatted again about old times in Chevalerie, avoiding any sensitive topics, and asked Alex question after question about being a mercenary. Philippe watched and listened as he ate. Emily was right where he always expected she would land. Girls like her, flouncy and stylish and set on a title, always managed to find themselves a suitable husband. It was true she had once pursued Philippe in that way, but he knew what she was after, so he never took her seriously. And after the debacle with Alex years ago, he had backed away from Emily at a hundred miles per hour, eager to forget everything that could remind him of what he had done.

Now there the women sat, so friendly with one another. The last time he had seen them together Alex had Emily in a chokehold that could strangle a troll. They were just so different, and he couldn't fathom the sudden friendship. Emily was formal and haughty, while Alex was quiet and unassuming. Even visually, they looked like they came from two different artists. No one would say Emily wasn't comely, but Alex, she needed no bows or ribbons or yards of lace to shine. Whether she wore a gown or breeches, he thought, watching her lips as she spoke, Alex was a symphony.

He wondered what in the world Emily had said to her that afternoon.

He'd really thought he'd broken through to Alex the night before, when they had stood bared before each other. But today she seemed distant again. He wasn't so dense that he didn't realize part of his fervor came from the fact that he never had to work very hard to bed a woman. But he didn't just want to bed her. He wanted... what did he want? His turmoil over her was so profound it was affecting this mission. Even now, as he sat with the Marquis, when he should have been focused on the task at hand, he couldn't help imagining what it would feel like to trace the skin just above the neckline of her dress with his tongue.

Alex, came the only answer to his question. He wanted Alex.

He stifled a sigh and looked down at his soup.

After the first course, tortured as it was for Philippe, the Marquis directed the conversation back to the pressing issue. "Philippe," he said, "I thank you for indulging my darling wife in this gossip of her hometown, but we have more important matters to discuss. Now that your guide is at your side, will you detail your plan to rid us of these problems with the raids?"

Philippe realized he had slouched down insolently into his chair. He sat up straight as he responded to the Marquis' question, relieved for the invitation to get out of his own head. "Well, as I've told you, we believe these agitators to be hiding in the caves west of here. Alex has personal knowledge of the area and we plan to use it to trap them, or at least the faction of them who are hiding. If they have discovered our intentions and they scatter, we will cut them off from their base and stall the attacks long enough to uncover their objective. Though I hope that's not the case."

"How will you trap them?" the Marquis asked.

"There is a third entrance," Alex jumped in, "tucked into rocks and vegetation. There is no reason to believe they would know the third entrance. Or, if they have discovered it, they shouldn't suspect that we also know of its existence."

"We'll have men stationed at each outlet," Philippe said. "We plan to make use of your guards."

"The caves," the Marquis said. "I never even considered..." he trailed off. He took a slow sip of champagne and swished it in his mouth. Then he spoke to Alex, "I am embarrassed to say you know my territory in a way that I don't."

"There is no reason to know these caves, My Lord," said Alex. "Unless you are hiding or running."

"And you?" Philippe asked her impulsively. "How did you learn them so well?"

"Perhaps I was doing both," she said, looking at him with an impish smile.

The Marquis flicked his eyes from Philippe to Alex and then back to Philippe. "And what of these men?" asked the Marquis. "What will you do once they are caught? I should like to have them to myself."

Philippe flushed with sudden embarrassment. It was unprofessional to inquire about his guide's experience, and the Marquis hadn't missed it. Philippe continued back on topic, he wouldn't let this misstep challenge his authority. "I understand," he said to the Marquis. "But we will take them to Chevalerie for trial. My father also wishes to avenge you and the people who have suffered."

"How does he wish to avenge me?" the Marquis responded, agitation growing in his voice. "Does he know the extent of the terrorism? Does he wish to pay the reparations to my people? It is my responsibility to support those who cannot support themselves, and I cannot do it alone. You may see finery before you," he waved to the room at large, "but it comes from a finite amount, and I can only stretch it so far. The region is in debt. Terrible debt."

"We do not mean to dismiss your challenges," Philippe said, his own voice becoming terse. "But the attacks are not confined solely to your territory," he said.

"You and I both know the majority of the damage has been done above the *Canyon de Cuivre* and that has traditionally fallen under my authority, *jeune homme*."

"And you, in turn, are under the authority of the Duke," Philippe said, not missing the jab at his youth. "I assure you, your strife will not be overlooked."

The two men eyed each other, nothing to be heard in the room.

The Marquis was the first to continue, his voice a tidal wave. "Ponce is not a city to be forgotten. We are the gateway to the North. We regulate commerce for all of Provence and, dare I say, France. The Duke has long concentrated resources in the southern part of the region and look what it has caused." His brows were turned down and his eyes fierce. "I will not be disregarded." He pounded his fist against the table, causing the dishes to rattle and the silverware to jump.

"*Etienne*," Emily said, calling her husband by name with surprising sharpness.

The Marquis looked at her, and he drew in an audible breath.

Philippe wiped his mouth with the napkin. "I assure you, *Monsieur*," he said evenly. "You and your territory shall be vindicated."

The Marquis took a breath, needing a moment to return to normal. "I trust your intentions, Philippe." He glanced to Alex and cleared his throat. "I just hope this is not a problem the Duke should have seen to himself." Then he crossed his arms and leaned back in his chair. "Please let me know if you require any additional resources while you are here," he said.

"Indeed," said Philippe. "We shall see what we are up against tomorrow."

Chapter Seventeen

A bird flying high above would never know this mountain was anything special. A person riding past its cracks and crevasses could miss its secrets entirely. The people in the nearby towns told tales of children being snatched into the depths and trysting lovers, never to be seen again. The rest of the passersby were either uninterested, unimpressed, or just plain scared of the dark.

Of course, many a foolhardy man had entered and lost his way, but no fantastical thing lurked like the rumors said. The only thing these caves had to offer was muck and dirt. The passages were known by some of the rougher mercenaries of the area. Alex, always on the lookout for shortcuts and hiding spots, had heard enough whispers in taverns to take her chances and explore the caves herself. She found them to be a benign, albeit smelly, way to skirt the distance around the mountain range. There were many parts inside that even opened into glorious caverns, giving light and air and making the spaces much more welcoming and accessible than they appeared to those who had not the spine to explore its depths.

And now, Alex was leading Philippe and his men into the depths of this secret territory.

They had set out at dawn and taken the two-hour ride to the first, most well-known entrance. Franc and Auguste, along with a handful of Ponce guards, had been stationed at the mouth. The party had then traveled along the north side of the mountain, where the grounds had changed from grassy meadows into rocky slate. There, they found the other known entrance and left more guards. From that point, the remaining members had continued around the mountain, across a deep canyon filled with thistle bush, over a rocky plateau, and back down to the sparsely forested base of the mountain, where they would find the last entrance, the one they hoped would give them an advantage. Their goal was to either flush the marauders out or trap them inside, at which point they would use whatever methods needed in order to extract their secrets.

The wind picked up and Alex adjusted her shawl around her head. This area of the mountain was difficult to read. Hundreds of cracks, clefts, and wormholes in the jutting rock falsely promised to lead them into the bowels of the mountain, but Alex knew where to find the only one that truly would. Had she not followed a little trail of water on a whim one time from inside the caves, she would never have found the hidden entrance.

Philippe was right behind her. She felt his impatience to get inside, but she knew he was holding back so as not to rush her. Alex scanned the rock as they narrowed in on a small clearing. A stream had cut a path in the rock long ago but had died many spring times before. Alex dismounted her horse, picked through the dirt, and felt along the rock wall. She followed a large crack running horizontally with her hands until it dipped into a crevasse. There she kicked away debris which disguised a triangle-shaped divide that opened to the dirt. There were trees rooted around it and into the dark rock which led up the mountain.

"Here," she said.

"This is it?" asked Henri. "This is nothing more than a crack in the rock."

Alex reached forward and pulled back a knotted thick of branches, revealing more of the opening. Light penetrated the dark space. "This is intentional," she said. "Someone has tried to obstruct and hide the entrance. I would bet this is their main entry point."

"Ridiculous," said Henri. "How could you possibly tell one of these holes from another?" He turned to Maurice and lowered his voice, "It probably doesn't go in more than ten feet."

Maurice raised his brows in agreement and Alex noticed a few other nods throughout the group.

"Ah, Henri, have I not earned your trust yet?" Alex jested, putting her hand on her hip.

Philippe alone seemed uninterested in Henri's comment. He pulled a few more tangles of root away and stood before the entrance. "And this leads us to the central cavern?"

Alex appreciated his trust in her. "It will come to a large cavern which collects water from several different springs and streams," she said, indicating the direction with her hands. "It then splits and heads towards the two outlets. There are several offshoots, but the water marks are easy enough to follow." She rested her hands on her hips. "This entry will lead us to the main cavern, where ten, fifteen men could comfortably sleep. The path from the back entrance is deeper and more dangerous, but that comes to the cavern as well." She toed a dead branch, and it rolled aside. "The main entrance connects too, but it is twisty and slower to travel."

The men stood staring at the little gaping hole. Alex could feel their reluctance about entering it.

"Well," said Philippe. "Let's hope we can ambush them in the cavern and be on our way back to Chevalerie tomorrow."

Alex watched as the men hesitated and kicked at the dirt, obviously not so thrilled about this leg of the journey.

"Torches," instructed Alex.

They took a moment to strike a fire and light several torches. Philippe dipped into the cave ahead of them.

"What will we find in there, Alex?" asked Maurice. "Animals, I mean."

"Bats," she said. "They'll get in your hair. And tuck your stockings nice and tight. I traveled with a man once who wore loose trousers and a snake scooted up and bit him in a very disturbing place."

She laughed to herself as the men hustled to check their stockings. It wasn't really true, but that's what they get for doubting her.

Philippe popped out of the cave, eager for movement. "Let's go."

Her eyes, sharp like a fox's, led them into the dark. Alex was confident, knowledgeable, and fierce in leading this group. In moments like this when everyone depended on her, Alex really enjoyed being a guide. She had a vast understanding of the countryside and of ways to avoid trouble. Plus, she was always eager for the chance to share her skills with people who needed help. But most of the time, the people who hired her just wanted her to stay mute and point in the correct direction, making her little more useful than a compass. Turns out, the direction she had chosen for her life was not particularly exciting and certainly less than fulfilling.

Over the years, she had met some good men and cultivated a few working relationships. But she was never free of worry, and she always had to be ready to protect herself. That meant she rarely found moments just to enjoy the people around her, which she had found herself doing with this crew. Alex often grieved for a different life. She remembered her time in Chevalerie very fondly, and though she felt guilty admitting it, every wish about her future ended up back there. Alex knew she had no right to go back. She had let her emotions run out of control when she was there, and there was no way she could ever make amends for bringing dishonor to the family that had cared for her.

But maybe—she still held out hope—if she did well on this journey. If she brought Philippe and the men to the rebels. If she aided in their chase and capture. Perhaps then, enough of her penance would be paid so that she could eke out a home for herself in Chevalerie once more. Maybe rent a room at a little farmhouse outside the city, and put poppies on her own sunny windowsill? The desire filled her dreams, day and night. She clung to that hope, which prodded her to do her best. With that in mind, she moved forward, with her crew behind her, into the dark.

With a few coughs and shudders, the group took their first tentative steps inside the cave. The ground was wet, and each step sank into the dirt with a *pop*. The first ten feet were the most disturbing, the ceiling only a few inches above Alex's head while the others had to crouch to fit. The musty smell of rotting vegetation was thick in their noses, and their eyes were reluctant to give up the light of day. But soon the passageway opened at least ten feet high, allowing them to wave their torches around freely. The cave constricted and grew like a snake digesting a meal, but even the narrowest parts could fit the men side by side. Water seeped through the cracks in the walls. In the spring, melting snow would create a stream that would thrash about through the caves, but at the moment it was no more than a trickle.

Alex led them, her eyes scanning every detail. The ground spoke of travel, with no distinguishable footprints but plenty of slips and ridges that wouldn't form naturally. The trail was faint, but it was there. Every ominous fork in the road tested her expertise, and she held her breath until she could confirm the trail again. As they moved further, the markings began to speak of panic. Clumsy boot prints, broken rock, every blemish told its own story, and Alex began to piece it all together the further they travelled.

She bent to observe a sharp edge of broken rock and made a quick decision about which way to continue. Meanwhile, Philippe's presence behind her was as thick as the stone around them. It could have unnerved her, but in fact, it made her feel secure. They were a good team, she thought. A strong team. And though she could never be many things to him, she was happy to know she had this opportunity to be his guide.

She slid her hand along the glistening cave wall and indicated to him a low stalactite up ahead with her torch. She felt him pass the information to the other men, and she moved her torch to the side, letting the shadows shroud her face. Even in this darkness, she felt the incessant glow that he caused. It burned so brightly inside her that she wondered if it was the torches or she herself lighting the way. The moment she and Philippe had been in the hot springs had been a revelation. He still wanted her. And it thrilled her. It absolutely thrilled her.

Emily, ironically, had told her to enjoy Philippe and what he had to offer. And, really, why shouldn't she? Even if she never had another lover, shouldn't she experience the act of sex at least once? Damn how she wished she could just sleep with that man. Her body reacted insolently every time he was near. Even at that moment, with dense earth around them and uncertainty in the air, his closeness caused delicious tension to pulse through her. And though he'd kept every promise he'd made at the beginning of the journey, she felt the gentle pressure he was applying. He knew what he was doing; she was the one who didn't know the rules of this game. She felt outmatched. Underprepared. Dangerously inexperienced.

She breathed a heavy sigh. She knew it was only fantasy. With every surge of longing and affection she felt for him, she felt a persistent throb of regret for an affair that she could never let happen. Indulging in him would undercut her dreams of moving back to Chevalerie. It would mean that she hadn't gotten stronger or smarter or better after all this time. She wouldn't deserve to be in Chevalerie any more than she did when she had shamed herself the first time. Plus, being that close and knowing his comings and goings—what he was doing, who he was with—she couldn't be sure she wouldn't humiliate herself again. She had to face it. He would always make her weak.

She followed the walls and ridges of the cave intently. Something caught her eye and interrupted her thoughts. She stopped, holding up her hand to signal the rest of her part. "Wait," she whispered. She crouched forward to examine a marking in the stone. It was just below her waist and tucked into a recess. If she hadn't been scanning the cave walls, she would have missed it. Three deep cuts, a few centimeters long, ran parallel to each other, creating white lines on the black stone. She ran her fingers over them. "This means something," she said. "But I don't know what."

"A trap?" Philippe asked, scanning up ahead.

She turned to him, working it out in her head. "They must have known we were coming."

They stared at each other for a moment in the firelight. Alex spun the ramifications in her mind, and Philippe looked to be doing the same, his eyes filled with contemplation. The answer was there. They just had to work it out.

"Why a trap so deep? Why not at the entrance?" he asked.

"They were rushed," she said. "The trail shows they were trying to get away."

"Then it's not a trap," he said, still watching her.

"It's a sign," she replied, catching his meaning. "Something is hidden."

"Something that can identify them," he said.

"That they want to come back for later. After we've left."

"So they've already gone," he said, glaring into the dark.

The men had been watching the two of them agog, heads swinging back and forth. Alex could have laughed at their expressions if she hadn't been so frustrated by the conclusion she had just reached with Philippe.

"Step carefully, men," Philippe said. "We have to figure out what this is."

No sooner had the words come out of his mouth than Sébastien stepped forward, hit a loose rock on the ground and tumbled forward. He fell against an indentation in the wall opposite the markings, releasing a sudden cascade of stones that poured out of the crevice like an angry river. Before she knew what was happening, Philippe had grabbed her by the back of the shirt and thrown her out of the way. Alex stumbled back, crashing to the ground, while the rocks pelted the rest of the men.

Dirt and debris filled their eyes and lungs while glowing torches gave no more light than embers in the sand. The men, full of fresh cuts and bruises, waved through the heavy air and hurriedly pulled Sébastien from the rubble. He grimaced, and closer inspection revealed a nasty gash across his middle.

"I can go forward," he said to Philippe through a wince.

Philippe pressed against the blood while Laurent ripped a cloth to tie off the wound.

"Take a second and see how you feel," Philippe said.

The dust was settling by then, and they could see now what the rocks had been hiding. A shallow cavern had been sealed up, but the avalanche had opened it. Philippe stepped forward, kicking several rocks aside. By his torchlight, Alex could see the loot, tokens they had acquired in their ransacks. Copper pots, farm tools, a few handfuls of coins. Somewhat valuable items, but certainly not enough riches to warrant the attacks. There was more to the attacks than the plunder.

"Such a strange assortment." Philippe waved the torch and leaned towards a large silver platter, revealing the markings of Peillon. He ran his hands over it, and Alex knew he was thinking hard.

"Are we going to continue forward?" asked Laurent.

"Yes," said Philippe. "But they're not here."

"How do you know?" asked Maurice.

"This is just a hasty attempt to hide their presence," Philippe responded. "Or perhaps to slow us down." He combed through the pile of rocks then picked one up. He pelted it down the corridor. "*Merde*!" he said as it clattered in the dark.

"Then they are on the defensive," said Laurent. "And the attacks will stop. We are in pursuit. We just need patience."

"Alex," Philippe said gruffly. "How far to the cavern?"

She perked up, ready for service, "We are near the end of this path," she said. "Perhaps ten minutes ahead."

Philippe paced, his frustration obvious. "We will go to the cavern and finish what we have come for. Perhaps they've left something of importance." He turned to Alex again. "Are there any more forks in the path?" he asked.

"I believe it is relatively straight from here," she said.

He turned and held his torch to the markings carved into the wall. He examined and touched it. "This may not be the only hoard," he said. "Step carefully from here on out. It was sheer luck we caught this warning here."

It wasn't luck, Alex thought. It was her.

"We are down a man, two because someone must stay with him," said Laurent.

"I am fine," Sébastien said.

But Philippe shook his head. "It may be for the best," said Philippe. "We will be less cumbersome with fewer people." He folded his arms and looked down in thought, his expression barely visible in the torch light, but to Alex his deliberation was captivating. She watched him closely, as she had when he matched wits with the Marquis the night before at dinner. He made decisions like he fought: fast, potent, and always sure. They may have lost their targets, but she now trusted him, as a leader, to put them on the path towards these men once more, and she felt a swell of pride and gratitude for being under such capable command.

"Alex," he said, snapping her to attention, "I will need you to stay here with Sébastien. The rest of us will move forward."

"Me?" she croaked. That's not what she expected.

"If the path is straight, there is no further need for your skills." He looked at her through the firelight. "And no need to put you in danger." He turned. "Move out, men," he said before she could protest.

She stared at the men, stunned into silence. Had she just made herself disposable? Did he realize the skill and instinct involved in getting them this deep into the mountain, or had she made it look like anyone could have led them there? No one wanted to miss the chance to see the spot from which the crimes spawned, but she most of all deserved to be at the front of the line. And, she thought darkly, the parallels she was drawing coming all too fast, if they were done with the caves, was he done with her?

The men passed by her. "Watch out for snakes," she called after them before turning grimly to Sébastien, who, in a panic, began checking the cuffs of his pants.

Chapter Eighteen

The dinner that night was subdued as Philippe recounted what he could with Ponce officials, who were all, more than anything, relieved to hear that the rebels had departed the area. Good and bad had come from their journey that day. The cavern had been empty, just as he suspected. Well, not exactly empty. The rebels had done a commendable job of obscuring their presence, but hasty dugouts revealed tobacco, flint, and other trappings. There were no clues about their new destination, however. It was good for Ponce and the other vulnerable towns. It meant they wouldn't sustain any attacks anytime soon, at least until these men could get their bearings. But it was frustrating for Philippe. His job was not over until this mystery was solved and justice was dealt. This mission was becoming more complicated and dangerous with every turn. His party had sustained its first injury, and the longer they toiled at finding these men, the better chance of another.

He was loath to tell his father they had made no real progress other than discovering an empty lair. He had counted on being able to trap them in the caves, but they had figured out his intentions minutes too soon. He was going to have to canvas the entire countryside in order to pick up a trail. His cousin had told him to be patient; the thought had twisted in him like a bad stew. Patience was his sore spot, and this could take months.

Something else was off. He'd already determined that these rebels had more backing than their crimes would suggest. Better weapons, better intelligence, perhaps even more men than he originally thought. Their spoils indicated unorganized looters, lowbrow men. But there was precision in their attacks. That meant someone smart was making the decisions. However, it couldn't last long because controlling unskilled men for hire was no easy task. Philippe hoped he could find a way to exploit that.

After dinner, the men went to bed early, no revelry in the air. Philippe, too, retired, but he lay in his bed, unable to sleep. He wanted to start off immediately, while any chance of a fresh trail still existed. Even then, he itched in his bed wanting to get moving, and he fought with every muscle not to jump up and rouse his men. His gut told him the rebels would not go far, but he had no way of knowing for sure. Still any hunch was better than sitting and waiting for their fate to change, and he would rather go anywhere than nowhere.

However, a few things required attention before they could leave. They needed updated maps of the region. They needed to consult hunters who knew the countryside and of any stand-alone structures that may offer shelter in the area. He needed to write to his father. He also wanted to send local men into the caves to catalogue the contents of the hoards, but they would need someone to guide them. Alex was the obvious choice for that, but he wasn't going to send her away with a bunch of unknown men unless he himself was present. Perhaps the cataloguing could wait as long as the entrances remained guarded. He sighed and rubbed his eyes with his thumb and forefinger. There was much to do.

But despite everything that was running through his head, the thing nagging at him the most was Alex. He'd really managed to piss her off when he made her stay behind. Truth be told, he was relieved to have a reason to get her out of harm's way. He was sorry it came at the expense of Sébastien but having her around was a burdensome tax on his own effectiveness. Alex's help in the caves had been invaluable—he could never have led that party himself—but the second the twists and turns ended, he wanted her out of the equation. Too much of his energy was spent worrying about her—would they have an encounter, would they be ambushed, would he be able to protect her? Alex may have been hired to guide, but he was no slouch at tracking himself. Her job was to take them through the caves.

That phase of the journey was over. Now what was he going to do with her?

He'd felt her resentment as solidly as the rocks falling from the walls. She was good at what she did, and he knew she had pride in it. He would never insult a man's good work by ending his contract before the journey was over. Was it fair to do it to her? What's more, he knew, indubitably, that if he didn't let her continue with this party, he would never, ever, see her again.

Despite the torture in his head and his heart, he eventually dozed off. But before sleep completely overtook him, clamoring commotion at the doors to the inn woke him like cold water to the face. He was on his feet in an instant and at the window of the room. He could hear horse hooves in the distance, but he couldn't make out the riders. He rushed into the hallway, haphazardly pulling on any clothes he could find, and ran right into Alex. He stared at her for a moment, forgetting what he was doing as he realized she wore nothing more than a long night shift with her sword belt around her waist. The shift clung to her body, and he was halted by the sight before she glared at him and pulled her own jacket around her. She, along with his other men, all in various states of disarray, rushed past him into the main hall. He shook his head, refocusing on the present, and followed.

The innkeeper and several attendants were already at the door, busy lighting up the room with candles and torches. The innkeeper paced nervously in his nightcap, holding a candle that shook in his hand.

"Open the door," demanded Philippe.

"But sir—" he said.

"Don't worry," said Philippe, drawing his sword. "These men aren't keen on showing themselves."

The innkeeper hesitated for a moment before he lifted the heavy wooden plank that secured the entrance. The door creaked open. The light from their candles poured ahead of them into the darkness, but Philippe could see nothing out of place. With his sword drawn, he took a tentative step into the night.

"Torch," he said, holding his free hand back.

The innkeeper gave a signal to one of the attendants, who jumped to grab a torch from a fixture on the wall and place it in Philippe's outstretched hand. Philippe took a few more quiet steps into the darkness, but there was nothing to be seen. He felt his men creeping out behind him. He took rapid analysis of the situation. He hoped Alex had stayed in the safety of the inn but knew she probably hadn't. He had to put that out of his mind. He looked out into the blackness. The moon only lit to the small bridge before the town square. Beyond that, he knew there was a stream, trees, and more darkness. He strained his ears, but even the rumble of horse hooves had gone away into the night.

But then the innkeeper broke the silence.

"My Lord? Perhaps we heard this?"

Philippe turned back to the entrance. There, nailed to the door, was a parchment. He walked back and ripped it from the nail.

Alex stood before him and held a candle near so he could read what it said.

"*Caverne de la Cathédrale.* Sunset." Philippe read. He turned to Alex. "Does that mean something to you?"

She nodded. "It's not far."

He looked around at his men. "I suppose we shall finally see their faces," he said, gritting his teeth with both relief and anxiety.

Chapter Nineteen

La Caverne de la Cathédrale was a section around the south side of the mountain range halfway between the main entrances to the caves. It was in a shallow bluff tucked inconspicuously into a chasm and flanked by a healthy arm of the river. Shades of color from dusty grays and reds to sandy whites and blues delineated ancient layers of earth compacted over a millennium and all at once exposed by a mighty earthquake. It created a wide-mouthed but shallow cave, nearly a hundred feet high. Heavy stalactites clung to the roof and large chunks of rock that had lived in their places centuries ago now littered the floor. It was a stunning creation of Mother Nature; to sit in the place was to feel her magical presence. But like many other wonders in this area, if one hadn't passed it before, it would easily be overlooked. Luckily for her companions, Alex knew just how to get there.

They arrived well before sunset to investigate the area and set up camp. Philippe had brought all the remaining men from their party plus several militia men from Ponce, making fourteen altogether. Six of those men were hidden in the trees along the path, with bows and arrows ready to fire at any trouble. Alex felt like the odds were in their favor and she was anxious to understand what was at stake. The strength of their enemies had come from their ability to remain hidden, not from large numbers. Now that they had been displaced, they would be looking to reach a deal. She did not know, however, how Philippe would respond.

The men settled in for a long evening, not knowing how prompt their adversaries would be. They were fanned out amongst the rocks with their weapons handy. Alex leaned against a large boulder with her knees up to her chest. Philippe sat nearby, whittling on a piece of wood. Though the men were jumpy and excited, Philippe alone seemed eerily calm. It was a glimpse into who he was as a fighter and a negotiator, and she was eager to see how he would manage this meeting. She was sure he hadn't wanted to bring her tonight. Luckily, they needed her to get to *La Caverne*. Besides, she wasn't going to let herself get cut out again. She was a part of this crew, and she would see it through to the end.

They had built a large fire near the entrance to the cave from chestnut wood, which, when it burned, tended to pop hot embers into the air. The angry pieces of ash would sometimes land on a body, causing the men to jump and jerk before brushing the biting embers away. They settled in, regardless, and soon they were passing around a canteen of liquor to help ease their nerves. She watched it go from one to the next, and finally Franc left his spot by the fire to hand it to her.

"C'mon Alex," Franc said. "Clears the head."

She smiled at him. "Thanks, Franc. I'm okay."

Franc nodded and tossed it to Philippe instead.

Philippe took a swallow with a grimace and looked over at her. "Why don't you have a drink?" he asked. "We may be here for several hours. A sip won't hurt."

"I don't like it," she said.

"It will help take the edge off," he said, nodding towards the foot she hadn't realized she was nervously tapping.

"I suppose you are right," she said, feeling irreverent. She took it back and took a swig. She cringed at the bitterness. "Ugh." She grimaced.

"Don't worry," he said, leaning towards her. "I'll protect you." He winked playfully.

She smiled at his ability to tease even with the current situation. As she watched the jug go from one man to the next, she felt a sensation of warmth she wasn't accustomed to. Despite the fact that they were moments away from meeting their foes, she felt secure among these guys, and their leader. Secure enough to try another taste when the bottle came around again. And then another a few minutes later just because she was bored.

"Easy there," she heard Philippe say.

Alex watched him as he worked his knife against the thick wood he was whittling in a solid, stroking motion. He glanced over as he spoke then looked back to his hands with an amused grin. It was rare to see him sitting so still and calm, she thought, studying him. He was usually pushing to go further, faster, practically vibrating with drive. She imagined his mind was turning fast, working a thousand scenarios for the night, as she'd seen him anticipate outcomes before. She should be doing the same, but she could think only of the heat from the fire that radiated off his skin and then warmed hers.

Oh no, what was she thinking? This was not the time. She shook her head and felt her vision wobble. What was this drink doing to her and how was it working so fast? She felt her muscles relaxing and her thoughts going places she didn't want to let them go. She ran her eyes over his long legs, thickly muscled body, strong arms and hands working his knife, and she thought about how they would feel roughly working her body in the same way. She shivered against the warmth in her veins. For once, her confusing feelings were not so confusing.

The drink came around again, but drinking the stuff didn't seem so bad anymore. She felt pleasant and tingly. Her head swam, and she stared at him, which wasn't polite, but who cared? Her mind worked hard rationalizing a reason to give in. She ached to give in to him, to give him what he wanted, but it still scared her to think of what the outcome could be.

The fire popped then and sent a spray of butterfly sparks into the air. Alex watched as one glowing piece of ash floated down towards her. She was happy for something else to take her focus, and she watched as it decided to land right on her knee. The small cinder glowed red at the center and pulsed out flashes of orange and yellow. She watched as it flaked off edges of white ash, realizing that she had seen dangerous fires, but had never taken the time to watch one harmless little ember.

But before she could finish the thought, the fabric in her pants gave way and the ember burnt right into her skin. Alex kicked her leg and smacked the spark away as sharp pain snapped into her. She patted her knee and examined the hole in her pants. She'd been able to brush it away before it had caused too much damage, but the stinging red welt cut into her skin.

"Are you okay?" Philippe asked. He was looking at her with humorous concern on his face, as were several others. She didn't know if they'd seen her entire display, but she wished she had burst into flames as fast as that ember.

Then, suddenly, as if by the grace of God, Philippe turned away. He'd heard something that she had missed. But it came again. A far-off call, three short hoots. The men snapped back to attention, jumping to their feet, the scene giving to immediate tension. Alex, however, sat rubbing her stinging knee, not quite remembering what that signal was supposed to mean. But seconds later there was a whistle outside the cave, followed by the approaching crunch of boot steps. Oh right, she thought, the *rebels*. She reached for her sword and instead lost her balance and rolled over the rock against which she'd been leaning. This was thoroughly funny, and she couldn't seem to stand.

Philippe looked down at her with wide eyes. "Alex," he hissed, "Get on your feet."

"I don't know how to anymore," she said, a giggle caught in her throat.

He stared at her in disbelief. Then he reached down and took her arm. He pulled her up like she weighed no more than a bird.

"Oh, that's how you do it," she said, staring down at her feet. She stomped twice to test out the ground. She looked up at him and bit back laughter.

"You had two sips of drink. How did you get this drunk?"

"I told you I don't ever drink because it makes-me-so-stupid." She paused, her words winding up like a top. "Am I slurring?"

"Just stay in the back and don't say anything," he said hurriedly.

She nodded her head and followed directions, sliding out to the edge of their covering. How did these men sober up so quickly? This is why she didn't drink. She should never ever drink. She leaned against the cool stone and tried to look casual. Wait, not casual. Intimidating. She bared her teeth at the dark wilderness.

Then, from the blackness of the night, emerged three men into the firelight. They were grimy and shaggy, the signs of their time in the caves very evident. The leader, a giant of a man with light brown hair that hung past his shoulders, held a wide, blunt knife out to the side, and the two men accompanying him held their weapons out to be surrendered as well. The three of them had light eyes, indicating northern roots. They wore ragged clothes, their breeches torn and faded. They approached with their hands up to indicate surrender, but nothing else about their body language was passive. The one in front wore scars that spoke of many battles and looked like pain would come to those who threatened him. Alex shuddered to think of tangling with him on her own.

"Take their swords," said Philippe.

Auguste and Luc sprang forth to take the weapons the men were holding out. The men didn't fight.

There they stood. Philippe's men with their backs to the cavern, the three rebels with their backs to the river. It was the moment they had been inching towards since they left Chevalerie, and Alex could feel the pressure radiating in the walls and centering on Philippe and the man before him. But she herself actually felt at ease, more interested in chasing a moth that had fluttered towards her than the meeting. She brought her hand to her mouth to laugh, but she passed it off as a sneeze. The eyes of the man at the center darted over to her. She coughed and looked away.

"I am sent here by my master to discuss a treaty," the large man said, in the formal language of France. The words were eloquent and respectful, not at all what she'd expected to come out of his mouth.

"I am disappointed that he doesn't come himself," responded Philippe. The same formal language fell off his tongue easily, not showing any surprise if he too felt it.

"He sends his most trusted lieutenant, *Monsieur,*" the man replied with a bow. "As I see the Duke has done."

They continued in the same formal language and navigated the introductions. No one paid much attention to Alex, far off to the side, and she congratulated herself for remaining inconspicuous. When they sat, she followed but sidled further towards the opening of the cave, the cool air feeling good in her lungs. The fire continued to pop and break, sending occasional hot sparks into the air and causing the men to jump and brush them away.

Despite the haziness in her head, she listened closely, eager as the rest of them to understand just what the crux of this problem was. She determined that the three men were not cut from the same cloth. The leader carried himself very differently from the two brutes who accompanied him, each of whom seemed as dumb as he did nasty, but the man in front had intelligence in his eyes. The leader went by the name Girard Giroux and had an ancient form of nobility behind his speech. Even his name, she felt, was historically significant, but she couldn't quite remember why. *Giroux.* She tried it on her tongue to see if it brought up any recognition. It didn't, but the sound earned her a sharp glance from Philippe. She shut her mouth once more.

The discussions went on for almost an hour, or it could have been ten minutes from her cloudy perception. Philippe had a keen sense of fairness marked with a demeanor that was not to be provoked. Giroux, likewise, was deferential but not a pushover either. He had an agenda and wanted Philippe to know his story. Giroux was from a small village known as Babin, one of a series of little towns along the banks of the Durance River. Alex knew of the town but had never visited it herself. The river towns were tucked into recesses in the canyon and are notorious for being inaccessible. Because of their isolation, there was very little trade, and the river, which was prone to flooding, had made it impossible to farm items that could be exported to larger towns. The townspeople were suffering, and Giroux explained to Philippe they felt forgotten by the Duke and their country.

They wanted to tax passage through the unregulated river. Currently, boats traveling the river paid no tolls. Babin sat at a critical bend, making it the perfect place to administer a toll, which Giroux insisted would be fair, bringing revenue and trade into the region. There was no reason the northern part of Provence should not benefit from the ships commuting to the South. And with no assistance or change to the regulations, their home was sure to die.

Alex didn't follow the politics of the region too closely, but she felt like this river was always causing problems. The Duke had refused a tax in the past, and, as Philippe explained to Giroux, he wanted the passageways into the region to be unfettered, fearing a tax would cause dissidence and fuel aggression towards these very people. The river was an important part of Provence and any alteration to the expected tolls could be felt throughout the region.

According to Giroux, the attacks had been intended to get the audience of the Duke, which, by bringing Philippe and his men to them, it had. Giroux and his master did not expect to be discovered and had hoped to meet on more even footing. Uncovering their hideout had disturbed their plan. They first thought to run but then decided it was in everyone's best interest to face up to their crimes now, before any more innocents were hurt. Nevertheless, Giroux argued, they had gone out of their way to strike areas that were not heavily populated. Though it was unfortunate for those who lost their homes, he claimed much thought was put into choosing areas that were economically prosperous and could absorb the losses.

"But more has been lost than homes," Philippe said to Giroux.

Giroux nodded and looked down. "The boy that died," he said. "I can say the attacks as of late have become more...impulsive. I take responsibility. And I grieve for his lost potential." Then he raised his head once more. "I did not dare say our plight was free from sin."

"Why do you hire mercenaries?" Philippe asked abruptly.

"*Monsieur*?"

"The men you command, they are mercenaries, no? Not your countrymen."

Giroux paused for a long moment. "We have hired some mercenaries to help us."

"But your attacks suggest the unskilled doings of men with no resources."

"*Monsieur,* I have expressed that the attacks were solely to gain your attention."

"And you had no other means by which to gain our attention? It seems a lot of preparation went into trying to hide the fact that you have a benefactor."

"There was a lot of preparation to be sure no one was injured."

"At that you failed," Philippe said, watching Giroux. "Someone gave orders to attack that house with the boy. But they were not your orders, were they?"

Giroux stood uncomfortably for a moment. "I don't know exactly what you are questioning, *Monsieur.*"

"An army can be built only on loyalty," Philippe said. "Or it is doomed."

Giroux stood mutely, clenching his jaw against Philippe's words.

Philippe watched the man for a long while. Alex could tell he was working something out in his mind after the strange series of questions. Finally, Philippe spoke, slipping into a stately, formal tone fit for a Duke's son. "On behalf of the Duke, we were not aware of the suffering on the banks of the river." He rested his hands on his knees in a sign of deference. "I assure you, they will be cared for."

"I thank you," Giroux nodded.

"But I can promise," Philippe continued, leaning back once more, "there will be no money or aid until someone stands for these crimes."

"That is understandable. Though I beg you, *Monsieur*, my countrymen are innocent."

"We shall find a reasonable outcome," Philippe continued. "The Duke is a fair man."

"Then with your permission," Giroux nodded to Philippe and then indicated to the two men beside him, "We shall take our leave. I will deliver this news. And you have my word, *Monsieur* Philippe. I will do whatever I can to ensure the peacefulness of your proposition." Then he shifted uncomfortably, "though I don't expect my leader will accept these parameters."

"If he sponsored these attacks in the name of his people, there should be no question that my offer is fair," Philippe said. "If he did this for himself, then it will clearly be unacceptable. Perhaps we shall both see who your leader really is."

The men rose then. Philippe shook Giroux's hand. Luc handed back their swords. Philippe directed Maurice and Auguste to go along with Giroux, to accompany his party back towards their camp to wait for communication. Then Philippe dusted his pants and returned to sitting, where he resumed his whittling. And like that, Alex realized the meeting was over. She was surprised that Giroux had been so humble. She was expecting a far more unstable bunch, but luckily, they didn't seem interested in causing problems.

As he turned to leave, Giroux hesitated. He slipped into that nearly forgotten dialect from the North they had heard in the *Sable Noir* and tried it on Philippe. "The girl," he said.

Alex's ears perked up, though she didn't lead on that she understood.

"What about her?" Philippe asked coldly, using the same dialect. She was surprised Philippe spoke it, but guessed most of the other men didn't. Giroux had been right in assuming a duke's son would be privy to the languages of his people.

"Before I go," Giroux began, "I must ask, why bring this woman with you?"

"She is our guide," he responded, not looking up.

"That is strange," he replied. When Philippe didn't respond, he continued, "If you wish to send a message of goodwill, I think my master should very much like a guide, as such."

Philippe's movements ceased. "She's not going anywhere," Philippe said with an eerie calm.

"It would be a very amicable gesture," Giroux pressed as his eyes flicked over to Alex.

"You have my answer," Philippe responded, his voice icy. The only other sound was that of his knife slicing persistently against the wood in his hand.

Alex felt like an idiot for drinking. Her heart thumped wildly while her thoughts and reasoning came hazily. Staying sharp was her survival, because she knew men, even otherwise decent ones, could flip at any moment. She knew Philippe wouldn't give her up without a fight, but Giroux was right. It would be a far better gesture on Philippe's part to send her away than to hurt the man with whom he negotiated. An immoral woman like her, after all, had very little value, and she knew she was more than expendable at this point in the mission. She leaned back, using the rock behind her to steady her body in case she had to jump into a fight. She just hoped her drink-riddled brain remembered how to use her blade...

Giroux gave a small nod with his head. "Unfortunately," he said, "My captain has heard of her already. He has asked that you send her as a token." Giroux shifted his weight. "To show that you are committed to moving forward without the need for more fighting."

Philippe was silent. He did not look up. The men around him started exchanging glances, as they began to realize the conversation between Philipp and Giroux had taken a turn. Alex noticed the men—her crew—were making their own subtle movements towards their weapons. Bernand pulled a dagger from his coat. Claude gripped his bow and positioned himself to ready an arrow.

Giroux was hesitant, seeming to notice the change in the men, but he continued. "I can tell you, *Monsieur*, he will not let up on the attacks if he does not have this assurance." He stepped forward, his hands held out in a beseeching gesture.

It was a long and resonant pause that followed in the hollow of the cave. Alex's senses had perked up against the wall of silence, and she breathed in the smoke from the fire, mixed with the sour smell of the filthy men who had threatened her. The two brutes puffed themselves out huskily, hands ready to fight with or without weapons. Giroux stood unflinching in front of Philippe, while Philippe's men galvanized behind him. Maurice stood up and cracked his knuckles. Luc took a heavy drink, stood up, and tossed the flask to the ground with a thud. Daniel drew his sword and snarled while the rest followed suit. Alex swung her head back and forth, watching the brawl unfold before her, trying to decide if she could help, but she caught the eye of Laurant. He mouthed to her, *Don't move.*

It was Philippe alone who did not seem agitated. He continued to play his blade against the wood, while everyone else stood rigidly around him. He was letting them fester, and the longer he ignored Giroux, the less significant his proposition became. It was an amazing feat, she was watching: this silent battle. And Philippe, dangerously assertive in his refusal to speak, promised to be more of a threat silent than with his sword to Giroux's throat. Giroux, suspended in his question, was unable to take it back or leave it behind, so he stood there, resolved to wait for an answer.

She thought the standoff may never end.

The fire broke the tension for them. It popped and sputtered like it had been doing all night, but this time a single spark spun into the air, much like the one that had burned Alex earlier. It floated down and landed on the back of Philippe's hand. Instead of striking the ember away, Philippe released the knife from his other hand, licked his thumb, and pressed the glowing spark into his flesh. It died with an audible hiss.

"You tell your leader," he said, brushing the black ash off his broken skin. "He will accept my offer or face the Duke's entire army. Not to mention these brutes behind me." His voice was steady, his tone was more than clear. "And if your benefactor comes near her or hurts her, I will take pleasure in ripping out his throat myself."

Giroux remained silent for a moment. Finally, he held up his hands. "I'm sorry, My Lord. I did not mean to offend."

"Bring our message to your captain," Philippe said, flipping back to the French they all understood. "We shall await his reply in Ponce." He stood up and folded his arms, indicating he was done with the conversation, the angry red wound visible on his hand.

Giroux nodded and took the cue. "*Au revoir*," he said. "I will send word." Not a moment later, they retreated into the darkness.

Philippe's remaining men held their positions. "Well," Philippe said after a moment. "We have survived our first encounter with these rebels, and they have survived their first encounter with us. I dare say they are far more lucky." A chuckle rippled through the men, and they were set at ease once more. They stretched and passed a congratulatory drink and began to prepare to leave. Everything had returned to normal just like that. The venomous threat in Philippe's countenance was gone. Alex blinked, wondering if the exchange she'd witnessed had been real.

Head still spinning, she rose to prepare her own horse, but the world seemed to trip, and she landed flat on her bottom. Everyone turned to her, and Philippe jumped to her side. "I can't stand," she said, looking ruefully up to him.

"You really should never drink," he said, a note of humor in his voice.

"I know." She frowned.

He directed the crew to go up ahead. "Check for any signs of danger," he said. "And be sure to clear the path for us. I'll wait with her until she can ride."

He led her closer to the fire then helped the men prepare to leave. She watched him, her heart throbbing with gratitude. They were to be alone, she realized, and the tingle that went through her left her gasping. As a lover or a fighter, he was even more dangerous than she had ever realized, and the thought made her thirst for him even harder.

Screw it, she thought. She'd blow up her life to be with him.

Chapter Twenty

Philippe finished preparing the horses and said goodbye to the last of his men. He turned to check on Alex and caught her eye. For a moment, he was taken aback by her stare. If he didn't know that she was drunk, he would have thought her look meant something very different.

He threw a final pack to Claude and smacked the back of his horse, then watched her for a moment. Alex sat on her bottom with her legs straight out in front of her staring back at him. Perhaps the firelight was tricking him into thinking he knew the look she was giving him, but he also knew better than to trust himself when it came to her.

The fire needed tending, so he stepped out to gather more wood. His eyes adjusted as he sorted through usable pieces littered near the water's edge. He had mixed feelings about the meeting. Instinct told him that Giroux could be an ally. The man's honor was apparent, but he was being manipulated by his leader. Philippe could tell that this situation went deeper than a mere stipend for the river villages, but did Giroux know? He could have taken Giroux and his grunts as prisoners. It would stop the raids and that was the goal, right? But with the leader still at large, the problem would not be solved. Philippe was trying to stay thoughtful and calm—sometimes through gritted teeth—and he felt like every aspect of his person was being tested on that front.

He felt he had handled the encounter with competence and honor. Then, Giroux had expressed desire to take Alex, and everything they had worked up to crumbled like a dam in a storm. In that moment, he knew that if he had moved, it would have been to attack Giroux. There would be no thought of justice or fairness, only maddening rage. The thing was, it wasn't that outlandish of a request. Giroux's leader may have thought the very reason they had brought Alex was as some kind of marriage treaty. Why else would they be dragging along this woman? Philippe had been frozen, not knowing how to proceed. Then he had felt the men gear up behind him, ready at his word to fight, and he was proud to have such strong fighters with him. For a second, all he could think was that this civil meeting was about to become an absolute slaughter, honor be damned.

But the fire had saved him and, perhaps, the entire mission. He'd ground the smoldering ember into his skin and the piercing pain refocused him. Giroux did not know how lucky he had been.

Philippe put his foot on a log and ripped a branch with a great *crack*. The force pulled at his charred skin, and he shook the pain from his hand once more. He took up a few more pieces of wood and returned to the fire. Alex stared at him intently, and he smiled at her. She was really funny when she was drunk, just a giant pair of eyes and absolutely no balance. He felt guilty for encouraging her to take the canteen, but he had never expected her to be so easily afflicted. He sat down next to her and added pieces of wood to the fire, stick by stick.

"So," he said, his voice soft. "We have begun our dialogue with the rebels." Though he did not look at her, he was acutely aware of her body and her movements next to him. She had bent her knees and was moving her hands up and down the length of her thighs, over those tight pants that he still couldn't get over. She was drunk. Very drunk, he reminded himself. He knew she was only acting like this because of the drink, but, *wow*, he couldn't imagine anyone more seductive.

"I'm cold," she pouted.

"I will put more wood on the fire."

"I don't need that," she breathed, while she strummed her fingers down his arm.

Now he turned to her, and they locked eyes. Her face was flushed and beautiful and before he knew it, he had reached out to tuck a piece of wild hair behind her ear. He scolded himself, but instead of her pulling away, she leaned into his hand. She closed her eyes, and he brushed his thumb against her cheek, warm from the fire. She looked at him again, and he understood everything. Alex wanted to get into trouble.

He cleared his throat and pulled back his hand. He poked again at the fire, thinking he may have to shove his whole hand into the center to clear his head this time. He would only stay here with her long enough to get her to stand, he thought with resolve. He wasn't going to do anything tonight that she wouldn't forgive him for tomorrow.

Alex wasn't making it that easy though. She slid the remaining few inches over to him, pulled up her knees, and rested against his side. "Do you remember the first time we sat near a river alone?"

"I do," he said, thinking of her lips, forever etched into his memories. "That was many years ago."

"It was the night before the competition," she said, still pressed against him.

"I remember," he smiled, still staring ahead into the flames. Her body against his was a timid invitation, but his own body was stiff with trepidation, afraid too much contact would be his undoing.

"The night before I *almost* beat you in the competition," she teased.

"You cheated, little fox." He leaned back to look at her and drank her in. Her thick hair flowed over her shoulders and down her tunic. A string tied at the top and crisscrossed down the center, the edge of her shirt tucked below the belt of her pants. He imagined what it would feel like to slip the silk off her skin.

"I still bested you," she said.

"You did," he whispered as he reached out to toy with the tie at her collar. He was feeling his body change: his breath coming quicker, his blood changing course. He could only resist so much; he was no angel.

"Do you remember when you kissed me?" Alex's voice turned husky. "That night? By the river?"

"I do," he said again. His voice was thick in his throat. He watched her mouth as she spoke, her words, each a drop of sugar that he wanted to lick from her lips. And for the second time that night, he knew that to make any move would be to lose control.

"I've thought about that kiss for many years," she said. "Often when I was alone." She paused and looked at him with trusting, open eyes. "I should like to experience it again," she admitted.

She was killing him. He knew it was probably wrong, but how could he refuse them both this pleasure? And if it were just a kiss, he could keep himself at bay. His heart pounded and he ached with want as he spoke before he could stop himself. "Then lie back, darling," he said, staring into her firelit eyes, "so that I may find your lips."

A breath escaped her as she reclined on the hard ground. Magnetism pulled him along with her, and he found himself balanced on his hands and knees looking down at her. Her lips parted and her eyelashes fluttered, and he realized he was about to taste her again. This was his chance to show her that things were different, that something had changed between them. He'd stolen all the other kisses from her, but this one, he decided, he would give back.

His knuckles ground into the dirt as he hovered above her. He watched her, worried his own need would ruin it, but then she smiled at him. He'd forgotten what an elixir her smiles could be, and he found himself grinning back. When he could hold himself back no longer, he leaned in, until his lips brushed hers. He was determined to keep some decorum, but she arched up to meet him and his instinct took over. He took her lips against his, first just the bottom, then both at once. They were soft and tender, peaches in the summertime. A powerful wave of desire shot through him then, and he nearly buckled above her. He kept the distance, though, and instead opened her mouth more fully so he could taste her more deeply. She accepted his kiss, and soon she was kissing him back, hypnotic movement between them.

Then her body was reaching for more. She bit her nails into his arms trying to pull him down closer to her. He responded by kissing her more desperately but at the same time straining his muscles to maintain some distance. This only made her writhe and whimper as she tested his resistance and reached for contact. It was too much. He had to stop before it went too far. He pulled back and looked into her eyes, assessing any damage he had done. She moved her hands to his shirt, more than content with their current situation, as she tried to pull him down to her.

"Philippe," she whispered, desperate. "Please do not stop."

He kissed her chin and lingered with his lips at her neck as she leaned back. "Alex, I don't think you know what you are asking for," he whispered against her skin.

"Yes, I do," she said. Still holding his shirt, she scooted up and shakily got on her knees in front of him. She pulled him up until he was kneeling as well, and she pressed her body against his. "Trust me," she said against his lips.

He felt a growl deep in his chest. He wrapped his arms around her waist and hugged her close. He felt the warmth and softness of her body separated from his by only a few thin layers of fabric. He fought back every instinct that said he had to take her there in the dirt. He couldn't do it. She wouldn't forgive him, and he couldn't forgive himself if he made love to her when she was not herself.

"Alex," he forced himself to say, "Please, *chérie*. We can't do this now."

She groaned and reached again for his lips, moving her body against him.

"Alex," he said again, his voice losing conviction. "We have to stop."

All at once she halted, the words sinking in. She looked at him and then scrambled back. She planted herself against a rock and put her hands over her mouth. "*Oh Dieu*," she said. "You just don't want me."

"No," he said, and he began to laugh. "That is not the problem."

"Then what is the problem," she said, anger rising in her voice. "I am here. I am ready. Why *now* are you not interested?"

"Darling," he said. "You are really drunk."

"I am not," she said. Then she hiccupped. "Maybe a little."

"I don't want to give you any opportunity to blame me for taking your innocence when you do not have all your senses."

She looked at him with her eyebrows knitted. "I don't believe you," she stated with stubborn conviction.

Without thinking, he snapped forward and grabbed her thighs. He dragged her roughly onto the ground beneath him. Instead of kissing her again, he moved down her body, and down her leg, to the little burn on the inside of her knee, barely visible through the hole the ember had burned into her pants earlier. He gripped the fringe of the opening and pulled the fabric apart with a loud rip. Then his hands were on her bare flesh and his lips at the edges of the fresh mark. He moved one hand up her inner thigh, until the fabric stopped him, but not before he brushed the border of her soft undergarments with his fingertips. Philippe shuddered as he ran his lips across her skin while digging his fingers into her flesh. Alex let out a cry, but then he released her thigh and was on top of her again, pushing against her this time, his kiss even more intense than before. Her lips, her tongue, her body, soft beneath him. When he broke away, he was gasping. "Don't mistake," he breathed. "I want to take your innocence. And if you should still want me in the morning, when nothing clouds your mind, I promise I won't let you leave the room until I have pleasured you thoroughly."

Alex, with a dreamy look on her face, drunk from the booze and soothed by the kiss, smiled languidly at him. "Then may I go to bed now to make that moment come even faster?"

"Yes, little fox," he laughed. "Let's get you back."

Philippe prepared the horses by tethering them together, then put out the fire and picked up the few items left behind while Alex sat quietly watching him. When he was ready, he asked her, "Are you sure you are able to ride?"

She nodded.

He helped her mount his horse then hopped on behind her. He snapped the reins and brought the horses to an easy trot. The night was clear, every star in the universe visible in the sky. Philippe grinned as he wrapped his arms around Alex, confident for the first time that she actually wanted his attention. He hoped that she would still feel the same tomorrow, but at least now he was convinced of her feelings. He just needed to find the right moment for them to come together. He was agitated and his blood hot, but he was content, in the moment, just to have her in his arms.

But then she spoke.

"Philippe?" she purred.

"*Oui belle*," he replied. He buried his face in her waves of hair and breathed her in. He wondered how she managed to smell so good, even when they had been out in the forest for the better part of an evening.

"Tell me what you would do to me," she said, her voice shy but also curious.

The small hold he had over himself broke in an instant and he felt his body go rigid again. She seemed to understand the change in him and arched back against him. He gripped her hips and breathed through his teeth.

"You are not making this night easy on me, little fox," he said.

"Tell me," she whispered. "If you were to take me tonight, what would you do?" Her words came, breathless.

The horses moved at a gallop and Philippe, realizing he was not concentrating on what he should be, slowed them back down to a trot. What was the harm? What trouble could they really get into on the back of a horse? He held the reins in his left hand, the pain from the burn ignored, and with his right hand he brushed the hair away from Alex's neck, exposing her balmy flesh to the night air.

He leaned into the crook of her neck, the smell of her more intoxicating than the bottle. "Well," he whispered into her ear, "I would begin by exploring your body. First with my fingertips," he traced a line with his fingernail from just behind her ear down her neck. "Then with my mouth." He kissed her along the same line. "I would like to learn every inch of you. But that's not something I could do in just one night. It would take me many, many more."

Alex shivered against him. "Then?" she sighed.

"I would like to go slow with you, Alex," he said. He moved his hand down and pulled the tie of her shirt open, exposing the top of her camisole underneath. He ran his fingers along the lacey edge, tracing the curve of each breast. "But you make me too hot, and I would take great pleasure in teaching you what those pants you wear do to a man." With that, he bit at her neck and moved both hands down to clutch her hips once more.

She breathed his name, urging him forward. He responded by wrapping the horses' reins around his wrist, so he had full use of his two hands. Then he deftly unlaced her tunic and at once her shirt was fully open to him. He found his way under the edges of her camisole and pushed his hands up her lean torso and across her fiery skin until her tight breasts were his. He was tentative at first, just daring to feel the soft weight in his hands, knowing he was going further than he should, but then she pressed herself into his hands with a cry, and he seized her possessively. He struggled to move gently. He had no grace or modesty left at this point and he knew the full force of his want throbbed hard against her.

"Alex," he said. "I'm sorry. I'm trying. But I can't stop myself."

"Don't. Don't stop touching me," she begged, arching back to put her arms around his neck.

He groaned in response to her yielding. He wanted her in a bed, or on the ground, or up against a tree, but this was all he had and he wasn't going to waste it. He released one breast then and moved his hand down lower, and for the first time since he had known her, he was disappointed she wasn't wearing a skirt. If she were, he could tease her far more effectively. Instead, he fumbled at the tie of her pants, looking for a way in. But with his head too foggy and his hand too clumsy, he couldn't figure it out. Instead, he grabbed a fistful of fabric and tugged the seam of the pants right up her center. She cried out and he did it again. And then again and again, until he controlled her rhythm, and she panted in his arms.

The poor horses were barely moving at all, Philippe having all but forgotten them. He kissed her neck and bit again at her shoulder. Alex gasped and as she did, he felt full of pride and possession. She was his woman. She was his. And he was seconds away from bringing her pleasure to its peak.

She let a delicious moan out into the night. Then she tensed up and jerked, bringing her hands down to grip his arms. Philippe squeezed her tight, burying his face in her hair, awaiting her moment, thrilled to be the one giving it to her.

"Philippe," she cried.

"Alex," he murmured against her.

"Philippe, Philippe. I need to—" she continued, breathing heavily. She writhed against him, and he held her even tighter.

"Come for me, *chérie*" he whispered, "and I promise the next time it will happen when I am inside you."

"Philippe, I think I'm going to—" she said again but couldn't finish her sentence. Suddenly, she pitched forward, broke out of his grasp, and dropped her head to the side of the horse. Then with one last gasp, she vomited right down his leg.

Philippe froze. Alex heaved again, spewing the rest of the alcohol into the dirt. The horses whinnied and sidestepped, causing Philippe to break from his shock and take control over them once again. Alex hung limply forward.

Cautiously, Philippe reached his free hand forward and pulled her hair back. Alex whimpered as she gripped the saddle, her head hanging low.

It took a moment for his brain to catch up. He touched her cheek. What just happened? He thought she was about to... Not... He arranged her hair and stroked her back. Then with a great burst of sound, Philippe threw his head back and laughed more fully than he had in a very long time.

"Why are you laughing?" asked Alex in a pitiful, muffled voice. "I threw up on your boot."

"Come here, little fox," he said, helping her upright. He pulled her hair off to the side and arranged her shirt so that she was covered once more.

"I'm sorry," she said, her head in her hands. "I'm so sorry. Everything is spinning."

"Try to rest," he said, stifling his laughter. "I will get you back." He held her tight, and she leaned her head against his shoulder. He was trying to be serious, but he couldn't break the smile from his face. He kicked his boot, attempting to shake it clean. What had this girl done to him? He was inside out and covered in vomit. He turned again to her hair and chuckled into it. He closed his eyes for a moment and breathed her in. And that's when he realized that he was in love. Utterly and madly in love.

Chapter Twenty-One

A few miles away, Giroux and his companions were racing to their outpost. The hooves of the horses pounded on the ground as they whipped through the trees. How had the young lord known so much, he wondered, feeling a pall hover around him. Their plan, which had been so carefully crafted, had been unraveled right before him. He didn't know what to make of it, but he knew his leader would not be pleased by the clever connections the young man had begun to make.

Giroux had been lucky that his benefactor desired to bring aid into the region. Giroux had long advocated on behalf of his village, but no one important ever wanted to listen. Until, that is, Giroux had stumbled upon the man who would be his champion and who gave him a willing ear. Suddenly, there was an objective and a plan. There was money to fund their actions. It may not have been a noble army behind him, like his grandfather had once led, but Giroux had been given a voice and was proud to be leading a mission to help his people like the great men in his lineage had done before him. Loyalty to his master—his *maître*—had burned in his chest.

From the beginning, however, Giroux wasn't always comfortable with the practices of his leader. The man was quick and brutal; he refused to use names and spoke to few. But the *maître* was a smart man, far more intelligent than Giroux himself, and Giroux had given up trying to understand the finer details in his reasoning. Though Giroux may not have always agreed with the tactics, his *maître* was much better at getting results than Giroux had ever been.

His *maître* had said that the Duke would not listen to reason unless he was forced, and that's when they began making the raids, even though Giroux was against it. His master had assured him that the attacks must match the desperation of the impoverished men of Babin, or no one would take their plights seriously. But the men with whom he worked were not his countrymen. They were mercenaries—as *Monsieur* Philippe had deduced—who had no honor. They stole, they pillaged, they killed livestock. Though Giroux had struggled to contain it all, several of the attacks had happened without his sanction. That was how the boy had died. Giroux always staked out his targets to be sure of the number of inhabitants and always made sure they had sufficient means of escape during the attack. But without his presence... Giroux had wept in solitude when he learned of the boy and requested humbly that they stop the raids. But his *maître* had spoken soothing words and promised it would serve the greater good in the end.

The five-man party approached a shallow bank of the river then. It was a good spot for a small camp and Giroux left *Monsieur* Philippe's two men there for the night. He would meet with them in the morning, and they would return to Ponce with the *maître*'s response. Giroux's own camp was not twenty minutes beyond the riverbank, but he wanted a moment for himself to collect his thoughts. He directed his two soldiers to return to their group, saying he would be along shortly, while he himself took a moment to travel a little ways downstream.

He traveled only far enough to feel the isolation, then dismounted his horse and plunged his face into the cool water of the stream. Tonight, he'd been given the chance he'd been waiting for. He'd spoken to *Monsieur* Philippe with sincerity and passion about the suffering of his people. And *Monsieur* had listened. Even after the brief meeting, Giroux felt he could trust the confident young man's word. *Monsieur* Philippe's one criterion in providing aid was that his leader would stand trial. Giroux laughed to himself as he wiped the water from his face. His *maître* was many things, but he was not a man who would face the public. He was also a man, Giroux knew, who could be very dangerous if he didn't get what he wanted.

Then, of course, there was the debacle over the girl, the strange girl who they had observed traveling with *Monsieur* Philippe's party. Giroux shook his head as he removed his boots and stockings, dipping his feet into the clear water. The cold cut into his skin, but it helped him to clear his chaotic thoughts. Being flushed from the caves earlier that week had come as a great hit to their safety and anonymity. The interactions with the Duke's men would have been on their terms as long as they had stayed hidden. Once they had been discovered, Giroux's *maître* had floundered to find new leverage. Then his leader had set his eyes on the girl. No competent leader would give up a comrade, any comrade, but if he happened to be in love with one of them... Well then, they had found a way to force his hand.

Giroux had adamantly refused to bring her into it at first, but once again his master's smooth tongue had convinced him to do something that made him uncomfortable. One mention of her tonight proved the theory correct. *Monsieur* Philippe's response was just what his master had predicted and, furthermore, had given Giroux powerful insight into just who the young man would be as an adversary. Giroux felt trapped. He didn't know which man would be a more devastating enemy.

However, he had a solution. One that became clearer as he sat with his sore feet dangling in the water: Giroux would be the one to stand trial in Chevalerie. Though the crimes may have not been his idea, he had been part of them. As long as he knew his people would be taken care of—his *maître* would be left to protect them—his own fate mattered very little. He just hoped he was putting his trust in the right man.

He remounted the horse and set off towards their camp. He rode until he came into range. He smelled the fire before he saw the outline of the small hunting shack that served as their marker. There were voices and the outlines of men he recognized.

He passed the corral where they kept their horses and came into the clearing. He jumped to the ground and asked, "Has *Maître* arrived yet?" in the northern dialect, which was the only language most of them spoke.

"He is among us," one of the men responded. He pointed in the opposite direction.

Giroux swung around and saw the hooded figure seated on a log at the edge of the clearing. He was surprised at first that his master would let himself be so casually among his soldiers, as Giroux was typically the only one to deal with the leader directly. He should have guessed the man would be eager to hear of the outcome.

"*Maître*, I come with news," he said, approaching the man. He returned to proper French as his master rejected the language of commoners.

"Indeed," his master spoke. He sat still, with his hands placed on his knees. His face was obscured by the cloak, but his bearing alone confirmed his identity. "I see he did not give up the girl."

"No," Giroux responded. "He became very aggressive when I asked of her."

"Hmm," was his reply.

"But I have his response," Giroux continued.

"Speak then. Tell me he abides."

"He said fifty francs per month per village, but we relinquish access to the river," explained Giroux. "And someone must stand trial for the loss of property and the boy."

"That is an insult." He did not break his rigid posture.

Giroux then kneeled before the man. "I beseech you, My Lord. The deal is not so bad." He lowered his head into a bow. "I will stand trial, *Maître*. If you will allow it."

"And then what?" the cloaked man asked, rising. He took a few strides away, staring off into the night. "The money will be sent to the towns?"

"Yes," Giroux rose from his bow and watched the man. "That is the deal."

"I just hope he keeps his word," he continued.

"I don't see why he wouldn't," Giroux said.

The man turned then and took three powerful steps towards Giroux. "Of course, you don't," he said potently. "Because you are an honest man. Honest men have trouble picking out liars." He held his hands behind his back, adjusting his posture once more. Giroux could just make out his jawline, and it was set in sternness. "My friend," he continued. "You do know that you are being manipulated, don't you?"

"I don't see how, *Maître*," Giroux responded.

The *maître* strode away again and waved his hand out towards the other men. "You or I or any of these fools could stand trial. Don't you see? Once the Duke can parade around his catch and show that he has found the man causing the trouble, your wishes will be moot. He will secure another generation of power while you and your people pay the price."

"I didn't think of that possibility," Giroux said stiffly.

"The tax on the river is the only deal we want. Do you trust that after all these years the Duke will suddenly reach into his own coiffeurs and begin sending tribute to your home? Your cast-aside, forgotten home? Just because you asked?" He laughed into the night. "My friend," he said, putting his hand on Giroux's shoulder. "The only way to control the flow of money is to control the river yourself. You know that. You also know a mere fifty francs per month is a pittance if you even get it. Do not let the Duke and his minions cheat you out of what you deserve."

"Then I will return to his men," Giroux responded, "to give *Monsieur* Philippe our answer. We will negotiate a more suitable agreement."

The cloaked man turned his head and watched out into the forest. He stared for a moment before replying, "I have a better idea."

Giroux heard the clamor of bodies in the brush before he saw them. He squinted his eyes into the dark. Had they been followed? He grabbed towards the sword on his belt.

He shortly realized it was unnecessary. It was his two men he had left moments ago. The tension in his body dissipated, only to come surging back a second later when he saw with whom they traveled. Tied at the wrists and gagged, were *Monsieur* Philippe's two soldiers, the ones Giroux had left by the river. They stumbled behind their captors, wild eyed and frantic.

The prisoners were shoved to their knees before the *maître*. They looked around madly, and when they saw Giroux, they spoke incoherent pleas to him through their gags. The other men from the camp were looking over and had begun to move closer, vultures to a kill.

"*Maître*, there is no need to bind them," Giroux said anxiously. He had not expected these men to be in danger. "They came with my approval."

"My friend," he said. "You must learn to take advantages where you find them. *Monsieur* Philippe wants my response?" He looked to the prisoners for a moment then nodded casually towards the one on the right. "Send his head."

The bound men sputtered panicked appeals into the night. Giroux stared at his *maître* aghast. "I refuse," he stated plainly. This was all a step too far, too dishonorable. Giroux just wanted to help his people, not murder innocent men in cold blood.

His *maître* paid no mind. "Who here will earn his position in the new regime we create together?" he said at large to the group, conceding to the commoner dialect.

The mercenaries looked at each other, snarls forming while a silent battle elected the bravest.

"I will," said one, stepping forward. He removed his blade from his belt and, in a remorseless motion, swung at the man's neck, taking his head off with two hacking cuts. Blood pooled at Giroux's feet as the body slumped to the ground. The other prisoner screamed behind his gag, pulling against his binding until he too collapsed, twisting in the dirt.

The hooded man approached the struggling prisoner and pulled him up by the shirt. He grabbed his chin and angled him up to his own obscured face. "I would like you to tell your leader what you have witnessed here tonight. Can you accomplish that?"

The man nodded his head violently, speaking terrified nonsense into this gag.

"Take him back," he said in dialect, and the two men who had brought them in, as of yet unfazed, leaned in to pick him up.

Then the *maître* turned coldly to Giroux and spoke. "You have followed my leadership thus far. If you choose to stop now, then all of these sins will all have been done in vain." He kicked the head to Giroux's feet. "Now, I believe someone is waiting for our reply."

Chapter Twenty-Two

Philippe rode steadily back to town. When he reached the stables, the attendants helped him get Alex off the horse. By then she had completely passed out. He tried to rouse her enough to stumble to her room, but her legs gave out. He solved the problem by picking her up and carrying her through the doors to the inn.

At the sound of guests, the innkeeper came rushing out to be of service. He looked at them questioningly. Philippe knew the humor in his expression had to confuse the old man.

"Is she alright, *Monsieur*?" the innkeeper asked.

"Yes, she's drunk," he said. "She will be fine. Would you mind sending a pitcher of water and a basin to her room?"

"*Certainement, Monsieur*," he said.

"And if you could find me a change of pants?" he asked, indicating his soiled leg.

"*Oui, Monsieur*," he said, scuttling off but not before giving Philippe another odd look.

Philippe maneuvered her down the hall to her room and got through the door with the help of several expectant attendants. He laid her on the bed and began to undo her boots. The innkeeper brought the water and Philippe directed everyone out. He pulled off her boots and stockings and rid her of her weapons. Though a little disheveled, with torn pants and a rumpled shirt, she'd remained reasonably clean, Philippe himself having gotten the worst of it. Her body was floppy and limp, making it easy for him to work, but she'd still crumple up her brow and let out a protesting moan every now and then. He worked quickly, having done this very thing for his brothers and his men multiple times in his life. Succumbing to drink was a common problem on the road, but he had never cared for a woman like this. Though he kept her modesty in mind, he worked with efficiency and purpose. Once she was laid out more or less unencumbered, he took a cloth, dipped it in the water and began washing her face. He leaned her forward and put a second pillow behind her, propping her up.

"Alex." He attempted to rouse her with a gentle shake. "Wake up."

"Mmmmm," she whined in protest.

"Come now," he patted her cheek. "Open your eyes."

"No," she mumbled. "My head hurts." She tipped forward and he caught her.

"Drink this water or you will feel worse in the morning." He held the cup against her lips.

"I don't want it," she said, shaking her head.

"Drink it," he commanded, titling the cup to wet her lips.

Alex grumbled but followed orders, taking a few gulps before she shut her mouth and refused any more.

"You are a terrible drunk," he chuckled.

She sank into the cushions and curled up into a ball. "I don't feel good," she whimpered.

"I know you don't," he replied. He sat next to her on the bed and again dipped the rag into the basin of water. He wrung it out and dabbed her forehead and neck, running his thumb along her cheek and the edge of her lips. He smiled to himself—she was certainly the prettiest drunk he'd ever cared for.

He left the rag on her forehead for a moment. As he was still waiting for pants, he decided to strip down to his undergarments and set the dirty pair outside of the room to be cleaned. He'd already decided that he would stay with her, as he would do for any of his men. Of course, the fact that it was Alex made the situation a little more delicate, but he hoped the closeness they had shared tonight would afford him her trust. He'd been a gentleman with her, mostly, and she was in no danger with him. Really, he'd take any excuse not to leave her side. He had realized he was in love with her, and everything had become clear. His lack of finesse around her, his inability to let her out of his sight, his uncharacteristically muddled head. The feeling had been growing inside him until it was a raging force and affecting everything he did. Even his more careful and prolonged pursuit of Giroux had gone painstakingly slow in part because he wanted to keep her safe and spend as much time near her as possible.

What a moron he was to not have realized sooner, but he'd never experienced anything like this before. His interest in women had always been... different, less complicated. To think, had he taken her the moment she entered Chevalerie like he had wanted, he would have missed all the enchanting moments between them, the ones, he realized, that had forged his feelings and, he hoped, hers as well. He didn't know what she would say to him when she woke up. Perhaps she would slip into his arms. Perhaps she would hate him again. No matter, because now that he had it figured out, he would chase her for a lifetime if he had to.

He watched her as she slept, more peacefully now, feeling warmth in his heart. He shook his head and chuckled to himself, the events of the evening having taken so many strange turns. He pulled a blanket over her and lay next to her on the outside of it. He rested his head on the pillow and crossed his arms across his chest. He closed his eyes and a satisfied smile worked its way onto his lips before he drifted off to sleep. He hadn't felt this content in a very long time.

He was unsure how long he had been asleep when a loud crash snapped him awake. He was disoriented at first and, looking to see that Alex hadn't stirred, he wondered if he had imagined it. The commotion outside the door told him otherwise. He jumped out of bed, threw on his jacket, and realized he was still in his stockings. There was no time to find pants now, so he buckled his sword belt and ran down the hall to investigate.

Out in the parlor, the innkeeper stood by the door with his candle, unsure of whether or not to open it in a repeat of last night's performance. Several civilian guests had poked their heads in, looking to see what had happened. Thankfully, Philippe saw Laurent, Claude, and Franc with their swords at the ready, and he heard the rest of his men coming down the hall.

"What has happened?" called Philippe.

"Something hit the door, *Monsieur*," said the innkeeper, "but we see no travelers from the windows."

Philippe drew his sword. "Let's see what it is this time," he said.

The innkeeper obliged, sliding the long plank of wood that barricaded the door to the side and jumping back into the shadows as the door creaked open. Philippe and his men held their positions, but nothing came through the door. Philippe hadn't expected communication until the morning. He felt deep in his bones that whatever message he was being given, would not be a good one. Philippe crept out into the darkness, but unlike last night, as soon as his vision adjusted to the dark, he saw something in the dirt, just a few yards away. His eyes couldn't make it out. His spirit, however, knew it was ominous and his stomach lurched in anticipation. He moved closer, cautious of the darkness, the feeling of foreboding as thick as blood. He was nearly upon the object before he understood what he was looking at.

He kneeled down and bowed his head at the ghastly scene. Then he reached out and closed the dead eyes of his fallen comrade.

"What is it?" he heard Laurent ask behind him.

Philippe continued to stare a moment, unsure of what to say, but very sure of the blazing anger pulsing in his chest. His men crept up behind him, and he heard the silence change as they too realized just what they were looking at.

He took off his jacket and covered the blood-caked mass. He tucked the sides under, feeling overwhelming remorse. He had let this happen. Maurice had died because he had misjudged the situation.

Out in the distance came a cry. Philippe looked to the sound as Laurent and Franc whizzed by him. There, in the field that bordered the inn was a shadowed figure, stumbling into view.

"It's Auguste!" Laurent shouted.

Philippe could see Auguste's hands had been bound as Laurent and Franc cut the ties. They helped the man to his feet and walked him to the rest of the group.

"Get some water! And a blanket!" Philippe rose and called out. "Does anyone have any booze?"

Bernard stepped forward and handed Auguste a small flask. “Here, brandy, here ya go,” he muttered.

“Philippe,” Auguste said, panting and out of breath, before gulping at the flask. He was scraped and cut about the face and his breeches had been torn in several places, but he was standing. “They ambushed us.”

Philippe grasped his man’s shoulder. “Do you need to sit?”

“No.”

“What happened?” Philippe asked.

“They pulled us into their camp. There weren’t very many. Eight, nine. Giroux was there. And there was another man. He was cloaked. He was the one in charge.”

“Did you get a look at him?”

He shook his head.

“Did he say anything?”

Auguste licked his swollen lips and shook his head again. He took another drink from the flask. “They stopped talking before we got there. And then some of it was in the Northern dialect. I didn’t understand everything, but he told Giroux they needed a new advantage, and then he looked at us and said to send Maurice’s head.” He swallowed hard. “I don’t know why him and not me.”

Philippe continued. “Who did it?”

“One of the grunts.” He squeezed his eyes shut and rubbed dirt and sweat from his eyes. “Then the leader told me to come back and tell you what I saw. They dumped me off a horse a half mile back.” He looked down at his hands. “Philippe, I have a wife in Chevalerie. I’ve got a baby on the way.”

Philippe gripped him on both arms. “You’re okay,” he said. “You’re alive.”

Auguste nodded and took another drink.

The innkeeper rushed out then and covered Auguste with a blanket. The inn and nearby buildings were coming alive as people realized something had happened. More attendants came to assist and help make sense of the tragedy, while Auguste was led inside. Philippe stared off across the dirt, past the square and into the open wilderness. He had played the patient negotiator long enough.

“We go after them tonight,” he ordered.

"Philippe," said Laurent. "It will be exceedingly difficult to track them through the night."

"I don't give a damn," he said. "We go now before they have time to regroup."

He turned and stormed into the inn to gather what few supplies he needed. He was sick to his stomach with guilt, rage, and impatience. One of his men had died, and it was his fault. Not wanting to put Alex in danger may have been the catalyst for his uncharacteristic patience in unraveling these crimes, but he had truly thought that endurance would be the key to this campaign. Had they taken out Giroux or his men sooner, would they have learned of the problem at the river? If they took them out now, would they ever discover the identity of the leader? If they didn't isolate the leader, would the problem even be solved? He loathed the waiting and hated not knowing the solution. But of all the variables, he did know one thing for sure: Giroux was the key to discovering their true enemy.

He made arrangements with his men and delegated tasks to the staff, each of whom busied around helping to prepare for the sudden departure. He gathered his own things and with permission, sat behind the innkeeper's desk. He rubbed his fingers across his forehead. Alex would never forgive him for leaving her behind. He had been so close to unlocking something wonderful with her, he thought with a knife of regret to his heart, but he had to go. This was his duty, and she had fulfilled hers once they had finished with the caves. He needed to write to his father about his progress as well, but that could wait. Right now, he would leave a note for Alex. He rustled in the desk until he found what he needed and spread a piece of parchment out in front of him. He took a deep breath and wrote across the page, *My Dearest Alex.* All he could do was hope that she would forgive him once more.

Chapter Twenty-Three

Birds were chirping, singing, and twittering pleasantly as Alex awoke. There was light on her face and the air she breathed was warm. Alex's eyes fluttered open and she stared at the ceiling of her room for a moment, listening to the lovely sounds of the morning just outside her sun-soaked window.

Wait. What?

She sat up like she was spring-loaded but had to grab her head as a dart of pain ran through her. She sank back into the sheets. It had been years since she slept past sunrise. What had happened? Why did her head hurt? Was she sick? No, she wasn't sick, she realized with dread. She was hungover. Her stomach curdled, filling her mouth with saliva and forcing her to swallow hard. Very, very hungover.

The memories of last night began to come back to her. Philippe had threatened the big man who wanted to take her. He had protected her, she thought, warmth growing in her chest. They had kissed, she'd just about *begged* to sleep with him, and then he had gotten her on the horse and she...

"Oh my god," she said aloud. She covered her mouth with her hands, then buried her face in the covers. "Oh my god!" she whimpered.

What the hell had she done last night? She tried to have sex with

Philippe, then she threw up on him. What kind of tricks of fate were being played on her?

She sifted through her memories and tried to determine just how bad her actions had been. Had she really thrown herself at him, and he had rejected her? No, that wasn't quite right. He wouldn't sleep with her because she was drunk. She attempted to sit up again and brought her knees up to her chest, realizing she still wore the clothes from last night. Then she saw the tear in her pants and remembered the kisses they had shared, and she began to melt all over again. They had reached a whole new level and his hands on her body had nearly killed her. If only she hadn't been such an idiot, perhaps they would have...

Wait, hadn't he sworn to bed her once she was free from the grip of drink? Suddenly, her focus changed. She was right back where she was yesterday. She still hungered for Philippe and, at the thought of him, her body was coming alive again. She would find him and demand he make good on his promise, so maybe she could go back to normal and stop this obsession. With new determination, she threw back the covers, pain in her head be damned.

That's when she saw it, the note on the bed stand, leant up against the cup of water she vaguely remembered him trying to make her drink the night before. The letter had her name on it.

She reached forward, hand shaking, knowing that whatever was in this letter was not something she would be happy about.

She leaned back against her pillows and opened the parchment. *My Dearest Alex*, it began.

It is a cruel joke that I must leave you tonight, but our enemy retreats and I must follow. We cannot wait until the morning. If they escape into the Alps, it will be nearly impossible to make them pay for their crimes. I hope the soldier that lives inside you will understand.

But it is the woman in you I must beg for forgiveness. Please do not run away, Alex. I have so many things to say to you, but I cannot possibly do it here. In one week's time, I believe you have promised to attend the Marquis' ball. I don't know what dangers await us, but I will be there, looking for you. I shall pray every night to find you. Please, I beseech you to meet me there.

Your servant,
Philippe

P.S. As I write this, I am waiting for a clean pair of pants. You are dangerous even when you are drunk, little fox.

Alex clutched the letter and read it two, three times before she sank back down against the pillow. He was gone, and her role in this mission had ended. She had been trying so hard to disconnect her feelings from this man, but she felt a sense of sadness that gripped her right down to her toes. She had *just* decided to explore what could happen between them, to let this maddening desire take over, and now the opportunity was gone. She didn't know the circumstances of their departure or to what places they now traveled, but she did know a week was a very long time, and surely by the end of this one, he would have found someone new to entertain him. She had basked in the attention that he gave her for as long as she could—the feelings he evoked, so achingly sweet—but she always knew it was only temporary. At least if they had indeed slept together, he would have given her a memory that could warm her for years. It would have been a gratifying way to say goodbye. Alex stared up at the beams in the ceiling and closed her eyes. With a terrible sense of disappointment, she realized she would probably never see him again.

Chapter Twenty-Four

The men had ridden hard throughout the night and were near the point of exhaustion, but Philippe did not want to stop until their targets had stopped as well. He had given his troops mere moments to water the horses, but he was determined to move fast, faster than their opponents. With every step away from Ponce they took, it was more likely that they would lose their adversaries, that their purpose would fizzle out into the forest, and the inciter of these crimes would get away. Not to mention the further he had to travel, the more likely it was that Alex would be gone when he returned. He was going to crush this bastard with his hands when he found him.

He was down to eight fighting men: Sébastien, wounded in Ponce; Henri, not great with a sword; and of course, Maurice, gone. Auguste had refused to stay behind, and Philippe admired his tenacity. With seven good fighters behind him, Philippe felt confident he could take on this group. If he could find them.

Philippe still believed that Giroux was sincere in his desire to help the people in the villages. Though he'd doubted this leader of theirs would easily give up his position and agree to stand trial in Chevalerie, Philippe had thought it was possible that he could win Giroux's loyalty after a few more meetings. He had anticipated more negotiations, not the violent reaction they had gotten instead. Their leader obviously had some greater hold over Giroux than Philippe had thought.

They had been chasing three men on horses, allowing the smaller group to be much swifter than Philippe's crew. The trail had grown thinner and harder to read for the last few miles. They had gone through an open valley, over a section of the river and back into the trees. Hard dirt and scant underbrush gave few clues. Philippe had hoped with the new morning light he could track them more easily, but by mid-morning, he had to concede that the trail was dead and the rebels had moved out of range. It was time to stop and re-evaluate their next steps. It would do no good, tearing into the wild with no direction.

They approached a rocky hill and to the relief of his men, Philippe ordered them to stop and told them to throw down their bedrolls at the base of the hill. He left them to hike the incline. The summit was twenty minutes away, and when he reached it, he could see out across the far expanse of wilderness. To the East was the valley they had crossed after leaving Aliette, and further south would be the town itself. The morning was clear and he could see all the way to the rocky beginnings of the mountains they had left behind. Further south, back towards Chevalerie, he saw the rolling tumble of forest reach out until the green trees melted against the blue sky into a hazy ash-grey infinity. Their prey was out there in the hundreds of open miles, tucked somewhere deep in the whispering forest that stretched as far as he could see. He would wait atop the hill until he saw some sign of their movement.

In his military career he never had a chase like this. As a lord, he was often involved in the political parts of battles, this being the foundation of his easy diplomacy. However, he preferred the tangibility of fighting; in fact, his consummate skill had come to the detriment of many a foe. He was happy to leave the political aspects to his brother Michel, who delighted in unraveling puzzles, or even Serge, his other brother on the seas, who flat-out refused diplomacy and got what he wanted through intimidation. Philippe liked to *act*, to make moves. This slow chase was torture.

Who was this man, their leader? What was his motivation in this scheme? Philippe wished for his father's council in that moment. But as his father was not there, Philippe himself would have to find the leader. First, Philippe would find Giroux and his camp. Philippe would then get Giroux to lead him to their captain, somehow. Until then, Philippe would stake him out. Watch. Wait. Once again, his endurance would be tested, this time all the more stinging because of how badly he wanted instead to pursue the inimitable woman who had captured his heart.

Philippe sizzled in the sunlight, frustrated and obstinate against the delay. He had barely slept in the last twenty-four hours, but he was too keyed up to feel the deprivation. He would sit and watch as steadily as the rock against which he leaned until he knew where his targets had gone. He needed his next move to be in the right direction. He needed the land to give him a sign. He crossed his arms, stared across the expanse, and waited.

Two hundred miles south, the Duke sat on the second floor terrace that looked back towards the North. The sun had almost fully risen for the day, and it was warm, though the days themselves had been cooling off. His lovely city of Chevalerie bustled in the valley just south, but he was caught up in his tower, mulling over what could be happening with the rebels. He had yet to receive any communication from his son. He stared out, down the grassy slope, into the trees that obscured the road, willing a messenger to appear. It was not really so much time gone, and he understood that many things could happen to delay a note, but in his gut, he felt that something had gone wrong. The Duke had hoped the mission would be swift and sure, but the duration indicated it had become more complicated. He trusted his son to execute a plan of which he would approve. He just hoped they had not come up against more trouble than anyone had foreseen.

He twisted his fingers around the arm of the chair, squeezing and releasing his fists in an effort to relieve his irritation, though what he wanted was to get his hands on someone, whoever was causing this problem. Even now, at nearly sixty years, he struggled with controlling his anger, and in situations like this, all his emotions were converted into ire. He'd learned ways around it, for the sake of his family, for the sake of his people, but it had never gone away, and it was a problem that continued to plague him.

Behind him, the door opened as soft as a kiss and his tension began to disperse like smoke in a breeze. His wife's honey scent which he loved so much announced her arrival. She had always acted as an opiate to him, her presence calming him in the worst of times. He felt a hand on his shoulder and reached up to squeeze it without turning, still unable to pull himself from his worry.

"Guillaume," she coaxed. "It is time for your lunch. You must stop ruminating over the situation."

"For such a small-scale problem, *Bleu*, there is a great deal at stake," he said. He pulled her around to face him.

"There is indeed," she nodded. "But your worry will do nothing more than make you ineffective when action must be taken."

"He should have sent me communication by now," he shook his head, feeling the tension tighten across his chest. "He knows I have no patience."

"Of course he should have. But you know Philippe," she said. She sat on the arm of his chair and leaned against him. "He won't tell you what has happened until everything is done. It does not mean there is any problem."

"Aye," he said. "But there is a problem. I can feel it in the way the wind blows. I now must decide if we storm the territory in greater numbers or continue to wait."

She sighed. "Don't tell me you intend to send Michel now."

"Perhaps just to make sure everything is going smoothly. Philippe may be happy for the reinforcements."

"As soon as I get my sons back here, you always find a way to get rid of them," she teased him. "Next you will pull Serge off the seas and send him as well."

"I would go myself," he said, still staring off, thinking for a moment how good it would feel to fight someone in that moment. To grab whatever culprit was causing these problems, put his hands around their neck and squeeze and squeeze—

"You will do no good if you do," Laure said, interrupting his thoughts. "You will upset any progress he has made by trying to take over."

"Are you not the one who always insists I talk out my problems? Trust me, I'd much rather rip the door from the hinges and throw it over the balcony as a means of distraction." It was coming. He felt it begging him. It was just irritation at this point, but he knew where that could lead if left unchecked: the heated blood up his neck, the reddening patches of vision, stinging tension in his chest. He'd gotten much better at maintaining his countenance, but his temper had cost him in the past and nearly destroyed him more than once. It was not something to be discounted, and it was why he deployed his sons when he did. He was not so old that he couldn't fight or command; he was not feeble in mind or body. But really, he had grown tired of dealing with the struggle to keep himself in check, to avoid detriment to his soldiers and citizens on his behalf. He squeezed his fist until his fingernails bit into his palm.

"Darling stop," his wife said on the brink of a laugh as she pressed her palm against his cheek. Almost immediately, her voice and her touch cooled the burning behind his eyes. His mind spun back into place as he looked at her—dark blue eyes, black hair barely touched by age, more beautiful every single day— and took her hand to kiss it.

"Ah *mon coeur*," he said. "You know I look to you."

She repositioned herself to face him. "I don't think it is a bad idea to send Michel." Then she looked out along the same line his eyes had been following. "But I wouldn't send the whole infantry. This is still a delicate matter."

"I am not ready to do it yet," he agreed. "But I believe Michel should be prepared. I have a feeling that when we do hear from Philippe, he will be requesting more men." They sat in silence for a moment, staring off into the distance. Guillaume closed his eyes and sketched an addendum to the plan that involved his eldest son, if need be. The resolution soothed his agitation.

Then, feeling better, he smacked his wife's bottom, "Come now," he said. "Let us have our lunch and see how Michel feels about the possibility of heading out."

"I'm sure he'll be thrilled to jump on a horse and ride into danger like the other two."

"We have bred fine boys," he said. He put his arm around her waist and they walked towards the door. "I am lucky to have them at my disposal."

"You just wait," she said. "Once they each find a woman, they won't be so willing to leave."

"Please, *Bleu*, let me worry about that another day. I have bigger things to think about right now."

Chapter Twenty-Five

Alex had been having the laziest day of her life. She'd spent most of the morning in bed dozing on and off. Her head hurt, along with her stupid heart, and she had no motivation to do anything. At about noon, she got up with no idea about where to go. She felt a little better but wouldn't ride today, at least not until she could get a meal down. How did the men do this so well? She decided she would never *ever* drink again.

She had roamed the town market and wandered the stalls. Many were still closed, but a few had wares out, and she was thankful for the distraction. She ended up at a bakery where she bought a hunk of bread. She took it to the main square and nibbled on it while she watched the people go about their business. Her job was done, and she had no immediate prospects. She had been hired to lead a party into the caves, locate the rebels and help create a map of the area. When she woke up to find the company had moved on without her, she realized she had outlived her value and that she was once again alone.

She'd heard the rumors, too, about the horrific message in the night. *Ah, Maurice, Maurice.* She dropped her head into her hands in mourning. He didn't deserve this fate, she thought, a sob of remorse coming up her chest. Had she contributed to it by being impaired the night before? If only she had stayed alert, perhaps she could have teased out an indication of this danger. She knew that Philippe had no choice but to lead the men out in the night as he had done. She had let herself lose focus, and it had cost her the chance to be of service to the mission. She had let her crew down. She had let the Duke and Duchess down. She let Maurice down. She felt ashamed.

Philippe's letter also caused grief to sit in her heart. Whatever had happened between them the night before had been something special. But, of course, she hadn't been clear-headed so the connection she thought had been there was probably an illusion. He had asked her to wait for him. It seemed sincere, but how many years of her life had she spent waiting for this man to return? How many times had he come back into her life as she had grown and ignored her? She had spent her life trying to overcome her insecurities tied up in him. And with this last encounter, she learned decisively, she couldn't. Her only option was to go far away.

She tossed the last few pieces of bread to the birds causing them to flutter around her. She decided her next move would be back to Chevalerie, to collect her payment and to see the Duke and Duchess one last time. Then, she would need to get very far from Chevalerie and Philippe, because he made her act carelessly, to the detriment of those around her. She would leave Provence, maybe France altogether. She could go past the Alps and make a new life for herself, one where no one knew her. She'd find a town where she could live out her days blissfully ignorant of Philippe's doings and far away from anything that would remind her of him, the place she once called home, and all the ways that she had failed.

For a moment, it struck her hard that she would not see him again, but she buried the pain. It was better this way. Even though she had decided she would like to indulge in knowing his body, if they had come together on this trip, either last night or another, it may have haunted her for the rest of her days. No, she was lucky to have escaped that torture.

She would leave Ponce as soon as she felt able. As soon as the headache went away and she could ride. She imagined it couldn't last for too long. She'd seen enough hungover men to know that they came around after a day or so. The sun dipped behind the buildings around the square and a shadow reached across her. She watched the birds aimlessly as they pecked at crumbs before being startled by a passing man and flying off into the skies. Perhaps later that afternoon she would go, or the next morning. Just as soon as she felt better.

At the same moment, in the deep western regions of Provence, Philippe's obstinacy had paid off. He had located the rebels. From his vantage point, he had caught sight of their movement. The birds told the story, and for a large part of the afternoon, he'd watched plumes of feathers take off into the sky in a directed path of disturbance. Then, just as the sun was drooping to kiss the canopy of the forest, Philippe's patience was rewarded with the smoke of a distant fire curling into the sky.

The men, by then ready for his signal, were riding again in minutes, and it took less than a half hour to discover the rebels' trail once more. It was feeble at first, their targets still taking cautious steps at that point. But soon the trail spread out, relaxed and ambled in an apparent sigh of liberation. Philippe and his men moved confidently, over knotted hills and craggy streams, towards their target.

A few hours later, the night had yawned across the forest, but the fire gave the rebels away. As soon as Philippe saw the glow, a mile or so out, he stopped all verbal communication. They canvassed the area, built a base for the horses, and circled around to the southern side of the rebel camp. It put them downwind and on a slight incline. Geographically they were closer to Aliette than Ponce, having traveled quite a ways since the night before, but the rebels had chosen an obscure location with no major landmarks. Surely, they wouldn't be expecting any intruders this deep into the woods.

Philippe and his men made their own camp in total silence and with careful precision. They wouldn't know exactly what they were dealing with until the morning, but for now, Philippe was confident that they were in a safe place to survey their enemies. His first instinct was to charge in while they slumbered, but that still would not give information about their leader, in addition to being foolhardy and dangerous. Instead, he would hope that the leader would soon join his crew. Either that or Giroux would leave to meet him, and Philippe would be there to follow.

For now, it was time to wait.

There would be no fire that night and very little communication. They had a sad dinner of cold cheese and bread before stretching out to go to sleep. Luc offered the first watch, which was a good thing because, as Philippe laid his head down, he realized he had not slept since dozing beside Alex in her bed. His gut clenched with remorse as he thought about leaving her in Ponce. It had been the worst possible moment to leave her, but he needed to go and do the job he had come to do. Part of him believed she would understand and miraculously he would find her, but another, stronger part felt she was already gone.

All he had was hope. She had promised Emily she would attend the Marquis' ball, so perhaps, even if she believed him to be the worst of scoundrels, a sense of duty would keep her there. No matter what happened in the upcoming days, he would be at that ball like he promised in his letter. If he could find her there, he would no longer hold back. He would take that woman and make her his once and for all.

If she was gone, he would spend eternity searching for her.

Exhaustion had won by then, and he felt his consciousness slipping away. As he lay there, he fought off the moment of sleep just to imagine her beautiful face and the way her body had felt in his arms for a little bit longer. He stared into the infinite sky, his heart heavy with a mixture of longing and anxiety. Just before he lost the battle with sleep, he could have sworn that he found her name written in the stars.

Chapter Twenty-Six

Emily was frustrated. The party was happening at the end of the week and nothing was ready. Of course, she began planning weeks ago, but everything seemed to be only about eighty percent finished. These ridiculous raids were keeping her husband busy, so he was no help—not that he was ever any help when it came to domestic matters. The baby was sick, and her oldest was going through a very clingy phase, which made it difficult for her to get any work done. The staff was preparing the household to shift into their country estate a few miles south, so they were very busy indeed. Usually, the family and the staff would have already been settled in the estate for a few weeks before the Marquis' birthday, and she had counted on that solace in order to prepare, but the problems in the region had kept them anchored in town. This year, she would have people from Chevalerie, used to the most lavish and exquisite parties, as her guests. She could not disappoint. And on top of everything else, she'd learned that her head housekeeper would need to depart due to a family illness, leaving Emily with no one to help her plan. She was at her wit's end.

It was late morning as she sat in the parlor of her home with notes written on cards spread out around her. She couldn't believe how much she still had to get done. A maid stood near her, fidgeting with stress because Emily had been snapping at her all morning. Of course, it wasn't the girl's fault, but Emily had no one else to yell at. Just then, the footman entered, announcing the arrival of a guest.

Emily waited for a moment, then turned to her maid, exasperated. "Well, go to receive the guest, then. Don't stand there without a thought in your head."

"Yes *Madame*!" The girl shrieked as she ran towards the door.

Emily shook her head. She needed competence in this moment. People who could think for themselves and not force her to make every little decision.

After a few minutes, the girl returned to the room. "Miss Alexandra de Foix to see you, *Madame*."

Alexandra! She hadn't realized she'd stayed behind.

"Yes, yes, let her in." Emily stood up excited to greet the woman. When Alex appeared in the doorway to the parlor, Emily dragged her to the sitting area.

"Alexandra!" she said, pulling her friend down to the couch. "You cannot understand how happy I am to see you!"

"Oh, Emily," said Alex, "I'm not worthy of such a greeting."

"I need help. You can help me with the party while we wait for the boys to finish this silly fight and get back to normal life!" She was thrilled. It was as if God in Heaven had answered her prayers.

Her guest didn't seem as excited as she was about the idea. "Actually, Emily," Alex began. "I was coming here to thank you for your hospitality and bid you goodbye. I shall take my leave soon."

Emily stared at her in disbelief. "But the ball is on Saturday."

"I know. I'm so sorry. But I need to get moving," she replied.

"Will you be returning for it?"

"That was not my plan, no."

Emily stopped for a moment and stared hard at Alex. "Did something happen between you and Philippe?"

Alex opened her eyes wide. "No, I just, I need to get going—" she stammered.

"Mm hmm," tsked Emily. Emily knew a woman scorned when she saw one. "What did he do?"

"Nothing!" Alex played with the tie on her shirt. "It's that... I need to get back to Chevalerie. I, um, I have another job waiting for me there."

"Really." Emily watched her skeptically and Alex crumpled under her gaze. Emily paused and crossed her hands delicately in her lap. "Well, if you don't plan to be here for the ball, the very least you can do is help me prepare."

"Um," said Alex, looking at her blankly. "What?"

"Whatever 'job' you have waiting can surely be put off for a few days. We'll just send word that you were fighting some robber baron and got stuck in a swamp or something."

"Stuck in a swamp?" Alex echoed.

"I don't know. Whatever happens when you traipse off into the forest," Emily waved her hands. "Come now. You must help me. I have no one else, and I don't know a woman in the world better at making decisions than you." She continued, a little more gently, "Besides, whatever has happened, helping me will help to take your mind off of it. You know, you may need someone to talk to more than you realize."

"I am not made for these types of tasks, Emily," Alex replied as she eyed the notes Emily had spread around her.

Emily felt a moment of triumph. She had begun to wear Alex down. She reached across and took the hand of her new friend. "Alexandra, you are capable of far more than you give yourself credit."

Alex sighed. "Perhaps I can stay until the morning."

Satisfied, Emily picked up a stack of papers and dumped them into Alex's lap. "Step one," she said. "Finalizing the menu."

Chapter Twenty-Seven

The next days were some of the most tortuous of Philippe's life. He was racked with ineptitude and impatience as he held his crew in the brush, surveying the rebels. He had been horrified to find, the morning after they had set up their own camp, that Giroux's numbers had doubled. This whole time they'd been tracking two groups of six and eight each, and now there were sixteen men together around his enemy's fire. Philippe didn't know where they had come from or how they had assembled so fast. At the very worst, Philippe had always thought his party could overwhelm Giroux and take them all prisoner, but now he realized that would not be possible. Instead, he held out hope that Giroux himself would depart to meet his captain. But now that, too, seemed unlikely.

There had been no sign of their leader and no sign of movement from the rebels. In fact, every day Philippe watched their camp become more and more established. They had built a fire pit with a spit. They toiled to create semi-permanent shelters and hung the kills from their hunts out to dry. They dug out banks and inlets from the river for washing. Philippe and his men, on the other hand, were hardly living. They were dirty. They were weary. They were hungry and tormented by the smells of cooking meat each night from the camp below. Other than trading off to go back and tend the horses or replenish supplies, they moved very little. Philippe's muscles were tight and tired from the complete stasis. His party was deteriorating while the men below them rested and regrouped.

The one good thing that had come of this waiting was that Philippe was forced to think out the situation. In these moments, he began to formulate a theory about what exactly was going on. The lack of food and movement had catapulted his mind into a clarity he had rarely experienced. Giroux wasn't the only one being manipulated, he realized.

He'd finally sent a communication to his father. Though a letter could reach Chevalerie within just a few days from their current position, it would take time to arrange a party and he could not count on reinforcements to help their current situation. It was time to reevaluate what he was going to do in the present now that he didn't expect any change in his enemy's position. He could not make his men wait like this forever. They could not be sustained without proper meals and exercise and then expected to fight if they waited much longer. Nor could he. Their energy stores were not infinite.

He looked across his men. Their faces were hard, but he could tell they were fatigued. Their eyes had gone sallow and their skin papery. It would be wonderful for all of them if they could attend the Marquis' ball in two days' time. For nothing more than to get their minds away from the tragedy of losing their fellow soldier. Philippe's heart ached at the thought. Looking back, he realized what an unrealistic promise it had been to make it back in time. He closed his eyes and rubbed his forehead. He had to follow the right path or he would lose everything he had worked for.

When he opened his eyes again, his decision was made. He gathered his men and explained the new strategy. He saw light in their dirty faces. They began then to work out new positions and tactics. He was thankful for the high standard of training demanded of Chevalerie's soldiers, as such an outnumbered attack could never work with mere thugs. It would be slower than he would have liked, and they'd still need a little luck. He may not be able to get them all at once, but they could take them out one at a time.

For Chevalerie. For Maurice.

The Duke was standing in the gardens when he saw the messenger tearing across the road toward the palace. The sun had almost left the sky for the evening, and he was glad he had not yet gone in for supper. As the man came closer, he recognized the colors of Peillon. Guillaume braced himself for the news. The messenger galloped to the gates, and at once Guillaume saw the guards respond and direct the man to the gardens. Guillaume walked swiftly across the gravel to meet the man, the palace footmen and stablemen jogging behind the horse, ready to be of service. When the messenger was within a few meters of the Duke, he jumped from his horse and fell into a bow.

"My Lord," he said, struggling to catch his breath. "Lord Philippe has sent post. Messengers have been riding nonstop to deliver this parchment to you." He thrust his hand into his wainscot and pulled out the letter. The Duke recognized his family stamp.

"Please rise," the Duke responded as he took the letter. Then to the nearest footman. "Get this man some water."

"*Oui, Monsieur*," he said, rushing off.

Guillaume popped the seal and turned to get the light from the last moments of sun.

Father,

I regret to inform you that the situation is not yet contained. Though we have flushed them from the caves, their leader remains in hiding. They have retreated to a hidden camp in the forest northwest of Aliette, where we have set up our own surveillance. We are outnumbered, and I fear an outright attack will do no good...

As Guillaume continued to read, his face changed. His fears about this mission getting out of hand seemed to come true. In his letter, Philippe had asked for more men, which Guillaume had already anticipated, but the most interesting thing of all was Philippe's theory about who was behind the problem. When he finished reading, the Duke sighed and refolded the letter. Could it be true? As he let the idea settle for a moment, he realized he didn't think Philippe was wrong. *Of course*. In his mind, he was finally able to close his hands around someone's neck.

He turned to the butler who was a few steps behind him. "I need to get post to Aliette. Ready a messenger."

The man nodded.

"I will let Michel know he must prepare at once," Guillaume continued.

"*Oui, Monsieur.*" His butler turned and began directing the footmen. In seconds they were all running to complete their tasks. The Duke hurried to find his eldest son. There was much to do that evening.

Chapter Twenty-Eight

By morning, they had already captured three of Giroux's men.

They were bound and gagged and back with the horses while Philippe's men held a complex cascade of positions that allowed them to triangulate an effective attack on any enemy who stepped out of bounds. Philippe was working on the idea that the only one with any brains down there was Giroux and that the rest of them were hired dolts that may have been able to hold up a sword but were not military-trained. From the looks of it, he was right.

During the night, they had rearranged themselves along the path the rebels seemed to use to relieve themselves. While Giroux slept, they took out the first. The man barely balked in his surprise and sleepiness. He was easily stilled and removed by the quick coordination of Philippe's own men. Just as they reconfigured themselves, the next one was out and went down just as easily. And then the next.

It was the fourth man who was going to give them trouble, and Philippe knew it as soon as he saw him shuffling into the trees. The sun was just coming up by then and the man was fully awake. Philippe had hoped to make more progress and get five or six of them throughout the night. He was now sure that their plan was about to be figured out.

Just then the man stepped into the range of Franc and Auguste.

Philippe watched from the tree where he had himself banked as they leapt at the man from both sides. The brute turned to run but saw Claude with an arrow aimed at his heart. He raised his hands, but not before he let out a balk that signaled his position. That earned him a quick left hook from Auguste before the other two gagged and subdued him. Philippe turned expectantly to the camp, where he watched Giroux pace the clearing and call the man's name. Once. Twice. Then, with new realization coming into his posture, Giroux swung around and called the three other names in apparent recognition of their absence. That was it, Philippe thought. Their time was up.

Philippe dropped to the ground and announced the second part of the plan with rapid signals. The men spread out to surround the camp as best they could while Philippe himself went to charge right down the center of it. The rebels were fed and rested but also half asleep. On the other hand, Philippe's men were keyed up and eager for action. Whatever happened, outnumbered or not, Philippe knew his boys would fight with their hearts as well as their bodies.

He took a breath. And then he ran.

The sky in the East had lightened from purple to pale blue, but the shadows were still working in their favor. Philippe ducked a few trees, his feet pounding hard over the earth. For the first time in nearly a week, he made himself known as the war cry coming from his throat drew attention away from his circling men. He swept through the brush, jumped a fallen log, and crashed into their camp.

As expected, many of the men were still rolling frantically from their bedrolls looking for their weapons. Philippe dodged one man not fully risen and struck another on the side of the head with the hilt of his sword, knocking him clean out, but it was Giroux standing at the fire who had his attention. They locked eyes, and Giroux drew his sword. Philippe, coming fast, had to duck one last feeble attack from a wobbly man before reaching his target. He swung his blade hard at Giroux, with all the power from the charge and the frustration from the wait coming out in one mighty blow.

Giroux took the shock of the attack against the strong of his blade and swung powerfully from above. The clang of their swords reverberated through the quiet forest and signaled his own men to attack. Suddenly, a chorus of shouts and whistles hailed down on them as his men descended from their positions onto the now-alert rebels.

Giroux pushed Philippe off and looked around to assess the situation, while men from either side paired up and attacked each other.

Before lunging again, Philippe called out to him, "I have waited the better part of this week to catch sight of the man you call leader," he said as they squared off, swords out. "But I believe you are waiting, just like us." Then he raised his sword again. "Before I take you apart, I give you one last chance to reveal him for your own safety."

"I will not betray him," Giroux responded.

Philippe nodded. "Then you will be my prisoner."

"Don't be so sure, *Monsieur*." Giroux swung again as he spoke. Philippe dodged the blade, but Giroux caught him hard with a foot to his shin. Philippe stumbled back and Giroux leapt forward to swing at him again. Philippe felt twitching in his muscles, a strange combination of adrenaline and lack of calories, but he wouldn't go down so easily. He caught Giroux's hacking steel from above and managed to push the man off once more. Giroux was on his feet again with his blunt blade at the ready in seconds.

He danced around two more of Giroux's strikes, taking quick stock of his men. Though they had come out strong, he knew that their small burst of energy could not be maintained. Auguste had been engaged by two hulking brutes, blood had soaked through Claude's shirt, Daniel had already lost his sword and was fighting with a dagger while Bernard had taken a hard fall before getting up to fight again. But none of them were down and that encouraged Philippe. He turned back to Giroux and, with two quick steps, lunged right towards the man's trunk. Giroux narrowly jumped aside and came back at Philippe with immense strength. Philippe took the blow against the weak of his blade and felt the shock of it shoot through his muscles. Giroux was a beast and fought aggressively. His thick sword was made for slashing and splitting wounds into its victims, while Philippe's sword was military grade and served best when there was distance between the opponents. Philippe was losing his strength. He struggled to keep Giroux at a distance.

In the few minutes since the encounter had begun, the sun had crept higher into the air. Now morning shadows flickered across the scene. Suddenly, Philippe thought of how little time he had left to fulfill his promise and get back to Alex, causing strength to rocket back through his limbs. Giroux rained blows down on him, but Philippe was still able to get a violent kick into Giroux's middle, causing the large man to stumble back and double over. Just then, Philippe felt another man grab onto him from the behind. Philippe slammed an elbow into the man's gut in an attempt to break away. But the man's grip on Philippe was too strong, and together they crashed to the ground.

Philippe dropped his sword to wrestle the man off of him. All around Philippe, the well-timed and controlled back and forth of the swordfights had deteriorated into confused mêlée attacks as men from both sides lost their main weapons and resorted to fists and daggers. Philippe maneuvered himself on top of the man and pounded his face with a hard, closed fist, causing blood to spurt from his nose. He hit him again and the man slumped to the side. Philippe reached to grab his sword when a boot crunched down on his hand. Philippe winced as he looked up to see Giroux standing above him.

Not outdone yet, Philippe reached up with his free hand and pulled Giroux down on top of him. Philippe had lost his sword, but the surprise of the fall caused Giroux to lose his own weapon. They were both off balance, but equal now, and Philippe did a quick catalog of his weapons. Two daggers in his belt and a smaller blade inside his boot. He and Giroux continued to struggle, the fight heavy and desperate, having devolved to close-in weapons and fists. It would now be a battle of will. One of them would lose, and it would happen before the sun had a chance to make it all the way into the sky.

Chapter Twenty-Nine

The candles were set. The food was prepared. The musicians plucked at their strings. The staff ran fitfully back and forth across the freshly waxed dance floor, dodging men on ladders who were themselves busy lighting each of the hundreds of wicks topping the chandeliers. The rugs had been beaten, and the deep violet ceiling-length drapes were opened and secured with golden tassels. Alex stood with Emily in the immaculate great hall of the country estate. Everything was ready, and Alex had been part of making it all happen.

Emily directed the butler to buff out a spot left on an ivory banister at the entrance to the hall, then turned to Alex. "Now, we take a moment for ourselves," she said with a calming breath. "The maids will bathe you, and then you *must* choose one of the dresses, Alex. No more delays." She looped her arm through Alex's and continued. "Be down again by five to help me do final preparations."

"Yes, General," Alex chuckled as she saluted.

"Please stop calling me that," Emily wrinkled her nose. "It's so unfeminine."

"I will when you stop acting like one." Alex teased.

They unclasped their arms and went to separate parts of the mansion. Alex returned to the room where she had been staying to find a bath had already been prepared for her. She delighted in the pampering and all the fancy soaps and oils Emily had at her disposal, so different from what she was used to. In the days she had spent between Ponce and Emily's country home, working to orchestrate this ball, she had seen a side of life that she'd never even acknowledged. There was great pride in running a household. And the work was exhausting. It was mental work, while the tasks she was accustomed to were very physical. She wasn't quite ready to trade in her sword for a dustpan, but for the first time, she recognized that there was a lot more to domestic life than eating candies and gossiping.

She disrobed and stepped into the warm tub and asked the ladies to give her some privacy while she bathed. The maids didn't know quite what to make of Alex but had grown used to doing what she asked as a guest of their mistress. The warm water was soothing to her skin. She sighed and then pulled her knees up to her chest.

When she had walked into Emily's home earlier that week, she had truly been on her way out of town. She saw no need to stay any longer, but Emily had sucked her right into this process. Alex had been too baffled by the request to fight back too hard. She was glad she had agreed to stay. She had grown very fond of Emily in the time that they had spent together. Emily was prissy and emotional, but she got things done and wielded her household just as violently as Alex wielded her blade.

Alex had needed a little support too, though it was hard to acknowledge. A few times over the course of the week, Emily had prodded, having understood instantly that Philippe was the reason Alex needed to escape, but Alex had remained mute on the subject. She just couldn't admit that she had fallen for him *again* and that she had welcomed all those same crushing feelings he inspired so well: attraction and affection, followed by excitement and hope, only to be beaten by disappointment and desperation. How did she keep letting it happen? Had she not, after all these years, learned her damn lesson?

She hadn't had contact or word from him since he left. Not that she really expected it. In his note he had promised to be there for the ball, and now the ball was only a few hours away. She had little faith that she would see him. Even if he did arrive, even if he showed up tonight, was there really any hope he would still be interested in her? She couldn't hope to maintain his attention. She was just a silly girl who liked to wear pants and went against everything society expected from a woman, like she had always been. Though they had shared some moments, he was still a handsome son of a duke with a country of willing women before him. Even knowing all that, she still wished to take him as a lover, even if just for a night. It was a desire she could not escape.

Just thinking of him awakened her body once more, and she submerged herself in the water with a groan.

Two hours later, Emily had to be summoned to Alex's room.

Emily had been in the middle of having her hair done when one of the maids ran in and begged for her help.

"The missus," the girl sputtered. "Doesn't like any of the dresses."

Emily waited for the last curl to be placed before she rose with decided calmness from her vanity. She marched through the hall, across the landing, down the steps and past the auxiliary entrance into the guest quarters. When she arrived, she threw open the door to find Alex clad in nothing more than undergarments, white-knuckle gripping the footboard of the bed like an angry orangutan with Emily's own exquisite wardrobe surrounding her. It was a battlefield of tulle and silk.

"I can't wear any of this stuff," Alex lamented. The three exasperated maids who had been assisting her were trying to straighten and hang the rejects.

"Alexandra, don't be a child," Emily said, a snap in her voice. "You may not wear pants to the ball."

"I'm not trying to wear pants to the ball, Emily," Alex said indignantly. "But I can't stand looking like a pastry either."

"I have offered you some of my finest gowns. You are lucky I like you, *chère*, or I should have you thrown out on your ear for such disrespect."

"You're right." The anger left Alex's voice and, defeated, she held up her hands in surrender. "You are absolutely right." She slumped down onto the foot of the bed. "It doesn't matter, anyway. Anything will be fine."

"That's a terrible way to think when you are getting ready for a ball. Ladies," she said to the maids waiting anxiously by, "please leave us for a moment."

The girls scuttled out, and Emily sat next to Alex. "It does matter what you wear, and it matters how you wear it. You are one of the hostesses of this party, and I won't allow you to look like I pulled you out of a ditch." She paused. "This is about Philippe, isn't it? Will you please tell me what happened between you two?"

Alex was quiet for a moment before she buried her head in her hands. "I threw up on him."

Now it was Emily's turn to be quiet. "Well, I wasn't expecting that," she said.

"I got drunk and we kissed, and then I threw up on his leg." Alex shook her head with her eyes closed as if trying to erase the memory.

Emily stared at her for a moment. Then she shrugged. "I've come back from worse."

Alex swung her head and looked at Emily. "Really?"

"My goodness, Alex, you are in desperate need of female companionship." Emily smiled and fiddled with the lace of her dressing gown. "You know how I met the Marquis? Not the story we tell people, but the real story," she said, feeling her voice go up a few notches with a tinge of shame. She didn't like to tell it, but she owed Alex something for her help.

"I haven't heard either story, actually," Alex said.

"Well," Emily began, still twiddling the lace in her lap. "We tell people that he saw me in the marketplace and before the sun went down that day, he had found my father and asked for my hand. But—" She cleared her throat and held her chin up. "The first time he saw me, I was in... a compromising position with his travel companion. A young lord from Aliette."

"Wow," Alex replied, eyes wide.

"Um hmm," she nodded. "The Marquis walked right in on us. The lord had his hand up my bodice and everything." She sighed. "It was embarrassing, and I thought it would be the end of my days, that my reputation would never recover. That I'd *never* marry." She smoothed the lace she had been tugging on. "You know, I'm the first to admit, I didn't always have the right ideas about how to maintain a suitor's interest. But I never let anyone make me feel bad about it." Then she turned to Alex. "So, do you know what I did?"

Alex shook her head.

"I kicked that lord off of me and held my head high. I regarded the

Marquis like I was the Queen herself from that point on. I even scolded him for not knocking before he entered a room."

"What did he do?" Alex asked.

"He apologized," Emily said haughtily, jutting out her chin. "And it earned me his notice, that's for sure. He asked to see me the next day and the one after that, and before his time in Chevalerie was finished, I was his betrothed."

Alex continued to stare at her for a moment, the shock in her expression apparent. "What happened to the lord from Aliette?" she asked.

"Who cares?" Emily shrugged. "I landed a marquis."

Alex, open mouthed, stared back, then brought her hands up to her face. She let out a peal of laughter and dropped back onto the bed. She laughed whole-heartedly for a moment and didn't show signs of stopping.

"Alright, that's enough," Emily said, bristling.

"Oh Emily," Alex said, slowly recovering. She sat up again, tremors of laughter still running through her. "You are amazing. Truly." She looked at Emily and then towards the beautiful gowns. She sighed. "I'm sorry for this." She shook her head. "Without my sword, I don't know." She trailed off for a moment. "I know it's silly," she continued, "but as beautiful as these gowns are, they make me feel so... so exposed. And useless."

"Alexandra," Emily said. "In a skirt or pants, there is no creature on earth stronger than a woman. Do you think I don't know what goes on in my city? Because I spend my days in silks?" She tutted and continued. "I am every bit as involved in the politics and the welfare of my people as my husband." She brought her finger up to make a point. "I'm just more subtle about it." She nodded. "Why am I throwing this ball?" she asked. "Because I like parties?"

"Um," Alex responded, shaking her head.

"Because my people need it right now," Emily asserted. "They need to see that the heads of this community are still strong and capable of protecting them. And the region needs time to breathe. There will be no resolution until we stabilize. My husband, Philippe, the Duke." She ticked them off her fingers. "They need a chance to find their footing. And I can help by offering diversion and distraction." She paused. "You know, the boys may run headlong into battle or do whatever they do, but we," she waved her hand back and forth between them, "we are the ones that make things happen. And we don't need swords to do so."

"I never saw it from that perspective," Alex smiled and looked down.

"Listen," Emily continued, putting her hand on Alex's knee. "I say this to you as a friend. Grace and confidence will take you far. You worry about staying strong? Never ever let someone think they've gotten the best of you."

"It is not so different than what I practice when I am at battle," Alex said.

"Whoever told you that social etiquette was not battle?" Emily raised her brows. "It's a dangerous sport."

Alex sighed. "Thank you, Emily. That does make me feel better." She shook her head. "I'm just in knots wondering if he will be here. I don't like feeling like this."

"This night is not about Philippe," Emily said, holding a finger up. "It's about Ponce." Then she said more softly, "It's also about you. Alex, you have power, more than you know. You just have to figure out how to use it." Emily stood then and looked Alex up and down. "The colors of the other dresses were wrong for you. What was I thinking? With your dark eyes and hair." She pressed her lips and put her hand on her chin as she thought. After a moment, she continued. "I have the perfect gown for you," she said. Emily called to her maids, and they poked their heads into the room like nervous chickens. "Ladies, I will need you to do some digging through my garments. And it will have to be done with haste."

Chapter Thirty

At six sharp, the arrival of the guests began in the main entrance of the Marquis and Marquise's country estate. The people had anticipated the Marquis' birthday and the arriving carts decorated with flowers and ribbons lined up and down the drive to prove it. Footmen were ready to receive each family, and Emily stood at the entrance, on the arm of the Marquis ready to greet their happy guests. They made such a handsome couple, and Alex admired them from down the hall. Emily looked beautiful as always in a golden silk dress that matched her hair, and the Marquis, tall and distinguished in his adorned jacket.

Alex had been stationed at the entrance to the ballroom and was meant to show the arriving guests inside. She took her post very seriously and was pleased to greet the happy people. She'd been humbled by the talk she'd had with Emily earlier, and as she watched the faces of each guest turn to awe when they saw the ballroom, she understood Emily's actions even more. Though Alex still would have liked to be tracking alongside the men, she was proud to have helped put together this event.

Emily had also been right about having the perfect dress for her. Alex was dressed in a beautiful dark navy gown that went straight to the floor. It had been a gown of Emily's mother and part of her dowry. It was somewhat out of fashion, not having the poof and yards of fabric that were popular at the time, but it had been crafted so well, and it fit Alex's body so perfectly, she felt more like a woman than she ever had in her life. It had a straight neckline that *just* captured her breasts and small capped sleeves. Her hair was twisted back from her face with a simple mother of pearl clip, her free dark waves still spilling down her back. She felt at once elegant, sophisticated, and indeed a lady. It surprised her how much she enjoyed the feeling, and secretly, before leaving her room, she'd spent a few moments delighting in the swish of her skirt across the wooden floors.

Within an hour, the ballroom had filled with excited guests, already indulging in their first dances of the evening. Against the dark wood panels and golden fixtures, the decorated guests, in marvelous fall shades of honey yellow, blush wine, glowing tangerine, lustrous chartreuse, ignited the great hall in color. Even the staff wore their most refined uniforms, mauve frocks with ivory collars for the women and ivory jackets with mauve embellishments for the men.

Off to the side, was an alcove that held the refreshments: exotic fruits, hors d'oeuvres almost too pretty to be eaten, crystal flutes of champagne and little cakes decorated to resemble the lavender and white poppies that Ponce was known for. Alex thought to try the little pink tarts or the pastry with puffed cream, but there was a tightness at the top of her stomach that wouldn't allow her to do so. Besides, she was much too busy to think about food.

Guests continued to spill in from the main doors into the ballroom. The strings of music built and swelled as each dance gave way to another. Alex glanced occasionally at the doors, feeling the tightness in her stomach creep through her chest. It knotted her as the lords and ladies around her continued to relax through sips of champagne and unrestrained laughter. Emily had been clear in Alex's duties for the evening: solve problems and have *fun*. Well, Alex couldn't exactly have fun with her stomach in knots, but she could do the other half of her duties. Alex looked around the ballroom for anything out of sorts. She summoned a footman to clean a spill, helped a lady locate her husband, and adjusted the collar of a maid who seemed particularly stressed about maintaining her uniform. Despite the nagging tension inside her, Alex was enjoying being quite helpful in the exuberant scene. Never had she worked in this capacity before. It was a thrill indeed.

Just then, a fancy girl bumped into a footman carrying a tray of colorful drinks at the edge of the dances, and Alex leapt forward to stabilize the footman and smooth the dress of the girl.

"Thank you," the girl whispered shyly, as she seemed to realize she'd almost gotten herself covered in liqueurs. They shared a smile before the girl rushed back to her dance. The footman nodded his thanks, and Alex looked up to see Emily gesturing to her from the dais at the head of the room.

Alex took a breath and called a maid to wipe a handprint from a window and then ventured out across the floor to the patroness. She tried to avoid the waltzing couples and stay off the dance floor, but it enveloped almost the entire room at that point. Soon she was weaving between twirling bodies and gliding feet. She'd made it only halfway across when suddenly someone grabbed her arm and swung her forcefully around. Before she knew it, she was crushed against a chest, impaled by a masculine smell and looking into intense, gold-ringed eyes. It was Philippe, it was him, sprung to life right on the dance floor.

When had he gotten there? What had happened to bring him back to her? Though she had made the decision not to spend the night wondering about him, as she looked at his face, into his eyes, she felt the tension in her chest, her stomach, her heart, surrendering in the most wonderful way.

He towered over her, and she was reminded how small she was in comparison. They stood there posed for the dance, but not moving to the music. He held her one hand in his, with his other arm wrapped around her waist. He leaned so far into her that she had to arch her back over his arm.

"I feared I wouldn't find you," he said, his voice deep and gravely and filled with magic she couldn't quite comprehend. He continued to search her eyes. "I thought I would have to travel all of creation to get to you."

Alex was so awestruck she couldn't speak at first, but words finally came to her mouth, "I did not think you would come back."

"Haven't you learned to trust me yet, little fox?" He grinned, then twirled her around and brought her back. She landed against his chest again, feeling her breath caught in her own. She was in his arms. She couldn't believe it was happening, but she was in his embrace once more.

The dance continued, and she could do little more than stare at him. His face was clean-shaven, his hair swept back and his eyes—all of it, all of him caused extra beats in her heart. But then she noticed that his eyebrow was split, an angry scrape ran up his jawline and across his ear, and his bottom lip was swollen under the scar she had given him long ago. She blinked, guilt rushing her. She realized that she knew nothing of the status of their objectives. One thing was clear: while she'd been enjoying herself here, he had been at war. And she'd spent all this time doubting his word. Repentantly, and in a movement of complete scandal, she stretched up and, very gently, kissed his scar.

She didn't know it was possible, but he crushed her even closer to his body, until she had trouble taking full breaths. She laughed his name as she saw his eyes heat even more.

"I can't breathe," she sputtered.

"Neither can I," he replied.

That's when she realized the song had ended. People around them were clapping. Suddenly, there was a man next to them.

"Excuse me, *Monsieur*, may you have the next dance with my daughter?"

Alex looked at the man who had a pretty young thing standing next to him, the reality of the evening interrupting her fantasy. Philippe stammered for a moment then looked back at her. Alex backed out of his grasp. She knew he could not deny such a request. Before she could depart, Philippe grabbed her wrist desperately and whispered, "Don't drink too much." He grinned and winked at her as he was dragged away.

Alex smiled, still dreamy and hazy at his sudden appearance. Turning from the dance floor, she saw Emily waving her over. Alex floated to her, the smile unshaken from her face.

"You see! You had nothing to worry about." Emily beamed when Alex reached her.

Alex just grinned. Out on the floor, Philippe danced with the girl, but kept looking back to Alex, his eyes filled with distress. He stumbled, not paying attention to the dance. He caught the girl, whom he had almost knocked over, then looked back pensively to Alex.

She brought her hands up to her lips in a mirthful laugh.

"You know," said Emily, "It will be a busy night for him. As the unmarried son of the Duke, he will be expected to dance with every unattached maid here."

"What does it matter," Alex muttered, staring at the man. "I've lived through worse."

Emily coughed delicately and cleared her throat. "You should find another partner to dance with," she said. "Or you shall be tormented this whole evening."

"I will be fine," Alex said, still smiling.

When Emily had said Philippe would be expected to dance with every unattached female in the room, Alex hadn't expected that there would be so many. She thought maybe nine, ten, but it seemed like this whole stupid region was made up of girls without suitors. Did they come from their mother's belly in full bloom ready to attack the son of a duke?

Alex's revere quickly faded as she realized she would have no more time with Philippe that evening. What a terrible joke this was. She had spent mere seconds in his arms and then had to give him up, once again. She took a few dances from the brave men who would approach her but could feel how it agitated Philippe. Even through his own dances, she saw in his brows the same frustration she felt in her own expression.

After seeing him be drawn into yet another dance, she realized it was pointless to stay there and watch him. It was upsetting her and unnerving him. Emily's trained staff had settled in, and the party was running quite smoothly. Alex decided that she had done her duty. She was done for the night.

She regarded one of the footmen on her way out. "When Lord Philippe is free, please tell him that I have retired for the evening but should be happy to receive him in the morning, if he so wishes."

"Yes, *Mademoiselle*," he nodded.

Trying not to draw attention to herself, she slipped out one of the side doors. Free from the ballroom, she moved through the parlor and out into the courtyard. Once outside, she lifted her skirts off the ground and ran across the lawn to the guest housing. She could still hear the strings play with rumbles of conversation and laughter tumbling out into the night. Alex entered the back door to the guest rooms and was happy to find that the hall was empty and silent. She walked past a few closed doors and entered her own quarters.

It was frustrating, that was sure. She'd try to deny it, but she had been so tortured this week, wondering if he would be there or not. Then, fate of fates, he had shown up and she could not have any contact with him. And, oh, the lovely women he danced with. Surely, he would find one he wanted more than her. She flung her shoes onto the floor, then remembered she shouldn't be so crass with Emily's things and instead arranged them at the foot of the sitting chair. Emily had been so accommodating, she felt a little bad for leaving the party early, but she was no longer needed and couldn't stand to wait around for him another minute.

She turned to the mirror where just a few hours before she had been primped and arranged. She let her hair down and it fell over her shoulders and past her breasts. She combed through it with her fingers and gathered it to the side. Then she began the task of unlacing the back of her dress. She watched herself in the mirror as her undergarments came into view. When she had seen Philippe, she was too taken by emotion to think out the night. She hoped to pick up right where they had left off, with his hands on her body and lips against her own, a panic that she would lose him again forcing her to seek the easiest connection. Something that could make him a permanent part of her, long after their time together had ended.

But he had obligations, she knew, and many, many options. Her dress dropped to the ground. She picked it up and laid it over the back of a chair. She put her hands on her hips and looked at herself in the mirror. She wore a black chemise over short, fitted bloomers, both of which were sheer and soft against forbidden skin. Her breasts pressed against the silk, and she wished he could have seen her like this, so pretty and feminine for once. She did not know how to inspire a more long-lasting connection to him. But she did know their bodies could come together like magic. She groaned, feeling like it was never going to happen.

Just as she was spiraling into despair, she heard a muffled voice on the other side of the door.

"Alex. *Alex.*"

"Philippe?" she called back, her heart exploding in excitement. She ran to the door and threw it open, forgetting for a moment that she was just about undressed.

There, in the middle of the hallway, he stood. His eyes opened wide when he saw her, and as he came to stand before her, Alex's body reacted with pulsating tremors that were so intense she nearly collapsed to her knees. She didn't know how he did it to her. In fact, she didn't know how he had found her or even gotten back to Ponce. But upon seeing him, handsome and clean, dark and scarred, and in her doorway, none of it mattered. It only mattered that he had come for her.

They continued to watch each other for a moment. Then she saw as his eyes moved down her body and up again. With the boldness of his stare, she understood how defenseless she was to him.

"You left," he said, a spark of anger in his voice.

"I'm sorry," she whispered. "I didn't think it would ever end."

"I didn't know what room you were in."

"I left a message with the footman."

Philippe didn't say anything more, just continued to stare at her. She noticed they were both out of breath, and her skin was aching to be touched. "I haven't had anything to drink," she said when she could think of nothing better.

He smiled wickedly, her words spurring him into action. He took a heavy step into her doorway, dominating her space. "Then I suppose there is nothing to stop me this time," he said, before closing the door behind him.

Chapter Thirty-One

Philippe felt like some other force was guiding him as he moved into the room. He was barely aware of his body, just his eyes, which were filled with her. Alex shuffled back as he came into the room, but he pressed towards her knowing the only way to awaken himself from the half-life he'd been living was to get closer. She was perfectly ripe, like nothing he'd ever seen, and he had waited far too long to devour her. Her luscious smell floated around him, and though his body raged for contact, he was determined not to rush a single second of the experience.

When he had arrived at the mansion, he had searched for her in a panic. He tore into the ballroom without ceremony and scanned the crowd. It had taken him mere seconds to spot her, with her back to him, across the room; she was the only woman dressed in winter colors and the only one not dancing. If he hadn't been so relieved to see her, he could have laughed. Alex would always find a way to not quite fit into high society but damn it if it didn't make her all the more alluring.

He touched her cheek and his heart came alive, and with his other hand he traced a line up her side, slipping over the silk. His heart thumped in his throat and his muscles strained to get close to her. Her raspberry lips parted as she looked up at him so sweetly, and he lost the battle to take it slow. He planted his palm in the small of her back and dragged her to him, her body against his causing sparks of life to shoot through him. Alex gasped and he kissed her as power and vigor washed through him. It was as if he hadn't existed until that very moment.

In a second, her arms were wrapped around him, pressing their bodies together. But it wasn't enough. Even now, he worried she would escape, so he picked her up and backed her to the wall behind them. Now cornered, he kissed her again, his mouth parting her lips, and he indulged himself in their tender wanting while he grasped the lace at the edge of her undergarments. His fingers twisted in the fabric in concentrated frustration. Then, he pushed his hand upwards, taking the chemise with it. He was too rough, he knew it, but her skin was smooth and creamy, and he wanted to leave bruises on it. *Slow down*, he thought to himself. He had to remember that Alex had never done this before and though he wanted to mark her as his own, he could not forget that she was innocent.

"Will you have me here? Against the wall?" she asked breathlessly.

Philippe groaned. "*Chérie*, the first time is in the bed," he said through gritted teeth. She never made things easy.

With that, he pulled the chemise up over her head and she was bared before him, wearing only her little drawers to cover her bottom. Her breasts were full and perfect, her hair falling just below them. She was so much more delicate than she seemed when she was clothed. She looked up at him coyly. He liked having her so vulnerable before him.

He tore at his clothes, managing to get down to his own undergarments, eager to feel her skin pressed against his. When he felt the curve of her breasts against his chest, he quaked inside. He kissed her with new intensity, his hands on her cheeks, in her hair.

"I am trying to be gentle with you, *belle.* But you make it so difficult," he said against her ear.

"Who said I want gentle?" she whispered back.

The small claim he had on his body was challenged as his instinct took over. He grabbed her ass to pick her up again, and he dropped her onto the bed. His breath was ragged and torn in his chest. He felt frenzied as he watched her from the foot of the bed, lain out, waiting, smiling before him. For a second, he paused and took a breath to calm himself. It was so much more than it had ever been with anyone else, and he didn't know if he could ever get enough of her to feel satisfied again. She propped herself up on her elbows and watched him. She smiled and bit her bottom lip and even wiggled her toes in anticipation.

His heart thumped so forcefully, he clutched at his chest as he stared back at her.

"Are you alright?" she asked, still amused.

He nodded, but he couldn't speak. Words would come at another time. Instead, he would show her just exactly how hard he had fallen for her. He bent down then and leaned into her body, in pure wonder. He needed to touch her, to be sure she was real, to connect, to claim her. He ran his hands up the outside of her calves, pausing to press the inner smoothness of one against his cheek. He kissed her skin, his hands working upward. When he reached her knees, he heard her breath catch as he moved them apart, but it only made him more bold, more eager to seize her. He flung one leg back over his shoulder and gripped handfuls of flesh while his lips explored the inside of her thighs. His palms reached to her backside, and he tangled his fingers in the silky fabric of her garment and squeezed. It made her yelp. He liked making her make noises, and he looked up at her with a grin, before teasing his tongue along her contours where soft material met softer skin. Alex gripped the sheets and dropped her head back with a groan.

The scent of her desire urged him on, and he found himself caught in a growl as he nipped at her skin. Soon, he was kissing her belly and his hands were moving up her torso while he balanced himself between her legs. She arched to meet his touch. He watched as she followed his hands with her eyes, her lips parted. Then he moved his greedy palms up to her breasts. She jerked towards him at the contact, and in response, he gripped her firmly into his hands, his arousal ready to overwhelm them both. He hovered above her and teased his lips against hers. Then he dropped his head to her breast and sucked tender skin into his mouth, making her cry out as he did so. She threw her arms across his shoulders, drawing him closer. He felt her body moving beneath him, her hips rocking up towards him. He used his knees to spread her thighs open wider, and he pressed himself against her, sliding the length of him along her most sensitive area.

Alex dropped back onto the pillows with a shudder, thrusting her breasts out for him as she did. He sucked and grabbed hungrily at her. Her body was so wild and sensitive. He had to go further, he couldn't wait any longer. He released his hold on her breasts and situated himself so he could move his hand lower and paint the outside of her drawers with his fingertips. After a moment, he reached beneath the fabric. Her eyes shot open, but he moved his other hand up to her hair and angled her for a kiss. He took her mouth as he touched her, working his fingertips over her silky skin. He drew large circles across her sensitive flesh, slowly opening her up. There was tension in her body, but he felt the moment when she submitted. He dipped into her to drag out some of her own wetness. Then he found her delicate pebble and teased it, her legs now falling willingly apart.

Alex broke their kiss, panting. She closed her eyes and wrapped her arms around his neck, her body telling him things words couldn't. He watched her, marveling at her form, her body moving like a melody. He wanted to give her everything, and he wanted more and more and more from her. He moved his hand more firmly against her now as his own need refused to be put down, and soon he felt her body reaching towards the end. But then he pulled his hand back. He wasn't done with her quite yet.

In realization, she snapped open her eyes and looked at him accusingly.

He smiled and shook his head. "I told you," he teased. "This time I would be inside of you."

She closed her eyes and half laughed, half groaned.

Philippe rose then and stood at the foot of the bed. With both hands, he eased the garment off of her legs. He watched her sex, pink and wet and ready for him, as she watched him. Then he moved his own undergarments down. Alex's eyes widened when she saw him bared, thick and wanting, and the feeling he had to finally make her his woman overcame him. Taking her knees and moving them apart, he kneeled before her.

But instead of lying back and letting him take the next step, Alex came up onto her knees. She looked up at him and ran her hands over his body, which until that moment, he'd forgotten was bruised and beaten. Over his muscles, across his skin, the feel of her lips and her breath on his wounded flesh was so satisfying even as it made him all the more desperate. She stretched up to kiss his lips, but her hands moved lower, over his abdominal muscles, past the angling of his hips, and to his surprise, she took the sturdy length of him into her palms. Philippe nearly crumbled. She moved her hands up and down, spreading his own wetness across his shaft, watching as she did so. Then she looked back to him with a bold smile before reaching down to feel the throbbing weights beneath him. He clenched his jaw and felt like he may buckle.

"Alex," he growled.

"Not until you're inside me," she said with big eyes.

It was over. He grabbed the back of her knees and dragged her into position. She flopped back onto the pillows with a delighted shriek. He moved her legs roughly apart and took his cock, pressing in just enough to meet the resistance of her maidenhead. She bit her lip at this, but then he decided to bite her lip for her and with one skillful thrust, they were finally joined.

Alex let out a small cry and stilled. Philippe stilled as well, giving her a chance to soften against him once more, though the slick sensation of their connection had ripped pleasure into every corner of his body. He knew he had to hold himself back, but his own desire was a dangerous force, and he watched her desperately, waiting for a signal that she still wanted more. "I'm okay," she responded to his searching eyes. She smiled and put her hand against his cheek, and it nearly undid him.

He began to move then, carefully, and as he did, he entered another world, a world of utter bliss. He gripped her legs to wrap them around his waist, allowing him to press more fully into her wetness. She trembled and held close to him, her quickening breath and delicious whimpers soon telling him she was ready for more. He picked up his rhythm, moving more deeply into her and Alex responded by moving back against him, her hips opening to take as much as she could bear. He pressed his face into her hair, her neck, rocking her forward, lifting her backside off the mattress. "*Mon dieu,* Alex. *Mon dieu,*" he whispered. A deep and unrestrained moan escaped his lips as he fully indulged in the sheer pleasure of bringing their bodies together.

He wanted to watch her, and fall into her eyes as everything happened, so he pulled back to look at her. But Alex had turned away. He nudged her to face him and nibbled at her lips and her chin, waiting for her to look back at him. "Alex," he whispered.

He repeated her name and tried again to catch her stare, but she kept avoiding his eyes, until he realized she was doing it on purpose. *Goddamn her*, he thought. She was still keeping him at a distance. He wasn't going to let that happen. He'd waited too long and fought too hard to get back to her to let her run away from him now. He'd get her to open her eyes.

He began moving faster, throwing new sensations at her before she was ready. He needed her to know that if she was going to retreat, then he was going to follow. He grabbed her leg to spread her open, grinding himself against her. Alex gulped a breath of air and blinked surprised eyes beneath him, but she still didn't look at him. Instead, she squeezed her eyes shut again and grabbed onto his shoulders to stay steady. He responded by angling himself up higher and pressing in again, sliding himself firmly against her front wall. Alex gasped and fell back onto the pillows, but she kept her eyes closed even as her body opened up, wanting more. His own breathing was coming quickly now, and the sensation of her tight form was enough to cripple him, but he wouldn't let either of them boil over until he got what he wanted.

"Look at me," he said through gritted teeth.

Her eyes remained sealed.

"Alex," he commanded. "Open your eyes."

Her eyes fluttered open, but she still looked away.

"Look at me," he said huskily. He leaned in this time and bit the soft spot just above her collarbone. Hard.

Alex cried out in surprise and her eyes snapped open. Her expression was a mix of shock and anger, but once he caught her eyes, finally, he smiled at her, and he felt her melt around him once more.

"Don't look away," he whispered.

And this time she didn't. Now, he could see in her eyes everything he wanted. He continued moving her back and forth, their bodies in perfect rhythm, and he let himself completely succumb to her. He lost control, driving into her forcefully, recklessly, the music of her pleasure in his ears, a thousand words in her eyes, and he knew they were undeniably bonded. He felt her body coiling up as he worked her harder, faster, giving her whatever she needed to feel release.

In a moment, she arched back and her breath caught. Her legs widened for him and he plunged frantically inside of her. He was tripping over the edge himself and he held on to her madly, the pleasure almost too powerful. Finally, she tensed up and cried out his name, clinging to him closely. Her body gripped his cock tightly and he felt the strong pulses of her satisfaction as she quivered and panted for breath beneath him. It was all he needed to erupt himself, a firecracker explosion that left him gasping her name in jagged ecstasy.

Alex... Alex... Alex...

It was the most intense sensation of his life, and as it slowly subsided, he found her eyes once more. He couldn't imagine a more perfect moment. He leaned in to kiss her, while their bodies continued to cling to each other in waves of desperation. She would rule him until the end, he thought with hazy recognition, the absolute end.

It had been too much.

It had been far more than she expected. Alex lay in bed wrapped in a sleeping Philippe. His chest was pressed against her back, and he held her tight with his strong arms. His heavy muscle rested against her backside. She was a little scandalized at the intimacy of it, but had to admit, with her head on his arm, and the soft sound of his sleep in her ear, she'd never felt more secure or satisfied in her life.

The night was just *full* of new sensations.

He'd fallen asleep kissing the back of her neck and whispering about his happiness in finding her, as her own body came down from the heavens. But she now lay awake, fighting away the moment of sleep, convinced that no beautiful dream could outdo this.

She had expected to connect with him physically. They had danced with each other in many ways, and she had known she would feel the pleasure of him with her body. But what she hadn't counted on, what she never expected, was the way he looked at her, and kissed her so tenderly, and the way he opened up all the feelings in her that weren't meant to be spilled. She had closed her eyes when it all became too much, but even that he wouldn't allow. He forced her to give herself to him completely, and in turn, she had felt a connection that was far beyond what happened with their bodies. Was this the game of sex? Was this what addicted people so? If it was, Philippe was the master. There was no part of her being left untouched by him that evening.

Oh, how would she go on now? How would she move forward in life knowing that experiences like this one existed? No happiness she'd ever known compared to the feeling of him against her skin. Perhaps she should take heart in knowing that she had given herself to the only man in the world she could ever desire. That would have to sustain her until her heart closed once again.

But those were thoughts for tomorrow. Right now, she was too filled with the sensual sensations of the evening to let herself think about anything different. She snuggled against him, happy for this opportunity to fall asleep in the arms of a man—of *the* man—who would forever possess her heart.

Chapter Thirty-Two

It was the sun coming through the window that woke her up. It landed on her face and she opened her eyes lazily, seeing the curtains flutter. She sighed, a wonderful sense of peacefulness settled in her body. She blinked her heavy eyelids, and his form came into focus, sitting on a chair across from the bed. He was fully dressed and smiling at her.

It all came back with a crash, and she snapped awake. She grabbed the blankets and pulled them up to her chin as she sat up rigidly in the bed. But a sharp pain went straight up through her middle, and she doubled over with a groan before reaching out to pile more blankets in front of her. She looked up sheepishly to see the amusement in his expression and then buried her face in the covers for a moment before sitting up and addressing him.

"Is it late?" she asked. She straightened her hair and tried to appear calm.

"Just after dawn," he said.

"You look awfully smug this morning," Alex said.

"Why wouldn't I?" he said, still grinning.

She felt that rush coming over her body again as she looked at him, but this time it was so much more intense because she knew where it could lead, what he could do to her. She ached with a desperate desire against that new soreness deep inside her as far too many feelings bubbled up. But she fought it all down and changed the subject.

"So now you must tell me," she said, trying to compose herself. "What came of your adventure? I know nothing of the success or failure of the mission."

"Alex," he said, his tone changing, "I am so sorry I could not wait—"

She cut him off, "I understand why you left. I do. I am, however, interested in your progress."

"Well, we did not capture the 'leader'," he said. "We tracked Giroux and his men to their new camp and waited for him to show until the last possible moment. But I had made a promise," he said, leaning forward in the chair, his eyes turning smoky again. "I couldn't miss the ball. And I was indeed rewarded for making good on my word." He grinned arrogantly at her, and Alex, overcome, looked down at her hands.

"Yes, yes," she said, feeling herself flush. "And there shall be a band of minstrels playing for you when you leave my room." She cleared her throat and adjusted her pile of blankets. "But the men? Is everyone okay?"

"Everyone is okay," said Philippe. "Tired, beaten up, but well. Franc and Luc are in Aliette with wounds, but they should be fine."

"And what transpired to give you your scars?" she asked.

Philippe finally shifted his focus, much to her relief, and gave her the details of the last week. After a rough fight, they had indeed overwhelmed the rebels. They brought the captured men to be detained in Aliette, where they waited now in holding cells. Philippe planned to take them back to Chevalerie. There they would be interrogated. The leader was still at large, but Philippe indicated he had some ideas about where they might find the man. Until then, he was fairly confident that the problem would abate, now that the captain was cut off from his lackeys.

"So, it's back to Aliette and then Chevalerie?" Alex asked.

"Yes. I have sent Claude and Auguste ahead. Laurent and Henri will travel with us."

"Our party has dwindled," she said.

"But I am very happy to have recovered our guide," he said with a grin.

Within the hour, Philippe had finished the rest of his own preparations. There had not been a band playing for him when he walked out of Alex's room. In fact, everyone he came across was too tired from the night before to really notice. But he would have liked it. He indeed felt deserving of an award.

Emily sleepily bade him farewell before she and Alex embraced and shared promises to stay in touch. The Marquis was absent, having already left for his morning ride. Philippe would have liked to talk with him again, but nothing had changed since they'd spoken the day before. The problem had not been solved to satisfaction, but it had been contained for the time being. He could get his troops back to Chevalerie and decide on a new plan with his father. He felt at least with Giroux and the others in captivity, they had bought themselves enough time to refresh and reorganize.

They would return to Aliette that day, wait for reinforcements to take over the prisoners and then get back to Chevalerie as soon as possible, which, as long as they did not linger, could be achieved in just a few days. At that point, another phase would begin in which they would need to get information out of these guys, and that could get brutal. Though he felt more and more confident about his theories, he had yet to share his thoughts with anyone but his father. If he was indeed correct, the situation would have to be handled with extreme care. He needed council. And he needed to regroup.

The morning was still young, and as they rode towards Aliette at a gallop, he breathed in the fresh air. He felt reborn. He watched Alex just ahead of him, with pride filling his heart. Her hair flowed behind her as she rode, and he remembered how it had cascaded across her naked skin the night before. When he woke up that morning, with her body still pressed into his, he had to restrain himself. He wanted her again, immediately, with a violent desire. But he didn't want to overwhelm her. There'd be plenty of time for that later, he thought smugly.

He wondered what she was thinking. Was she as relieved and excited as he was that they had crossed this boundary between them? She was flustered, nervous, and adorable that morning, and he knew it may take her a little while to relax in his presence again, but they had buried so many obstacles, he could stand to be patient a little while longer.

Presently, they approached a tight canyon and the group slowed.

Philippe angled his horse next to hers as Laurent and Henri stretched out up ahead. Alex looked back at him playfully. His body began to respond. She was thinking about it too, he thought as he sidled his horse closer.

He could not *wait* to get her home and all to himself.

"Hey," he said, coming up next to her. The closer he got, the more heat he felt under his clothes.

"*Monsieur*," she responded.

"*Monsieur*?" he asked. "Have we not put away the formalities?"

She just smiled and looked away.

They continued down the trail, guiding their horses over the rocks. It was strange that after all that had happened, he felt at a loss for words. He continued speaking, refusing to let any awkwardness creep between them. "Are you as pleased as I am with the events of last night?" he persisted.

"It was nice," she said quietly.

"Just nice?" he coaxed, looking for some sign she would welcome him into her bed again, preferably very soon. But she stiffened, and it was his first indication that maybe Alex wasn't thinking the same as he was.

"You can be satisfied with your performance, if that's what you are asking." There was still a teasing tone in her voice, but he felt the distance coming back, an earthquake threatening to rumble a chasm between them.

"Well, I'm glad for that Alex, but it's not what I'm asking." He turned his head so he could lower his voice. "I'd actually like to hear that you like me a little more than you did before last night."

She gave a laugh. "Well, you did not go down in any estimation."

"I suppose that's a start," he smirked, gratification running through him again. His voice softened. "Was it what you'd hoped for?" he asked.

"Philippe, we shouldn't talk about such things out here. It isn't proper."

"What we did last night wasn't proper."

"Yes, but now we are in the open."

"I don't care," he said.

She blew a strand of hair out of her face in frustration. Then she turned to him. "It was far more than I expected," she smiled with her eyes cast down. "It was wonderful. And I thank you for treating me so well."

The pride her words caused was almost out of control. She was his woman now, and he had pleased her. It was enough to send him to the moon. He could have soared in the feeling for the rest of the day. That is, until her next sentence brought him back down to earth.

"It shall be a memory I treasure throughout my life."

He paused for a moment, wondering if he was detecting the correct tone in her voice. "I had hoped," he caged, "to give you many more memories."

She laughed. "You don't have to patronize me."

"What do you mean?" he asked.

She shrugged. "I asked for the experience, and you gave it to me. Surely, you have your next conquest in mind already."

"What conquest? Do you think you were a conquest?"

She looked at him, rolled her eyes and then laughed again. "For once, I promise I am not upset with you. I knew what I was getting into. I wished to know what sex would be like. And who better to show me?"

His heart was beating too slowly. Or maybe her words were coming too fast. "No, no, no. Alex," he said. "That was not just sex."

"Philippe," she deadpanned. "Of course it was."

"Alex." He stopped his horse. "Alex," he called again. She stopped and looked at him. The men up ahead shot curious glances at the two of them, but seeing Philippe's contorted face, they hid their stares and continued moving forward.

"I—I," he stammered. He didn't quite know what to say. He hadn't even considered the possibility that his intentions were unclear. She stared back at him. He felt that if he just found the correct words, he could make things right, but he didn't know what he had done wrong or why she was acting so coldly. So, what could he say to fix it? "It wasn't just sex," he said. "For me."

She looked at him squarely. "It has always been 'just sex' for you."

He took the words to the gut. "In the past perhaps," he trailed off.

"This is not about the past."

He could not understand why she continued to push him away. It turned him suddenly defensive. "Then what is it about?" he snapped, his voice rising. "You clearly still aim to make me pay for what I did six years ago."

"I am not still mad about that," she said. "But I cannot see where this will lead." Her voice matched his. "What do you want, Philippe? Do you want me to go be your mistress? So you can have me when you wish, and I can die on the vine wondering when you will come visit me again? I have seen you do it to other girls. You forget that I watched you play for many years. I do not wish to get tangled up in that game."

"I never said that's what I wanted," he said, his voice low.

"Then what do you want?" she shot back, exasperation evident.

He had an opportunity, he knew it, right there to tell her he wanted to bring her back to Chevalerie and make her his forever, in any way she wanted. But he was sure anything that came out of his mouth would be wrong. Did she want to be married? Did she want to run away together? He just didn't know, and before he could say a word, she turned her horse in the opposite direction.

"This is ridiculous," she scoffed.

"Where are you going?" he called.

"Back to Ponce. I will find work there."

"You are not relieved," he shouted, unbelieving that she was turning away.

"I think I am," she said. "I'm sure the Duke's son can find his own way home."

"You won't get paid," he sputtered, trying to think of any reason to get her to stay.

"I'll take last night as payment," she said over her shoulder as she kicked her horse into a gallop.

"*Alex*!" he shouted after her.

Chapter Thirty-Three

He was infuriating. Absolutely infuriating, she thought as she raced her horse away from him. She darted through the woods at a quick clip, zipping through the trees as fast as the obstacles would allow her. She needed distance, lots of distance. Her horse jumped a fallen log and she ducked a branch as she entered into denser coverings. She'd *tried*. She'd tried to accompany the party and be of service in the final leg of the journey back to Chevalerie, but how could she deal with his pseudo-sweetness and her lingering feelings, feelings that were so much more profound than she had imagined they would be? How dare he say that it had meant more to him; what game was he playing? He'd gotten what he'd wanted. Why did he continue to play with her so cruelly?

He didn't understand. He couldn't. She had spent so many years hopelessly in love with that man, fighting with her emotions was like second nature to her now. After last night, that amazing night they spent together, how in the world did he think she could watch him chase after other women? It would be an agonizing death, worse than any slow bleed caused by a sword. Instead, she would let the pain dull itself out to rebuild herself once more.

It wasn't his fault. He wanted what he wanted. Part of her was gratified that he at least would like to have her again, but she couldn't be so close to him anymore. When he had approached her just before and began speaking in his sugary tone, her breath had gotten stuck in her throat. It was useless trying to fight her desire—the only solution was to be as far from him as possible. The path ahead of her darkened with dense trees and brush, and she knew very well what was on the other end of it. There would be work, she would travel, she would continue living a life in which she stuffed one appropriate dress into the bottom of her bag, below a stack of maps, her book on tactics, and some biscuits for the road. It was a trifling and unfulfilling path. How she was ready to be done with it all, but what else could she do? She would not make a suitable wife to anyone, especially now, even if she could stomach getting close to another man. And what other options did she have?

Her horse galloped while she continued to mope. Her mind flicked back to the night before, when he had stared so deeply into her eyes. Was there any chance he truly wanted her and that she was being unreasonable? She took a breath and tried to think about the situation as objectively as possible. He'd had the opportunity to sleep with her the night she'd gotten drunk, but he hadn't taken it. That was an indication of his intentions, was it not? He'd all but begged her to stay in Ponce when he left. He'd come back from chasing their enemies to find her. He went after her and left countless women behind to find her in her quarters the night before. He had followed her wherever she went, actually. She groaned and dropped her face into her hands, tugging on the reins of her horse. He hadn't been cruel to her. He'd been... really wonderful. And it had felt like so much more than sex. But what did she know? She'd had nothing to compare it to, only the stories she had heard from randy men on the road. The bond she had felt the night before was indescribable and she could have died fulfilled in his arms, but she didn't trust herself. When it came to Philippe, her instincts were absolute shit.

She closed her eyes and tried to clear her head. She slowed her horse and weaved through the thick trees. Was it real, what had happened between them? Did he want her, or was this a moment's diversion? Alex paused in the thought, wondering about Philippe and his intentions like she had a thousand times before. This time, something was different. There was another feeling, swirling among all her questions and insecurities, like a firefly dancing through the mist. Alex clutched her hands against her chest, trying to draw it out. The feeling was feeble at first, but there was power in it, and she knew that it carried something that she had been missing. She squeezed her eyes shut and turned off her ears to the forest sounds around her, using all her senses and intuition and strength to call upon what was inside her. The feeling began to grow, more fireflies sparking to life. The light spread throughout her body and the thought buzzed in her ears. Her mouth flooded with sweetness now that she was paying attention. She took deep breaths to let it all settle, and she realized it was taking the form of Emily's words. They were telling her something—something she should have been saying to herself for a very long time:

This was not about what Philippe wanted.

For once in her goddamn life, it wasn't about what Philippe wanted.

A lightning bolt exploded inside her and she finally understood. In all this time, she had never asked herself what it was that she wanted. Without shame or guilt or any of the other feelings that had prodded her along for so many years: what the hell did *she* want? The realization opened her up like a blooming flower to a burst of sunshine, and her body flushed hot and cold all at once as she processed feelings that had, until that moment, never had anywhere to go. She took a breath and asked herself, what *did* she want? She knew it, immediately, and the answer was quite simple.

Alex wanted everything.

She wanted to forgive herself for ever feeling weak. She wanted to be able to be vulnerable and scared. She wanted safety. She wanted a home and to be welcome back in Chevalerie. She wanted someone to rely on and for those she loved to be able to rely on her. And, she could admit, she wanted Philippe. All the wants and desires rippled through her in a wave of energy as though a dam had been broken. And just like that she realized there was nothing stopping her from having all those things. She just had to let them happen.

She opened her eyes. The wind fluttered the leaves around her and suddenly everything looked different. She had to get back. With a thrill inside her, she urged her horse around, full of purpose. She would not wait another second to begin her life. The horse neighed and raised its front feet as it responded to her jolt of energy. Before Alex could get the beast up to speed, a familiar voice called out to her.

She turned and watched the hooded figure approach. "Hello dear," he said. "Where is your company? It is dangerous to be out here alone."

"Marquis?" she said, slowing to a stop and reaching forward to calm her horse. It was odd to see him there; it wasn't right. "I have just stepped away," she said. "But I shall rejoin them directly."

"So, they are not far?"

"No," she said, slowly reaching toward her blade. "Just down the way," she lied. "What do you do out here by yourself? Surely the Marquis has an entourage to accompany him?"

"I do," he said, lowering his hood. "They are with me now."

One by one, she saw them. Giroux, along with, she assumed, the rest of the men Philippe had captured, now free from their imprisonment. She didn't know why or how, but she knew she was in trouble.

"I'm sorry it had to happen like this," said the Marquis. "I know how very fond my wife is of you. And for the record, she is quite unaware."

The thought comforted Alex. She hoped her friend was spared any problems at the hand of this traitor, but how mad she was at herself for not seeing this sooner. Her mind had been far too clouded to recognize that he was a threat.

She unsheathed her blade. "It will not be easy to capture me, Marquis. I hope the outcome you desire is worth it."

"Desperate men need little provocation," he said.

Well, she thought, adrenaline charging her up like an electric storm; she would cause as many injuries as she could before going down.

Chapter Thirty-Four

Philippe had stood brooding by a small stream since after Alex had left. Laurent and Henri were paused uncertainly up the way, waiting for him to make a move, but Philippe was stuck, kicking rocks into the water. What in the world had just happened, he wondered. How had she gone so quickly from his arms to the road leading away from him? He felt like she was still punishing him for what had happened so long ago, though he had tried and tried to make it clear that he could never want anyone else.

He took a stick and chucked it as far as he could. It ricocheted an echo across the mouth of the canyon. She was so damn stubborn that she wouldn't even listen to him. He folded his arms and looked down the stream, deeper into the canyon. Well, he supposed, he hadn't actually *said* anything to her. But couldn't she tell how he felt by his actions? He'd given himself completely to her, and he knew she had done the same. Yet here they were again. Would it really matter if he spoke the words to her and told her that he loved her?

This was absurd. Why was he letting her get away? Maybe he hadn't paid his penance yet and won back her trust, but he would not give up. What mattered in this life if he could not spend it with this ornery, difficult, crazy woman in pants that he was so in love with it hurt? If need be, he would spend his days proving to her that he was worthy of her attention.

"Men," he said, returning to the spot where they rested. "I am going to retrieve our guide."

Laurent grinned. Henri smirked. "Aye, hurry up then," he said, conceding a smile.

"Head to Aliette," Philippe said. "I hope to meet you there soon."

With that he was off. He hoped she had run straight and not left any difficulties in her trail, but if she escaped the Earth, he would trail her across the stars. He raced his horse hard, imagining what he would say to her. He would make her listen. He would make her understand. He would tell her that he loved her and that he would give her anything to stay by his side. How could she think that he could want another woman after everything that had happened between them? She was all he wanted and certainly more than he could handle.

He tracked her back across the road and deeper into the woods. With every moment and every step of his horse, he was more fevered, more desperate, more determined to tell her all the things he hadn't said. As he came upon one of the trails which led towards Ponce, he had to pause. He looked around. Something was strange. He moved the horse a few steps ahead, scanning the scene. There were no birds chirping. There were no insects buzzing. He hopped off his horse and looked to the ground. It was muddled and kicked about. He looked to the side and saw trampled vegetation, crushed stalks and leaves in the dirt. There had been a struggle here. There was hoof print and the tread of man as well. His heart began to pound. He stomped across the ground, following the progression of footsteps. She'd been gravely outnumbered.

Then he saw it—blood—splattered across a tree trunk. He touched it, still wet. He couldn't imagine a more helpless feeling than the one that settled in his chest. He looked down the path, rubbing the streak of blood between his fingers. They didn't try to cover anything up, which meant they expected no trouble, or they hoped to be followed. Either way, they would have a nightmare coming after them.

This was his fault. His fault for so many reasons. He hadn't done his job because he was lovesick. He'd let the Marquis think he'd gotten away with his crimes in order to trap him at a later date, but he'd misjudged the situation, and he'd let her go off into danger, completely alone.

Philippe mounted his horse and took off down the path, a demon screaming inside of him.

Chapter Thirty-Five

Michel had been in good spirits for most of the journey up the region, despite having had his little vacation home interrupted. He'd only been back in Chevalerie for a few days and was having a good time being taken care of by his mother when they received word from Philippe. It seemed that the simple mission to neutralize a civil rebellion had spun out in too many directions, and Philippe needed backup. He'd asked their father to send reinforcement troops to meet them in Aliette, where they could relieve the men and have extra support transporting anyone they managed to capture. It also seemed as though the ultimate enemy was still not detained though Philippe suspected the Marquis du Ponce himself as the one trying to control the rivers through the pawns he had hired. To "capture" a marquis was far more politically daunting than it was necessarily physical. Therefore, Michel brought with him not only troops to relieve the tired and beleaguered men with whom Philippe fought, but also the Duke's instructions on dealing with the Marquis situation.

His father had spoken with Michel regarding the journey, insistent that Michel or he himself lead the way. Michel felt like he would enjoy some adventure and thought it unnecessary for his father to leave the comfort of home. Michel had been on a tedious expedition in the East, maintaining trade relations with several of the Asian outpost merchants. His journeys were important to the economy in Chevalerie, but his time had been spent on diplomacy rather than physicality, and he found himself hungry for a little danger before he had to return to the Far East.

Plus, his mother couldn't pass the opportunity to gossip, so he knew Philippe was probably knee deep in some entanglement with little Alex. He didn't want to miss the opportunity to see what trouble his youngest brother had gotten into this time.

But when he had arrived in Aliette earlier that morning, the prisoners were gone, released in the dead of night. By whom? The Marquis du Ponce himself. The Marquis had told the magistrate he would take the prisoners to Ponce for trial, and the confused magistrate had signed the papers releasing them. Michel was severely irritated by the lack of standardization. Something like that would never have happened in Chevalerie. To think, the Duke's son brings captured men to be detained and a marquis from another town, releases them? Unthinkable. These smaller towns, with no nearby nobility and no uniform government, often lacked hands-on and competent leadership. Eventually, Michel would take over the Duchy and making sure everything went according to well-established standards would be his first order of business.

Now, as he led his company of men up to Ponce, he was annoyed. He was annoyed that the men Philippe had put away had been released. He was annoyed that he didn't know what kind of trouble he, his brother, or their men were facing. He was annoyed that the Marquis, sworn to his position by the King of France with the same proclamation that had made his father a duke, had turned on his country for money.

Michel pushed his dark waves back from his forehead and knotted them with a band on the top of his head. Then he slapped the reins of his horse, urging the beast on. He was ready for whatever would come.

He had no more the chance to hasten his party along than he saw two men on horses approaching from up ahead. He called for his own to slow.

"*Bonjour, messieurs,*" he called. "State your affiliation."

"We are of the same blood," said a man coming into clear view.

"*Bon Dieu*, Laurent," said Michel, recognizing his cousin. "Henri." He nodded. "I am happy to see you both alive and well."

"We are alive, cousin, but worse for wear," Laurent said, dismounting his horse. "What is the news from Chevalerie?"

Michel hopped from his horse to embrace his cousin. "I am afraid we may be in danger at the moment," said Michel. "Where is Philippe?"

"We were with him not long ago," Laurent said. "He has gone after Alex. Back towards Ponce."

"Of course he has." Michel sighed. "Well, mount your horse. It seems that you are unaware of the events that have transpired."

"Philippe has asked us to meet him in Aliette," Laurent responded.

"I have just come from there," Michel said, smacking his cousin on the back. "The prisoners have escaped with the Marquis, and Philippe probably fights them now."

"The Marquis?" Laurent asked.

Michel nodded. "I shall fill you in while we ride." He hoisted himself onto his horse. "Let us be off. We must find them before blood is shed." He paused. "Or at least our blood."

The party continued up the path from which Laurent and Henri had just come. Michel urged them forward. He hoped to see this through before sunset.

Chapter Thirty-Six

She was tied to a tree. And gagged! Did they take her for a screamer? Ropes were stretched around her middle to just below her neck. Her arms were planted against her sides and no amount of wiggling gave her slack. To make matters worse, she could see her sword, tossed aside and forgotten but well out of her own reach. Her hands burned to reclaim its hilt, but she could do nothing more than watch as the men before her strategized. They wanted Philippe, and they thought she was the answer. It had been no accident that they were upon her once she was alone. The Marquis claimed he would have snatched her sooner to draw out Philippe had his wife's event not gotten in his way. Once they had approached her that morning, they wasted no time knocking her off her horse, but Alex had made good on her promise and caused some pain before they took her down. She had nailed one with a punch to the jaw, kicked another hard in the stomach, and toppled a big one by binding his sword and knocking him off balance with a shoulder check. She even took a chunk out of another man's arm with her sword, leaving a perfect spray of blood across the trees. That was all before she was overtaken, being pushed into the dirt, bound and gagged, and not spared from the cheap shots and extra roughness they took with her.

It was him all along, the Marquis, that *scoundrel*. No wonder they had such trouble pinning down their enemies. The man they sought was the very man for whom they were fighting. After they had captured her and secured her to the Marquis' horse, she felt the hate boiling out of him—for the Duke, for the King. While they rode, he muttered about the Duke's capped taxes and sales regulations. The Marquis had had a brilliant plan to bring money into the area, he bemoaned, but now, he would have to use Alex to capture Philippe and thus regain his advantage against the Duke. He *hated* having his plans disrupted.

They had traveled a few miles deeper into the woods to a makeshift camp of his men. Alex was now secured at the far end of a small clearing while the men toiled before her. She counted twenty six, including the Marquis and Giroux. Up ahead, the Marquis was preparing for a confrontation in the midst of the thick trees. He was at once commanding and assertive, but he was rushed and giving hasty orders: sharpen your sword, place a lookout, clear the brush, grease your blade. He believed Philippe would discover her absence, gather what was left of his men, and come after her. Alex alone knew she had strayed and Philippe would have no idea she had been taken.

What would happen to her when Philippe didn't come? She did not want to think about what these men would do to her. At the hands of men with no control, no honor... she would fight and rip them apart as best she could, for as long as she could. She twisted in the ropes, embarrassed at her failure to escape. The fear was there, but it had been overtaken by her own fury at herself for not piecing this together sooner.

She had just been on the edge of so many wonderful things. Now she felt only remorse deep in her chest. In the end, she would perish, a silly little story of the woman who wielded a sword and finally got what was coming to her.

Up ahead, something was happening between Giroux and the Marquis. Giroux indicated towards her, but the Marquis met him with unyielding indifference.

"This is not the outcome that we discussed," Giroux said loud enough for Alex to hear. "Our objective can be met without any further bloodshed. I have told you that I will stand trial."

"You know nothing of politics," said the Marquis, dismissing his plea.

"I have it on the authority of *Monsieur* Philippe that the village towns will be cared for," Giroux said ardently. "Even in my imprisonment, he promised my people would be a priority. Why must we continue with this fight?"

"*Imbécile*!" the Marquis thundered. "I do not care about a monthly pittance for the villages. The river is the issue! I do this to control the river."

"I never agreed to fight for you to control the river," Giroux said, his own voice dark and passionate. "And I certainly did not agree to take hostages and kill innocents." He looked back to Alex, who was watching keenly. "She has nothing to do with this."

"You are wearing on my patience, Giroux. You served your purpose, commanding the village raids in my stead, but they are finished. I no longer need you." The Marquis cut an imposing figure, even though Giroux towered above him. "Soon, I will own the river and hire a hundred men in your place." He turned to the men at large. "Know this face!" he boomed. "This is the face of your lord and master." He said it in French then repeated it in dialect. "When this day is done, I will have all the leverage I need to secede from the Duchy. If you are with me now, you will be rewarded then."

The men cheered and bellowed their enthusiasm—dirty men, dishonorable men, men hired to be loyal. The Marquis turned back to Giroux. "I'm sure many here wouldn't mind doubling their salary to take out a traitor," he said. "And then perhaps tripling it for burning your beloved villages to the ground."

Giroux looked around, his hand on the hilt of his sword. One by one, the men drew their blades, showing allegiance to the Marquis. Alex jerked again at her ropes and eyed her sword, wanting just one more chance to fight.

That was when she saw a wink of movement in the forest, off to her left. It was just a slight rustle of leaves, but no animal would dare come so close to the noises of these men. Alex watched carefully, so as not to draw notice, but the rebels before her were locked in a standoff. Then she saw it. Philippe's angry face glaring at her from behind the leaves. She thought she must have been imagining it, but he looked so mad at her that he *had* to have been real. She almost laughed in relief; her joy at seeing him was palpable. Philippe nodded in the Marquis' direction as he brought his finger up to his lips, reminding her they were far from being out of danger.

Before her, rebel swords were still drawn, but Giroux had taken his hand off his blade. "I am your servant," he said with a bow of his head.

The Marquis put his hand on Giroux's shoulder. "Do not forget it," he said. And as quick as that, the upheaval was over.

Philippe, meanwhile, disappeared from her view as the tension in the camp broke. She hoped he wasn't alone, but she couldn't make out any other signs of life. Then, suddenly, he was right behind her, his presence thicker than the trees.

"I'm alone," he whispered, answering the question she couldn't ask.

Alex made no sound but felt her fingers wiggling in excitement that he was there.

"Calm down," he laughed and touched her hand. "We'll try to sneak back to my horse, but you may need to fight if we can't get you out before they notice."

Finally, she thought, she was itching to teach someone a lesson.

The tree was large enough that good placement allowed Philippe to go undetected as he cut through her bindings. He worked swiftly but delicately, so that she could feel the vibrations as he cut without hearing the sound of the fibers splitting. Thankfully, no one had paid much attention to her once they'd secured her to the tree. She hoped their ignorance would last just a little longer.

Then, as the Marquis scanned the various projects he had moving forward, he turned to her. He took a hard look and walked a few steps towards her position, eyebrows cocked and head tilted. He knew. She willed Philippe to slink away, but she felt him just freeze in place. The Marquis was upon them before she could even try to look like nothing was happening.

"It would seem that the lady guide's absence does not go long unnoticed," the Marquis said to Alex.

Alex held his gaze. She would kick him in the face if he were closer.

"I know you are here," he said, turning his attention from her.

She felt a final, forceful slice go through the ropes before Philippe stood up to come around and face him.

"You're a little early, Lord Philippe," the Marquis said. "We aren't quite ready for you, but we have numbers on our side."

"You had numbers on your side the last time I captured your men," Philippe said condescendingly.

"Well, their commander is here now." The words leached from his smile. "And you seem to be the one waiting on reinforcements." He scanned the trees. "I had hoped you would rush in foolhardy when you realized she was gone. It seems I was correct."

"So, what do you want?" Philippe asked, not responding to the taunt.

"Right to business?" The Marquis nodded through a complacent smirk. "Then I won't draw it out any further." He narrowed his eyes and called out to the men behind him. Alex watched as they became aware of the situation.

The Marquis continued, "I want you to write to your father recommending the tax," he glared potently at Philippe. "I will be the natural choice to monitor its distribution. Then you will tell him you have decided to remain in Ponce for a... vacation, perhaps? Maybe you got lost in a whorehouse." He shrugged. "I don't care. You will, of course, be detained. Killed, when it suits my situation best." He grinned, malice evident. "By the time the Duke figures it out, I will have raised my army."

"He won't believe such a story," Philippe replied.

"Well," began the Marquis, "it will be your job to make him believe."

Philippe folded his arms and leaned against the tree, studying the man. "That doesn't sound like a very good deal, Marquis," he said.

"I agree," the Marquis conceded. "But if you don't do what I ask," he unsheathed his sword and angled it towards Alex. He pressed the tip into the depression of skin just between her collarbones. "I'll let these savages kill her. And I'll tell them to make it hurt."

It wasn't the steel to her throat that made her panic, or even the threat. It was the look on Philippe's face that told her he was considering the Marquis' proposition. *No no no*, she thought, fear forgotten, she only wanted to stand beside him and fight. Philippe had cut slack in her ropes, but she was still bound. She tugged helplessly at the bindings while she watched all the spirit drain from Philippe's face.

"Answer me now," the Marquis said as he pressed the point more firmly against her throat.

"If I submit, you must not hurt her," Philippe said, his confidence shaken.

"I will give her to my wife," the Marquis oozed. "As a pet."

Philippe had no men behind him. He had no allies in this bunch or any chance of victory. Alex knew if it wasn't for her, he would have a chance to get away. She was flushed with gratitude that he would give himself up for her, but then, as she watched his wrist shift to surrender his blade, Alex snapped.

They weren't going down like this.

Summoning every ounce of strength in her being, she dug deep, through years of training and fighting, through everything that she had ever overcome or stored away because it was too painful. She became purely animal, a repressed beast brimming with willpower and grit. She bit into her gag, and with a deep and desperate growl, she ripped into her muscles and all at once tore through her remaining bindings.

The ropes coiled back like snakes against her surge of energy, startling both the men. She wasted no time and grabbed the Marquis' blade with her bare hands. She jerked him forward and used the leverage to take out his feet. He crashed down, dumbfounded, on top of her.

But he was off her in seconds as Philippe threw him back and attacked him aggressively. She pulled frantically at the rest of the ropes as one of the Marquis' underlings charged her. She braced herself against the tree, and just as he got close enough, she kicked his knee with her boot. She heard the snap of bone and the man crumbled before her with a scream. She dove across him and grabbed her sword. Power bolted through her as she reclaimed her weapon. She scrambled to her feet and ripped the gag from her mouth, the last of the rope falling to the dirt.

The Marquis' men were caught off guard, and not all at once did they realize the fighting had begun. Many of them had their sword drawn in the opposite direction, looking to the trees, waiting for the attack. It would be just moments before they realized Philippe had come alone. By now, Philippe was locked in a heated battle with the Marquis, but Alex had gained enough attention to do some damage herself. A short but thick man came at her, and she put a perfect gash right across his face. Another raggedy man swung his blade at her wildly, but she ducked his sword, swinging a powerful undercut that knocked him right off his feet. He landed in the dirt and rolled to his stomach. Alex stomped across his back as she ran to Philippe's side.

The Marquis had backed away, not having the stamina of the young lord, and Philippe was now skillfully slicing through two others at once. He dropped them both just as the rest of the men began to realize that no one else was coming. They approached the lord and his guide, snickering with the ease of meeting their objective. Philippe and Alex angled themselves so they were standing back to back. The Marquis caught his breath as the remaining soldiers closed in.

"Let's give 'em hell, eh, little fox," Philippe said to her.

"Just what I was thinking."

With him behind her, feeling the energy of his body, Alex felt comfort even though the odds were against them. He had come back for her, and she wished he could know just how grateful she was. She knew she was not invincible, she knew that this fight meant she would never get to say the things to him that she needed to say. But, here, she would stand her ground and she would fight with him, for him, for herself, until her very last breath.

Chapter Thirty-Seven

Michel led the group hurriedly through the forest. He tracked the signs along the trail with ease and brought the men nearer to the culprits. He controlled a respectable group of twelve men, but he was unsure of what they would meet up ahead. They had already come through the first clearing where there had been a struggle, but now the sounds of fighting were guiding them down the path to their destination. The clang of swords rang out above the forest and Michel was calmed by the fact that he wouldn't be hearing the sounds of battle if his brother had already been felled.

When he finally had a visual, it looked like Philippe was in the middle of fighting off a small army with... yep, that was Alex. He hadn't seen her in years, but she was doing well. The two were sorely outnumbered, but they were still standing. Michel signaled to the men to surround the camp. Luckily the Marquis and his men were engaged, so they had not much trouble moving into position, but it was still surprising no one was out there watching...

That's when Michel made eye contact with a lookout up in the trees.

"Reinforcements!" the scraggly youth called.

Michel sighed and hollered, "Attack!"

The Chevalerie soldiers rushed the surprised lines. They were still outnumbered, but upon a quick survey, Michel could see that the men they fought were not trained soldiers. They were unrefined and ragged. They took a moment to realize that they were under attack but quickly fell into their fighting stances. Michel rushed to his brother and Alex to help them control the center while the rest of the men fought around them.

"Brother," Michel nodded. "Alex."

"Brother," said Philippe, obviously relieved. "Very nice to see you."

"*Monsieur*," Alex said. "I shall greet you properly at another time."

"I shall hold you to that," Michel said as a man came at him. He lunged with his sword and dove into the fight.

Chapter Thirty-Eight

Michel's help had come not a moment too soon. Between the three of them and the rest of their company, they had laid out nearly half of the Marquis' men. Alex felt a new rush of excitement as she realized she was fighting with such talented soldiers. She lunged forward and caught a sour man with a dirty face across the trunk. He came back at her again and took a long shot over her head, but she ducked in time. She swung around and narrowly missed his head with the tip of her blade. He made a kissing face at her. She struck again and pierced him right through the shoulder. The man cried out and fell to the ground, writhing with pain. She jumped around, looking for someone else to fight. Michel fought Giroux while Philippe was back to taking it out on the Marquis. The rest of the men were holding their own. Philippe took a lunge at the Marquis and by the angle of his sword she could tell he was trying not to kill the man, just tire him out. He was beautiful when he fought, she thought, momentarily distracted by his form. He was beautiful when he did just about anything.

Just then she felt a strong hand around her ankle. It was Kissy-Face back from the dead. It startled her so much that she let out a cry causing Philippe and Michel to look over at her. In the split second that their attention was drawn away, the Marquis cracked Philippe hard across his side, and Giroux nailed Michel in the jaw with a solid punch. Alex panicked at the domino effect and kicked the man away from her, stumbling right into the line of fire between Philippe and the Marquis. The Marquis, wasting no time, jumped out and grabbed a handful of her hair, causing her to trip back across the dirt. Before he could get a decent hold on her, Philippe swung his sword violently and took a meaty slice across the Marquis' leg. The flesh burst open like a split sausage. The Marquis howled at the pain as he dropped to the ground, releasing Alex as he did.

With their leader immobilized, Giroux threw down his sword and put his hands up in surrender. The rest of the men took this as their cue and began to drop their stances. The Chevalerie soldiers raced around, collecting their weapons and controlling their forces.

Seeing the fight coming to an end, Alex smiled weakly at the two brothers whose matching grimaces directed at her made her laugh. They were fine. She couldn't believe it had gone in their favor, but they would all be fine.

Within fifteen minutes, the rebels were bound and plans were made to start back towards Aliette. The Marquis still lay in the dirt, howling in pain. Philippe looked at him in disgust. Quite the tyrant when things were going his way, and now a complete waste.

His comrades tied the hands of those who could pose a threat, while Alex went to the Marquis to begin wrapping his wound, as he sputtered and whimpered. She was kinder than Philippe would have been. He would like to see the man bleed out.

"Ow, be careful with me. I am old," the Marquis growled at Alex.

"I do this for your lovely wife and children, not you, you stupid swine," she said, knotting the bandages tightly. He grimaced.

Philippe chuckled.

Once they had a moment, Philippe approached and embraced his brother. "You came at just the right time."

"I was home barely any time at all, and you ruined it. Father was going to come up here himself to put out your fire."

"How was I to know that the contact he gave me was indeed the foe I was tracking?"

"This is why brains are important, Little Brother." Then he lowered his voice. "And not just women." He nodded towards Alex and gave Philippe an inquisitive look.

Philippe smiled and looked at Alex. "That story is not yet finished, Big Brother. I shall have to tell it another day."

"Fair enough," nodded Michel. "Now, let's get these men transported and locked up. Again."

It was then they took on the great task of getting everyone to Aliette. Many men on both sides needed medical attention, and everyone needed lodging for the night. The prisoners needed to be documented, the horses needed to be tended, and Michel and Philippe had a storm of letters to send up and down the region.

The day had not been easy on anyone. The whole town of Aliette had been on alert as the future Duke and his brother transported nearly fifty men through its gates. The townsmen erected a temporary barracks for the wounded, and the doctor ran from patient to patient. The magistrates were tasked with filling the prison cells and were threatened to be hanged themselves if someone were set free again without the explicit permission of either Philippe or Michel. The little inn was filled to the brim and several locals opened their homes to men who still needed a bed. Michel and Philippe were invited to stay at the Chancellor's mansion, and Philippe made sure Alex would have accommodation there as well. Aliette, that day, was busting at the seams.

Of all the prisoners, the Marquis alone had been given special accommodations. Even under arrest, his station required that he be treated with certain diplomacy. So, he too, it was decided, would be kept in the Chancellor's house, under strict security. The doctor explained to Michel and Philippe that he had lost a great deal of blood from his wound, which had filleted his outer leg from knee to hip, but he, for the moment, was stable. However, if he did survive, he was unlikely to walk on the leg again.

There wasn't a soul in town who wasn't exhausted. By nightfall, the activity had settled. Philippe had had a chance to clean himself up and sit for a brief meal between sending out correspondence and meeting with the magistrates. Michel was just as busy, and they had conferred only in passing throughout the day. He hadn't seen Alex, but he knew she was in the mansion, as he had paid a couple of footmen to let him know if she decided to leave. The day had given him many duties, but she wasn't getting away before he had a chance to yell at her for running... and to tell her how he felt.

After everyone had eaten and the poor Chancellor had said his goodnights, flustered as a pigeon with all the various forms of nobility and prisoners in his town and his home, the house was silent. Philippe sat alone in the drawing room, writing out a few last notes before making his next move. He wanted to get to Alex but was still weary and didn't feel like he could take another round of rejection after everything they had been through that day. He was at least thankful for the quiet, which allowed him to think out just what he would say.

But the resting night was destroyed before it began.

The clock had just struck ten, when a horrible ruckus hit the great hall. Philippe shot out of his seat, grabbed his sword and hit the ground running. When he reached the front room, he saw that Alex had the same idea, along with Michel and much of the house staff. Philippe quickly realized what the commotion was and saw that, for once, no one was in any danger.

Emily stood in the center of the space, screaming her head off as the frantic butler tried to quiet her.

"He is my husband!" she cried. "I have every right to see him!"

Philippe watched as Alex rushed over to her. Emily collapsed into her friend's arms. Philippe stomped over to the butler.

"Let her see him," he said.

"But he is under arrest, My Lord!" the man said with a disconcerted bow. "The Chancellor was very strict about not allowing anyone in his room."

"Well, I put him under arrest so I will dictate the terms." Philippe turned to Alex. "Take her to his room. I will join you momentarily."

Alex nodded and led the sobbing Emily down the hall.

The butler looked at him contritely, and Philippe spoke to calm him. "Good sir. I appreciate your attention to the situation, but as it were, I have little fear that the Marquis can escape through contact with his wife."

Michel spoke then, "I will speak with the Chancellor if this makes trouble for you."

The butler pressed his lips together and nodded in compliance.

Philippe marched through the hallways with Michel behind him. They entered the dimly lit room where the Marquis was being held. He was a sight, wrapped in bandages and moaning like a wounded animal. Emily stood over her husband, looking stricken. Alex stood in the corner.

No one spoke for a moment while the husband looked pitifully at his wife.

Michel ended the silence. "I know this must be difficult for you, Lady Marquise, but—"

Emily raised her hand to cut Michel off. She remained staring at her husband. "Etienne," she said to him. "Etienne, I hoped, I *really* hoped, it wasn't you."

"Me?" cried the Marquis, "I was manipulated by Girard Giroux," he said. "He wanted to control the assets for himself!"

"Lies!" she cried, seething. "I searched for every possible outcome that didn't place you at the head of this debacle," she said. "Do you know what this will do to our family? Our people?"

"*Mon choupette,* you must believe me. It was not at my hand!"

Emily fumed. She looked as though she would attack him and, for a moment, Philippe thought he would need to restrain her, but she took a breath to calm herself before continuing.

"I thought perhaps this game would fizzle out," she said. "But I realized you had really lost it this time. Do you know, Etienne, what it is like to make a decision between your husband and your country? I had sworn my loyalty to you. But am I more a wife than I am a marquise?" She thundered at him. "Do I let my husband profit at the detriment of the people we are bound to protect? Do you understand what you put me through?"

"I have only ever wanted the best for you," he said, pleadingly.

"No," she said as she whacked his knee with a flick of her wrist. The Marquis moaned woefully, but Emily continued. "You want the best for you," she said. "Do not blame your tastes on me." She took another breath to calm herself. "Etienne, you must know." She paused. "I wrote to the Duke. Shortly after I received news that the man was beheaded." She looked at Philippe. "Maurice," she said the name of the fallen soldier solemnly. "I'm sorry this escalated to such violence. I tried to intervene, but I was too late."

Philippe turned from her to Michel for confirmation.

Michel nodded. "It's true," he said. "We received her communication moments before I departed."

"You betray me to the Duke?" the Marquis said, his own anger resurfacing. He winced as he struggled to push himself up in the bed.

Emily straightened her dress and stood tall. "I merely stated that if anyone in my household—" she paused to clarify, "*anyone* in my household —were in line with the raids, that it was in isolation and did not reflect the dealings of Ponce." She stared daggers at her husband. "And that when found, the Duke would have my full support in that person's arrest."

Michel interjected. "Between her letter, and yours, Philippe, we were fairly certain of our culprit at that point."

Philippe folded his arms and leaned back, impressed with Emily's conviction.

"What will you do to him?" Emily said, all emotion gone from her voice.

Michel stepped in. "He will be tried and jailed in Chevalerie, along with the rest."

"Jailed, indeed," said Emily, still watching her husband. "But he will remain in Ponce."

"Excuse me?" said Michael.

"He is lame," Emily said. "He may die. I want him to be accessible to his children. They must understand where he has gone." Then to her husband, "I love you, Etienne, and you are still my husband. I will care for you as best I can. Now we will all suffer for your crimes."

Then she turned back to Michel and looked at him, with smoldering determination. "You have it on my honor as a Lady and the Marquise du Ponce, this man will give you no more trouble." She glared back at her husband, but still spoke to Michel. "Now, what will you do with him?" she said through her teeth.

Michel stared back, incredulous at her audacity. He began to speak, but Philippe cut him off.

"Give us a second," Philippe said. He grabbed Michael by the arm and dragged him out of the room.

"Michel," Philippe said, just outside the doorway. "Did father explicitly say he was to be detained in Chevalerie?"

"No, but am I to trust his wife to be his keeper?"

"Look at her," Philippe said. Through the doorway, they could see

Emily jerk the Marquis' head to the side as she roughly cleaned his brow with a cloth. Then she yanked at the sheets under him to examine his wounds. The Marquis writhed under her scrutiny. Before she was done, she smacked him across the face and told him to act like a man of his station. Philippe continued. "I dare say that she will provide worse punishment than the stocks."

Philippe leaned back in through the doorway and looked towards Alex. She'd been quietly observing from the corner, and now she was watching Philippe. They looked at each other for a long moment. Then he turned back to Michel.

"I've actually known Emily quite a long time," he said. "I believe we can take her at her word." He continued. "Besides, Michel, I owe her a few things."

Michel glared hard at his brother, then sighed through his nose. "It's my ass if Father doesn't approve."

"And these are the benefits of being the baby brother." Philippe grinned.

It took another few moments of deliberation in the hallway, but when the brothers returned to the room, all eyes looked towards them.

"Okay," Michel began, "here is what will happen."

Philippe felt good about what had been accomplished. It had been trying. It had been complicated. It had tested him far beyond his limits, but Philippe was convinced that the slow, weaving path he had traveled to get to this outcome had been the right one. They had stopped an insurrection. They had preserved a town and a family as best they could. There was a chance that his father would disapprove, but Michel could deal with that fire.

His pride in their political actions, however, was thoroughly outdone by something else. Alex was nowhere to be found, and he was pissed. In the flurry of maids and footmen that had to prepare accommodations for the Lady Marquise, and the next stampede of messengers headed to Ponce and Chevalerie, Alex had vanished. Once he'd realized she was gone, Philippe had torn off through the manor. He checked her room. He checked the dining room and the kitchen. No Alex. He went up and down the halls; he checked the gardens and the stables. Nothing.

But her horse was there, and the guards at the front gates assured him that every messenger had been identified upon leaving. He was comforted for a moment, but Alex had a way of disappearing. Was she still trying to get away? The thought made him furious. At her, at himself. Now he stormed through the once again dark manor with absolutely no plan.

There was a small study off the main parlor that he'd missed. He stomped across the floor and stood in front of the door. *She better be in there,* he thought, because if she wasn't, he didn't know what he would do. He threw the door open, and to his relief, curled up on a lounge chair near the fire, was Alex, sound asleep.

Philippe slammed the door behind him. She startled awake and glared at him while she rubbed her eyes. "Are you finished with the Marquis?" she asked sleepily.

Philippe crossed his arms, still smoldering. "Yes," he said.

She, sensing his anger, sat up. "Why are you mad at me now?" she asked.

"Because," he said, "for once, I'd like to find you where I left you."

She laughed and stretched her back. "I was not aware that you were looking for me."

He watched her carefully. He was relieved to find her, but still irritated. The truth was, he was wounded. She had wounded him. Why was she so hard to pin down? What they had shared the night before, when she had been so willing in his arms, seemed to have never existed. She'd become distant. She'd run away and hadn't even seemed particularly happy that he'd found her tied to a tree.

He was going to teach her a lesson, he decided.

"Draw your sword," he said to her.

"What?" she asked, surprised by his sudden hostility.

He turned and locked the door behind him, drawing his own blade. "You heard me."

Alex looked at him perplexed, but in an instant, she was on her feet, sword in hand.

The room was lit only by the fire and cluttered with furniture and decorations. There was a wide sofa between them, but Philippe couldn't be bothered. He took the quickest route towards her and thrust his blade over the piece of furniture. Alex ducked and returned the blow. He dodged her swing as she stepped up onto the couch. She swung again before jumping over the back, putting them face to face.

He backed up two steps and bumped into a heavy bookcase. Books rumbled and clattered to the floor. Alex came at him again, and he dodged, spinning around to give himself more room. She looked a lot more agile than he felt, but he lunged forward causing her to leap away and bump into a vase herself.

Philippe jumped forward and caught the thing before it fell, giving Alex the chance to whip him across the leg. He went after her and struck in kind. She winced and fell back against the wall, knocking a decorative sword to the ground with a heavy clang.

They paused for a moment, staring madly at each other and already out of breath, the fighting from earlier still heavy in their bones.

But the silence was broken soon as the doorknob to the study rattled. "I-I-is everything okay?" came the butler's nervous voice from behind the door.

"Yes, good sir. It is Lord Philippe. I shall be more careful. Please go back to bed." He glared at Alex, and she shrugged. Then he leapt towards her, with angst and exhaustion behind his blade. His moves were without any grace at all. Alex, on the other hand, was a vision of Helen come to life. Her body was tight under her bodice and pants and every move was a dance. She smelled like she had been bathed in fancy oils and he wanted to bury his face in her wild hair.

They moved back and forth, sending books and papers flying. Alex knocked a heavy stack of maps to the floor and Philippe tipped a chair. Meanwhile, the fire blazed between them. He tried to grab her a few times, but she was too fast for his sluggish hands. His muscles protested and his moves lacked precision, but he wouldn't let her get away. In fact, if he could just get his hands on her, he would never let her go again.

Finally, with his own feet heavy against the ground, Alex lost her footing as she slipped on a map. It was his chance, and he snapped forward and grabbed her by her shirt. He dragged her forcefully to him.

Alex, not balanced, struggled to break free, but his grip was cast in iron.

"You told me you wanted me for the experience of sex," he said through gritted teeth as he worked to hang on to her. "Is that correct?"

"That is what I said, yes," she replied. Her struggling continued, but her bad position kept her from making any headway.

"So, if you think to use me for sex," he said. He dropped his sword and wrapped his other arm around her waist. "Then *use* me."

He leaned over her and into her, hanging onto her tightly. They stood frozen in a stalemate for a moment glaring at each other—Alex, off balance in his arms; he, refusing to let her go. Then, to his surprise, she dropped her sword, threw her arms around his neck, and kissed him. Hard.

In that second, Philippe came alive. Whereas just before he hardly had the strength to keep moving, he was now filled with the energy of ten men. He picked her up and she wrapped her legs around him. He kissed her desperately while trying to make sense of the room they had worked to destroy. *The couch,* he thought. *Get her to the couch.* He made quick work of the floor, stomping through books and parchment, before she could change her mind or the roof could fall in, or anything else could happen. He dropped her onto the cushions before him. He pulled off his coat and tunic, bearing his chest, and then he went back towards her, unlacing her bodice with expert fingers as he kissed her lips.

He worked his mouth down her neck as her bodice fell away. He ripped her shirt and chemise over her head and pushed her back onto the cushions, her exposed skin glowing warm under his hands. He shuddered with desire and latched on to her nipple with his lips, teasing it with his tongue, while he ran his hand roughly over her other breast. Then he kicked off his boots, yanked off her shoes, and leaned back in to enjoy the feel of her bare flesh against his own.

Alex's breath was heavy in his ear as were the sighs she couldn't hide. In a moment, he planned to have her moaning like a beast. *Mon Dieu,* she made him crazy, he thought, as he took small nips at her skin and made his way down her belly. One second, he was pounding at her with his sword, and the next she was prone and willing beneath him. He leaned back for a moment to work on her pants. Still such an odd thing to be taking off a woman, but he would happily get used to it. He pried her belting loose and gripped the fabric, pulling her pants and undergarments off in one slick motion.

Her legs splayed before him and he put his heavy palms on the inside of her knees. He pressed them open and into the soft fabric of the couch.

Alex, alarmed by his movements, leaned up on her elbows, "What are you doing?" she asked, a note of panic in her voice.

Philippe raised one eyebrow, looking up at her. "Last night, I made love to you, but you didn't believe me. So now I'm going to fuck you, so you know the difference."

With that, he moved the palms of his hands up the inside of her thighs and leaned into her sex.

"Oh my god," he heard her say.

She was glistening with want and he couldn't wait to taste her. He leaned in and ran his tongue right through her weeping layers.

Alex tensed up, her body a tight coil, and let out a strangled moan.

He continued pressing her legs apart and dove more fully into her. Her syrup was sweet and he couldn't believe how good she felt against his mouth. He started by licking and nibbling her edges, working towards the sensitive swell at her center. Alex gradually relaxed against his hands. He liked the control he had over her, just for a moment, to feel her body dissolving under him as he teased her with his tongue. She thought she could handle everything, but she had no idea what door she had opened with him. He could work her slowly or strongly and for all her stubbornness and cool control, she had no ability to turn him away. She thought to use him for sex, then damn her, he would enjoy showing her just what she asked for.

Her body reacted to his touch, his lips, his caress. He reached up to grip her breast with one hand as he continued to devour her. She seemed helpless to control her movements, and he held her in place with commanding hands. He began moving quicker, zeroing in on the tender bud at her core, using the tip of his tongue to drive her mad. Alex squirmed wildly beneath him, alternating between tension and release of her muscles. She twisted and strained. Her back arched as he held her legs open, giving himself unlimited access. When he felt the last of her resistance to him finally melt away, he took one hand off her thigh and moved it to her waist, angling her more closely to his lips.

Alex's hands covered her face as she panted and gasped for air. He loved every second, his own desire causing him to get rougher and rougher with her. He would have been happy to do this for hours, but he knew it would end too soon. He felt her body begin to tense up and he continued moving in motion, punishing her with more pleasure than she could stand. Finally, she stiffened and held her breath. She reached down to his head and twisted her fingers into his hair. In seconds, he felt his reward, her ravaged orgasm against his lips.

Her moaning subsided into soft whimpers as he licked her more gently and moved his hands up and down her body. He kissed the inside of her thigh. He would give her ten seconds to relax. That was it. Then it would be time for round two. What a game he had discovered. He liked teasing her so. He smiled devilishly as he planted sloppy kisses across her belly. One... Two...

Chapter Thirty-Nine

Alex was still quaking from the sensations he had sent through her. Who even knew that what he just did to her was a thing? He had used his mouth on her in such a sensual way… she felt her face get hot again, and she reached with her hands to cover it up. She was slowly becoming conscious again and floating back into her body. The rafters high above her. The silky couch beneath her. The words Philippe had said to her. She shuddered at the obscene pleasure of it all.

Before she could bask any longer in the feelings of what had just happened, she felt his strong hands lifting her by her waist. Her eyes shot open, and she caught him winking at her before he flipped her over onto her knees. She had just enough time to catch herself and plant her hands on the arm of the couch. Philippe lifted her ass and in less than a second, she felt him slide into her still throbbing sex. Alex, scandalized by the position, could hardly protest because just as she thought to say it was too crass, he squeezed her hips with commanding hands and began moving inside of her. Then it felt far too good to complain.

He was so big and thick, and in this position, she could only just take all of him. She still ached from the last orgasm, but all she could think was that she wanted everything he would give her. She was aware that this was different than it had been last night. She felt it in the way he manipulated her body, the way he had taken her so aggressively. The way she felt him using her for his pleasure. She wanted to give him pleasure.

Just then he angled her up and ran both hands up her torso, across her breasts, pulling her body back to him. She felt his strong chest against her while he skewered her where they were joined. She could feel his dominance, over her body, over her. Then he moved one hand to her throat and held her firmly. His body burned into hers and she felt his breath on her neck as he whispered gruffly against her ear. "You're mine, Alex," he said and his hands dug possessively into her.

She about lost her mind. There were so many sensations, but she could do nothing more than surrender as he continued to feed her feelings that she didn't even know were possible. He was so powerful and so in charge of her body, she was lost to him. All she could do was gasp out, "Yes."

With that, he released her throat and thrust forcefully behind her, knocking her forward once again. He began moving faster and Alex tried desperately to keep up with everything that was happening. Was it embarrassing that he had this much control over her? She'd fought with him physically and mentally to keep things even between them, but here, now, she wouldn't even know where to begin. He was the master. He rammed himself deep inside and she let out a tortured cry. *Oh, who cares,* she thought, and she let herself lose control.

The intensity just kept coming and coming. Alex moved against Philippe, her body arching and reacting to his touch, his smell, and the thrilling moans he was making as he, what did he say? Fucked her. She never wanted it to end.

Then Philippe reached around with his hand to her front, to knead the needy spot between her legs. All at once, she was on the edge again. She felt the orgasm start deep inside of her this time. Her legs went watery and Philippe took the sign to break her apart. Her body's response was immediate to the rough, absolute penetration. Before she knew it, she was screaming and panting and rocking against him like the animal she had become, all the emotion she had wrapped up in this man, coming out in one great surge.

Philippe let out a savage growl of his own. His speed and force let her know he was just seconds behind her. He ripped into her, one hand digging into the flesh of her hip, the other pressing firmly against her front, drawing out her unyielding orgasm long enough to meet his. He froze and grunted as he lost himself, pushing every fraction of himself into her. She felt him swell and pulsate against her soft walls, as merciless waves of shattering pleasure rolled through her.

Once he could, he began sliding himself deliciously inside her again, extending every sensation until the last shudder, as they both still gasped for breath. Before he finally left her body, still trembling around him, he reached forward, grabbed a fistful of her hair, bent her back, and kissed her.

It was a few moments before either one of them could speak. They lay wrapped together, face to face on the couch, while the fire continued to crackle in front of them. Philippe had not stopped holding her or kissing her since they had collapsed, consumed, completely spent.

"Whatever you just did to me... whatever you call it?" Alex said.

"Yeah?"

"I liked it."

Philippe chuckled as he bit at her collarbone. His hands were still on her, moving up and down her body. She closed her eyes and sighed while he continued to make her tingle.

He brought his hand to her face and brushed her hair back. "You make me absolutely crazy, Alex," he said. "You always have."

"I could say the same about you," she replied with a smile.

The moment was a cushion. A deep, comforting softness after a rapid descent. So much had happened in the last few days. Alex was happy to lie there and not think about anything else except the sweetness of his lips on her skin and the way his arms felt around her.

But Philippe pulled back, obviously not so content. He searched her face with his eyes, and she understood that he had something he wanted to say to her. He pressed his lips together, took a breath, and then after one last pause, he spoke.

"You know, Alex," he said. He wrapped his hand around her waist and held her tight. "When I kissed you. The first time? And then I went to Emily?" He watched her intently. "You have to know," he trailed off. He looked away, then back to her, earnestly. "She wasn't the one that I wanted."

Alex paused, listening to him with her whole body. These words, she knew, had the power to recolor a pivotal point in her memories, if she understood him correctly. "You wanted me?" she asked.

"Of course I wanted you," he said. He closed his eyes and brought his finger and thumb up to rub his forehead. "I had always cared about you, but that night, it all changed very suddenly. You were growing up, I was growing up." He looked away and to the fire. She saw it flickering in his eyes. "I don't know what happened, but... all at once, it was just different. And I didn't know what to do." He turned back to her. "I just knew I couldn't have you then."

"No," she said. "I was too young. I wasn't ready."

"It was stupid what I did. I was—stupid and cruel." He took a deep sigh. "I only thought about what that kiss meant for me. I never thought about what it meant for you." He closed his eyes in a wince before continuing. "But then you challenged me and you knocked me out." He repositioned himself to lean above her. "You disappeared, Alex. You just were gone." He searched her eyes. "I didn't know what to make of everything that happened. I was upset. I was humiliated. And my mother wouldn't tell me anything about you or let me read your letters because she said I needed to write to you myself."

Alex blinked, taken aback. "I didn't realize it had affected you so," she said.

"Alex, I was devastated," he said. "I wanted to write to you, but I didn't know what to say." He sighed and dropped his head. "I never knew what to say." He stayed with his head down, but in a second he looked back at her, and she recognized new conviction on his face. "But now I do," he said. "Now I know exactly what to say. To you."

Those mesmerizing gold-ringed eyes were on her. She realized that something had been building in him for longer than she ever knew, and now she felt magic changing the space between them, an aura connecting them, lighting them up in a swell. Her stomach fluttered in anticipation, and she hoped she was prepared for his words.

"Alex." He paused and took a slow, deep breath. "I'm in love with you. I'm sorry I didn't say it before. It's been there all this time. I just needed to figure it out."

The words spiraled in deep, soothing wounds inside her that had never fully healed. She brought her hand up to his cheek and brushed a thumb across his lips, the scar she had given him, pausing to let the words affect her. He was waiting for her—anxiously, she knew—for some signal that she felt the same, but she needed to take everything in and to let his words settle inside her. Alex realized that all this time, it had never really been about whether or not Philippe wanted her. His intentions had always been there; they had been immature and misguided, and they needed time to evolve, but they were there. He'd set a mark on her years ago, but she had always been too afraid of getting hurt and too full of shame to let him get close. She looked at him now, his eyes burning with ardor and madness and she knew the only thing to do was to wrap her arms around him and tell him all the ways she loved him too.

Instead, she burst out laughing.

"*That's* not what I was hoping for," he said, exasperated.

"You just look so angry at me!" she laughed.

"Well, do you blame me? I'm trying to tell you how I feel!" He went to move back but she wrapped her leg around him and leveraged herself on top.

"Philippe," she said. She stretched across him, weighing her body against the length of his. She reached up to his face and put her hands on his cheeks. "I love you," she said. "I *love* you. How could you expect a different response from me?"

He looked at her with his brow furrowed. "You're a little hard to read sometimes."

"I know." She laughed, as she dropped her head to his chest. "I'm going to work on it." She looked back at him and bit her lip through a grin.

"So," he said, looking at her intently. "Is now the right time to ask you to stay with me? I don't want to keep having to capture you." He smiled now. "Though I certainly like what happens when I get my hands on you."

"I will not make it quite so difficult for you to catch me anymore." She looked at him coyly.

"Then marry me, Alex."

She watched him for a long moment, feeling the weight of the words floating in the air. "Well, first," she said, still teasing him. "First, I want a promise from you."

"Anything," he replied.

"I had always liked being your student," she said. She arched her back, as desire for him began to roll through her body, knowing for the first time that he was hers for the taking. "Teach me more," she said and she licked the scar on the bottom of his lip.

His eyes grew heated again. Suddenly, he flipped her onto her back, and he was poised on top of her once more. "I agree to your terms." He leaned in to kiss her. "Now do you say yes to my proposal?"

"Yes, Philippe," she said, smiling as she pulled him close. "Yes, of course, yes."

Chapter Forty

It was another week of official responsibilities before Philippe could lead the remaining men—both soldiers and prisoners—back to Chevalerie. Michel had taken the first group back a few days earlier, but Philippe waited on escorts from Chevalerie, who would oversee the Marquis' transport back to Ponce.

Michel had conceded to place the Marquis under house arrest in Ponce until he was well enough to stand trial in Chevalerie, but given his condition, the brothers recognized that this temporary punishment may be indefinite. Philippe knew this could invoke his father's fury. The Duke wouldn't be keen to let the Marquis evade a trial and sentence, but at the same time, Philippe understood the futility of marching a gravely wounded man across the countryside just to be thrown into some oubliette. The threat had been neutralized. Now, Philippe just hoped to provide Emily with some stability. The Marquis du Ponce would be stripped of his title and would be required to pay off debts, as well as fund the Chevalerie soldiers who would have to become a permanent fixture in Ponce. Emily's life would be very different from here on out. Philippe was troubled that she would now have to suffer the humiliation of her husband. Emily had proven herself to be an ally, so he hoped his father would provide her some consideration. At least for now, she would be occupied with the task of caring for her ailing and incarcerated husband. As for the Marquis, Philippe was sure Emily wouldn't let him forget that there would be no more balls under his roof.

The morning was full of early sunshine as Philippe and his party crossed the southern gates of Aliette. Though they were on their way home, his job was not quite over. In addition to the Marquis, Giroux had to be dealt with. Also, the river towns, blameless themselves, could not be forgotten. Though each task weighed on him, Philippe felt the excitement of a new adventure, the best adventure. It was the life he would embark on with Alex, and the thought of it made him as light as a cloud.

She was trotting her horse a few yards ahead. He watched her strong, elegant form, which he now knew so much more intimately than before. As he stared, she turned her head to him and smiled. It was a simple gesture but something that made his heart race in his chest. Who would have thought that just a short time ago, he didn't know what was missing in life, but now, with this wild woman at his side, he finally felt grounded. Solid. Terrific. He could take on the world.

He angled his horse closer to her. They were setting out on a two-day journey in which they would have to camp between towns. They would have no privacy, and he was already feeling antsy as his need for her was cropping up. Then she turned to him and spoke.

She turned to him and spoke low enough that no one else could hear, "You know that thing you do to me?"

Philippe smiled wickedly at her. "Which thing?"

"With your mouth?" she replied.

He shifted uncomfortably in the saddle, remembering her body spread open before him. "Uh huh," he said dumbly.

"I want to do that to you."

His brain moved slowly. "What do you mean?"

"I want to use my mouth," she bit her lip coyly, "on you."

It felt like everything in his body stopped. He couldn't speak or think. His pants became two sizes too small and he lost feeling in his arms and legs. He could recognize the smug satisfaction in her face as the realization of what she had said crept over him. She was just teasing him now. When he could function, he spoke. "You can do anything you like to me with that glorious mouth of yours, little fox."

"Then I think I would like to try that sometime," she said. She turned to ride her horse ahead, leaving him to his mutinous body. Okay, well, she won this round, he thought. But he would get her back, sooner or later. Now he just had to rush the men back to Chevalerie so he could lock her in a room for a few days and take her up on that invitation.

Later that week, Duchess Laure paced around the sitting room. Michel had been trying to calm her while her husband sat behind his desk with his head resting on his hand.

"*Bleu*," Guillaume said, tapping the tip of a quill pen across a page, making nothing more than a mess. "Please don't worry. The Marquis has been neutralized. There is no more danger."

"I shall continue to worry until everyone is safe under my roof and done with this terrible debacle. And all those prisoners with whom they are traveling? How can you say there will be no more danger?" She paced to the large window at the other end of the room.

"Laure, we knew that there could be danger," the duke said as he placed the quill back in the ink and left it there. "I wouldn't have sent Philippe in the first place if I thought it would be too much."

Once Michel had been dispatched to help Philippe undertake all the trouble that had come to him, Laure had become sick. Her cool composure for her husband's sake had begun to splinter. Two of her boys were now out fighting this foe who, as they had learned, was the Marquis himself.

Everyone kept hushing her and telling her that everything would be okay. Though in her heart she knew that Philippe was alright, she wouldn't sit comfortably again until she could hug him for herself.

This life with her sons fighting all over the place and defending the kingdom wore on her. On days like this she wished to relinquish everything, take all of her family, and go live safely in a cave somewhere.

"I still don't understand why you didn't bring Alex home with you," she bristled at Michel.

Michel stared daftly at her for a moment. "Uh, Mother, I believe she was free to make her own decision on that one."

Laure sank herself into the couch. "You're right, darling. I'm sorry. I just don't see why they are not home yet. They should have been here by now."

"Perhaps they took an extra night and stayed at one of the inns rather than make camp," he shrugged.

"Why would they do that?" she asked, both perplexed and frustrated.

Michel and Guillaume exchanged a look. Michel cleared his throat.

"Philippe and Alex?" Laure said, looking between them. "You don't mean..."

Her words were cut off as the footman outside began calling for help with the incoming party. Attendants whizzed by the doorway to the sitting room. The three looked at each other for a moment and then rushed to the front of the palace. The gates at the far end were opened and a cloud of dust rose on the road. Laure stepped out, farther from the steps of her home, to identify the riders. She raised her hand to her eyes to shield them from the sun.

As they got closer, she felt her heart go light. It was Philippe indeed, returning home. She scanned the riders and saw Alex by his side. They looked road-worn but as they approached, she could see that they were both beaming. Laure smiled back and stood in the sun, waiting for them to reach the steps.

"See Mother," said Michel, "I told you they were fine."

"I had to see it for myself."

"Hurry up, Brother," Michel called when they were in range. "Mother is anxious to have you home."

Philippe rode to them, the horses kicking dust high up into the air. "She is not the only one anxious to have me home." Philippe grinned. He settled his horse and jumped off, as the men behind him began to do the same. He hugged Laure as soon as he was steady on his feet.

"I was so worried about you and this company," she said.

"I am safe," he said warmly. "Though I admit it became a little more involved than we imagined it would."

She let him go so he could embrace his brother and father before Laure grabbed him again for another hug.

"Mother, I was fine," he laughed. "I believe your anxiety was made worse because of my companion on this journey."

With that he turned and took Alex's hand as she dismounted her horse. To Laure's delight, she saw that he didn't let it go.

Laure reached forward and hugged Alex around the neck. She was the same wild-haired creature that Laure had always loved, but Alex had a whole new essence about her. The restlessness was gone, Laure could see. She brushed a lock of hair away from Alex's face and welcomed her back to the palace.

"Mother," Philippe said after a moment.

"Yes dear," Laure replied, squeezing Alex's shoulders once more before turning to her son.

"Alex and I have something to tell you." They glanced at each other.

Laure stepped back and looked at the two of them. She couldn't have been happier at the match. It had been a long time in the making, but she'd always known, somewhere deep down, that these two would end up together. They looked so happy, hands enlaced. Philippe was handsome and held himself with pride. He looked more pleased with himself than she had seen him in years. And Alex had a softness about her that had disappeared in her youth. She was smiling, grinning, just like a young woman her age should be doing. Laure felt the happiness well up inside her until she had to dab at her eyes. Michel reached out and handed her a handkerchief. She accepted. They would be perfect together, she thought. Simply perfect.

"Well let's get inside so you can wash up. I'm sure whatever news you have, it will be wonderful," she said.

But the revelry was broken. Her husband, she realized, had not yet had his say.

"Hold on a second," said the Duke, stepping forward. "I am happy to see you home safely son, but we have some things to discuss before we can put this mission to rest."

Philippe looked back at Alex, and she released his hand. Laure reached out to put her arm around the girl, while Philippe went to stand before his father.

"First of all," said the Duke. "You went far too long without informing me of your progress. By doing so, you endangered yourself and your men."

Philippe stood eye to eye with his father, his jaw clenched, saying nothing.

"Second," continued the Duke. "You, along with your brother, made the decision to place the Marquis under house arrest without my permission."

Philippe's fists clenched. Laure hoped her husband wouldn't be too hard on him. She did not know the extent of Guillaume's anger, but she knew he struggled with it, and it could blow the palace apart if he let it.

"You made an outlandish request on behalf of his co-conspirator, this Giroux," he continued.

"On that," said Philippe, "I know I am right."

"I'm not finished," barked the Duke. Everyone from footmen to prisoners, the company men to her own family, stood in uncomfortable attention. Laure braced herself for the storm.

"Where is Girard Giroux?" the Duke asked, taking his heavy stare off Philippe and scanning the party.

"Here *Monsieur*," came a clear voice from the crowd. Laure watched as two of Chevalerie's men pulled a man, bruised but by no means broken, from a horse.

Giroux's hands were bound in front of him, and he stood tall as the Duke approached him. Laure noticed he was an absolute monster of a man, but still maintained a quiet dignity about himself.

"Unbind him," the Duke said.

The men at Giroux's side complied, cutting the bindings. Giroux rubbed his wrists as he watched the Duke.

Her husband continued. "You were flawed in your means. However, I feel you did what you did out of good intentions." He paused. "I have learned from my sons about your character, and I don't believe they misjudge you." He stared hard at Giroux. "And the Northern villages still need assistance."

"That was always my singular objective," Giroux said with a bowed head.

"You come from a noble family," the Duke said. "I remember your grandfather from my travels. There wasn't a more honorable man in the region."

"I have always tried to act with him in mind," Giroux looked down. "I am sorry to have failed."

The Duke pulled back and looked at the man with concentrated scrutiny. He folded his arms in front of him and began to speak once more.

"I am still waiting for an answer, but I have written a letter to the King's palace on your behalf. I have requested that your lineage title of *Comte* be reinstated. Regardless of his answer, you shall be my steward in the North. The one we will trust to receive and equitably distribute funds from Chevalerie."

Giroux looked up at the Duke, dumbstruck. "You would trust me to do that?"

"No," the Duke said. "Not quite yet. But I will give you the opportunity to earn my trust. Don't think you will be left alone up there."

Giroux stared at him, "I would be ever honored to serve you."

"Come." The Duke waved to the footmen. "Take him to a room and get him settled. He will continue his recovery here as my guest."

A ripple of words went through the onlookers. Laure was pleased with Guillaume's proclamation. She had counseled him in these days on how to proceed with all the stinging thorns left by the Marquis, but she didn't know which direction he would take. She was proud of him for leading with instinct, rather than protocol. It had always proven beneficial for them, for their home.

Michel and Philippe looked especially pleased with this announcement. They nodded at Giroux as he was led into the palace. Philippe approached his father, smiling, but the Duke turned to him, anger back in his brows. "The last thing you are guilty of," the Duke continued.

Philippe's smile dropped from his face, the dressing down not over.

Guillaume sighed and let his face relax. "You worried your mother." He clapped Philippe on the back of the neck and pressed his forehead against the young man's. "You did well, my son. You stopped an insurrection without the proper resources. You helped bring new leadership to the land. I am very proud of you."

With that Michel went over and grabbed Philippe around the neck, pulling him down into a headlock. "Come Little Brother, get settled. We have many things to discuss." They scuffled a moment before Philippe was able to push him off.

"*Excuses moi, Monsieur*," came a voice. It was Alex. She approached the Duke. "What is to become of Emily, the Lady Marquise? And her home?"

The Duke watched Alex for a moment. "Yes, Emily," he began. "She surprised me."

"She surprised us all," said Alex.

He continued. "Her husband, Etienne du Ponce, will no longer be a Marquis. He has lost that privilege and responsibility." He put his hand on Alex's shoulder. "But his wife, Emily. She will retain the title. In her own right. I would like to see what she does with it."

Philippe and Alex looked at each other. They grinned.

"I am happy to hear that," Alex said.

"I am too," Philippe agreed. "I think she is good for the task."

Guillaume grunted a nod and with that, movement started immediately. Philippe reached out to take Alex's hand. Guillaume lost himself in the crowd, organizing where prisoners would be taken and where the men would need to debrief before going to their homes. The attendants buzzed, ready to take care of all the additions to the palace.

Laure approached Michel. She linked her arm through his. "Michel. Michel my dear," she said.

"Yes, Mother," he replied.

"I am happy for this outcome. I am."

"I, as well," he said. "I believe Father acted quite fairly."

"Don't discount your influence on him. He trusts your opinion and recognizes your talent in such matters. Besides, these will be all your decisions one day." She sighed, content, as they continued the walk back to the front doors. "You know," she began, "we shall be planning your younger brother's wedding. And once that is finished, we must turn our focus to finding you a bride. And then after you, the much greater task of finding one for your other brother."

"I am happy as I am. I will take a wife when it suits Chevalerie."

"Ah, don't be so sure some young coquette won't catch your attention. You can't plan for everything, you know." Up ahead, Philippe struggled to keep his arm around Alex as attendants attacked them from both ends. Soon enough they were pulled apart, Alex being directed towards her room and Philippe to his. Philippe waved to her as he was led away. "You see that fool up there," Laure continued. "It will be you soon enough," she laughed. "It just takes the right girl."

Chapter Forty-One

That evening, after dinner, Philippe waited for Alex under a large sycamore tree in the East Garden. It was a place where they had played many times as children, way back when Alex first took to the sword. He had wanted to find a space where they could be alone, now that he feared he would have no time with her until the wedding. He had seen her not long ago in the dining room where they officially announced their engagement, and through the course of dinner it was decided that their wedding would happen in two weeks' time. His mother was already frantic, calling out a long list of everyone who needed to be notified and invited to the staff. His father lost interest in wedding plans and began discussing ideas for the newly established *Vallée de la Rivière* with Michel and Giroux, but all Philippe could do was stare at his lovely fiancé, across from him in a shimmering silver gown and wearing a smile more beautiful than the stars.

As he waited for her in the garden at their designated meeting spot, he began to feel uneasy. He wanted her in his arms; he wanted her close, without any hesitation. He wanted to be married before she could get away from him again. He began pacing back and forth, across the grass, staring impatiently at the path to the palace. What if she changed her mind? It wouldn't be the first time she decided to run away.

Just as he started to get worked up, he saw her floating towards him. She was a dream in her gown. The vision went in through his eyes and trilled out through his limbs. She was his woman, he thought, and there was only her.

In front of her, she was carrying a basket. As she came closer, he realized what she had, and it made him drop his head with laughter. He looked back up, anxiously waiting, and he watched as she picked up speed to jog to him, but Alex, not used to the dress, struggled to grip the panels of her skirts while holding the basket in front of her. Just before she reached him, she stumbled, tripping over the long fabric of the dress she wasn't used to controlling. She pitched forward and dumped a basket full of peaches all over him.

"Philippe!" she cried. "I'm so sorry!" She laughed. She dropped to her knees in the grass and grabbed at the fallen fruit. "But look what I found in the kitchen! Do you remember when your father brought these home from his travels years ago? I haven't tasted one since."

Philippe laughed as he helped her to gather the peaches rolling away from them. He went to his knees before her, and together, they put the fruit in the basket. "Of course, I remember," he said, grinning. He reached out to grab the last one and drop it in the basket. "Come," he said, standing and helping her up. "Sit with me here."

He led her to the base of the tree. They were perched high on a hill that looked down over all of Chevalerie. The stars twinkled in the sky while the fires and lamps from the city winked below them. He sat down and leaned against the tree, pulling Alex down into his arms.

"Is it strange to be here?" he asked.

"Some of my happiest memories are from this very spot. I am very glad to be back in Chevalerie." She shifted to put her head against his shoulder. "Though I feel I may miss the activity I am used to."

"We will find a solution," he replied. "I don't want you to get bored."

"I have a feeling you will keep me entertained," she said. "But," she continued, "do you know who I spoke with today?"

"Tell me," he said. He ran his finger over her lips and down her neck.

"*Monsieur* Perreault," she said. "Our teacher."

"He always enjoyed you," Philippe said. "Except for the day of the tournament."

"Well, yes," Alex said. "But Philippe, listen. He is getting older now and has expressed the desire to take on an apprentice." She angled her head to look at him.

It took him a second, but then it hit him. "It's brilliant," he said.

She grinned. "Do you think he would be open to it?"

"Who would be better for the job? Even now, down there," he indicated towards the twinkling town, "rumors spread of the brave woman who fought alongside the Duke's sons to protect our home. It would be a shame to waste such talents."

"I'd be really good at it," she said, a thrill in her voice.

"I know you would," he said. "And then I won't have to worry about you running off?"

She turned so they were face to face. "I've earned you, Philippe," she said. "I'm not going anywhere."

Philippe gripped her, feeling desire rise up through his body. He would struggle in these next weeks trying to find time for them to be together, but he knew he would find a way. Nothing could keep him from her now. "I couldn't ask for anything better." He reached into the basket and took a peach. He brushed it against his chest and held it out for her.

"Then I think Chevalerie will be a grand place to call my home," she said as she bit into the peach.

He leaned up to lick the juice from her lips, knowing it would be. But it didn't matter whether it was Chevalerie or any other place. Because from that moment on, *she* would be his home.

Thank you for reading! Did you enjoy? Please add your review because nothing helps an author more and encourages readers to take a chance on a book than a review.

And don't miss more from Florence A. Bliss's *Swords of Chevalerie* series, coming soon.

Until then, discover BOLEYN CURSE, by City Owl Author, Deborah Cohen. Turn the page for a sneak peek!

You can also sign up for the City Owl Press newsletter to receive notice of all book releases!

Sneak Peek of Boleyn Curse

BY DEBORAH COHEN

1514

Three hooded figures, hands clasped tightly, hurried through the winter night. A biting gale blew the snow in all directions, its swirling tempest a wall of white fury. The group leaned into the storm with the weight of their bodies, their heavy cloaks beating like bat wings in the wind.

The tallest pointed to a narrow close off the main street and they stumbled past tilted half-timbered houses towards it.

"Who's there?" a haggard voice called into the darkness. A dim lantern seemed to float mid-air.

The figures moved toward the light, their steps more certain in the murky glow of the flame.

"Who's there, I say?"

"'Tis Lady Boleyn," hissed the tallest. "Hurry, girls. We mustn't be discovered."

A door slammed shut in the alleyway ahead, but the group continued, edging towards the sound with determination now. At the entrance of the little cottage, a shadowy face emerged from behind a crack in the door.

"Aga... Let us in or we shall catch our deaths."

As the door crept slowly open, Elizabeth Boleyn and her daughters shuffled inside, the low light of the cottage wrapping itself around them like the fine strands of a spider's web.

An old woman stood by the hearth, a tattered shawl pulled around thin shoulders. Only two brown teeth remained in the dark hole of her mouth. A milky film clouded one eye. The other revealed a blue iris, a sharp pupil dancing with a life of its own.

"Elizabeth, it has been some time," she crooned.

"These are my daughters, Aga." Lady Elizabeth brushed the snow from her skirts. "Anne is sixteen. And Mary, not but a year behind that."

The old woman approached slowly. Scrutinizing the youth with her good eye, she dragged a thickened fingernail along each of their jawlines in sequence. Her eyes narrowed when her finger reached the eldest girl's chin. "This one I have seen."

Lady Elizabeth took the old woman by the arm. "Aga, I hate to rush an old reunion, but I come to you in desperate need."

The crone closed her eyes. "Yes. I wondered when you would come. But are you certain you wish to save him?"

"He is the father of my children." Elizabeth paused. "I love him."

"Do you really?" Aga sneered. "I have often wondered how a woman could love such a man. But you have risked great things in coming, so you must at least need him, if not love him." She shuffled to a chair by the fire. "Now then, what ails him? How many days has he been ill?"

The ancient Aga eased herself into the seat and gestured for her guests to join. Wide-eyed, the girls shuffled to the hearth. The cottage was but one room. Dried herbs hung from the exposed beams in the ceiling. A low fire crackled within a simple hearth and a black pot hovered over the cinders. Teetering shelves along the wall housed a dozen mismatched jars, each containing dark and unrecognizable things.

Lady Elizabeth wrung her hands as she paced the floorboards. "It began four days ago when Thomas came home from the hunt. He felled a deer but had not an appetite for it once it was served."

The girls sat perched, backs straight, along the bench by the table. They leaned forward to hear what their mother had to say.

"The next morning, Thomas said he was much refreshed but took little bread to break his fast. Later that day, he began to cough." Elizabeth turned to Aga. "He took to bed with fever and has gotten worse by the day. He does not eat. He barely drinks." She knelt down, grasping Aga's gnarled hands in her own. "I think he is dying."

The old woman stared into the flames for a time. "I have seen it. He will not last the week. But are you prepared for what is to come if you interfere?"

Elizabeth's face hardened, but she did not reply.

"You vowed fifteen years ago not to live this life anymore." Aga's lips twisted into a smile.

"I have no choice," Elizabeth finally whispered.

The old woman drew herself up with some effort, nodding as though she already knew the answer she would be given. She cleared away a surface on the careworn table and began pulling jars from the shelves.

"You will require assistance, Elizabeth. You are unpracticed of late and will lack the fortitude required to shift things."

Aga opened the first jar and pulled out two dried frogs, long since dead, hardened and black. "One frog that will never become a prince, one prince that will be ever more a frog." She tossed them into a wooden bowl, their dried bodies skittering across the basin's surface. Next she added four pinches of gray powder, filling the air with a pungent smell of fungus. "A pinch of wort for each day your husband has been ill."

Her fingers searched the top shelf, feeling for another vessel. She found a jar filled with thick red liquid and poured the contents over the other ingredients. A metallic scent layered atop the earthy one in the room, creating an odor consistent with that of a slaughterhouse.

"Blood of the pig, in place of the blood of your husband—although I'm not sure which one is more of a swine."

Lady Elizabeth interrupted. "Aga, I am committed to do this, but I will not involve the girls."

Aga sprinkled in some dried rosemary and rosewort, and gave the girls a knowing look. "Two innocent roses, two innocent daughters. Both will be required." She added a bit of fetid brown water from a jug in the corner, and then tossed in a pair of twisted bird's feet. "Crow's feet to help him claw his way back from death."

As she ran her fingers through the bloody brew, Aga pierced Lady Elizabeth with her dancing blue eye. "And finally, the spit of a witch..."

Elizabeth glanced at her girls and back to the clouded gaze of the woman. A pained expression pinched the fine skin along her nose.

"You must do it, Elizabeth. There is no other way." Aga's lips trembled in anticipation.

Elizabeth hesitated before moving to the table. Then, puckering her lips together, she bent over the bowl and spit fiercely. She stared down at the vile concoction for a moment before wiping the spittle from her mouth with the back of her hand.

"Mother!" exclaimed her eldest daughter, Anne.

But the two women took no notice, lost in their old ritual. Aga poured the contents of the brew into a jar as Elizabeth slid it into the embers. They held hands as they watched the small glass pot boil, mumbling a strange incantation as the elixir took form, a hot little wind swirling around them. Finally Aga pulled the glass from the flames with an iron poker and placed a stopper in the top.

"You know what to do from here. The moon has entered its healing phase. It will assist you."

Elizabeth nodded.

Aga wagged a finger in the air, still red with pig's blood. "You will require your coven. A powerful coven you have, a mother and two daughters. If you attempt this alone, he will die a painful, watery death. I have seen it."

"But I want my girls far from the Craft," said Elizabeth softly.

"Then why did you bring them? Why make them witness?" the crone shot back.

The two women stood face to face, one tall and elegant, one crooked and haggard. Their silhouettes cast an eerie shadow on the floor.

Finally, Elizabeth bowed her head. "I promise."

"There is one last thing." The old woman grabbed Lady Elizabeth's arm, turning her so her back was to her daughters. "I have seen your eldest in my visions. Anne... Anne... Anne Boleyn... You must send her away when this is done."

Aga's lips almost touched the lady's ear. "Your daughter bears the mark. I have seen it. In time, she will be a danger to herself and your family."

Elizabeth stumbled back, avoiding the dancing blue eye. She deposited the small glass jar into a hidden pocket in her cloak and gestured to her daughters. "Thank you for your help, Aga. But we must go."

Lady Elizabeth and her girls stepped into the night, back into the driving storm that brought them to this strange little cottage not but an hour ago.

Don't stop now. Keep reading with your copy of BOLEYN CURSE, by City Owl Author, Deborah Cohen.

And sign up for Florence's newsletter to get all the news, giveaways, excerpts, and more!

Don't miss more from Florence A. Bliss's *Swords of Chevalerie* series, coming soon, and find out more at www.florenceabliss.com

Until then, discover BOLEYN CURSE, by City Owl Author, Deborah Cohen!

When PhD history student, Ellie Bowlan, attends a séance, she receives a strange message: To end your family curse, you must save the life of the man who killed your parents.

Ellie has always believed her parents' death to be an accident, but this mysterious missive hints at a secret murder. As a skeptic of all things supernatural, she ignores this bizarre advice, until her research forces her to face the truth about her parents' murders and the astonishing connection between the Bowlan and Boleyn family line.

Long before Anne Boleyn was Queen of England, she was a precocious teen growing up in the French Royal Court. At the elegant Chateau Clos-Luce, Anne is tutored in witchcraft by artist Leonardo da Vinci and French royalty, Marguerite de Navarre. Drawn in by the alluring power of the Craft, Anne pursues her supernatural gifts with zeal. Then one night, she casts forbidden magic to kill the villainous King of France and leaves behind a terrible curse that echoes across the generations.

And Ellie is next in line to pay the price. Soon Ellie realizes that solving her parent's murders isn't enough. She must find a way to end the curse or fall victim to its dire consequences.

Please sign up for the City Owl Press newsletter for chances to win special subscriber-only contests and giveaways as well as receiving information on upcoming releases and special excerpts.

All reviews are **welcome** and **appreciated**. Please consider leaving one on your favorite social media and book buying sites.

Escape Your World. Get Lost in Ours! City Owl Press at www.cityowlpress.com.

Acknowledgments

Thank you to Embry for reading my earliest version of this with love, and to Jessica M. for letting me text her with writing victories and tragedies. Thank you to Heather L. for making sure I got my history correct. Thank you to Carye who always makes me feel talented and to Kareen for being supportive in everything I do. Thank you to Amanda for relating to my characters and cheering me on. Thank you to Mariah for being so excited at every step in the publishing process. Thank you to my talented friend John for critiquing a draft, even though you are my ex-boyfriend and it was probably super awkward. Thank you to Mandie for providing top-notch therapy through the writing struggles. Thank you to Jaclyn, who read every single draft and never stopped accepting my calls.

Thank you to Romance Writers of America for connecting me to so many talented people, including my publisher! Thank you to City Owl for welcoming my story. Thank you Heather M. for smiling when I pitched to you and Tina M. for being patient as I got you all my materials. Thank you to Jessica S. for editing my manuscript with a careful and sharp eye and helping solve problems I didn't know I had!

Thank you to my dad for never, ever reading this novel, but for filling my life with stories. Thank you to my sister for coming up with the tagline that got this book published! Thank you to my handsome Italian husband Gennaro, whose first language is not English so he doesn't always understand what I write (but don't worry, *amore*, there are scenes in here that make you look good). And of course, thank you to my mom, who listened to me agonize over this book, who combed through every scene for typos (even the dirty ones), and who cried every time I got good news. I really would not have stuck with it if it wasn't for you, Mom, and I hope to keep you crying over my writing career for a long, long time.

About the Author

FLORENCE A. BLISS is an author from Las Vegas, NV who has a keen eye for writing love stories full of drama, heartache, humor, and enough passion to light the pages on fire. With an MFA in creative writing from UNLV, Florence loves to write across genres but has found her home in romance. She lives with her fancy Italian husband and two children. Together they love to travel, explore the ghost towns around Las Vegas, and roadtrip up and down the Pacific coast. (Luckily her husband takes great pictures so she doesn't have to.) Florence is an avid people watcher and strives to understand why people do what they do, and she never tires of imagining the stories of what couples have had to overcome in order to come together.

www.florenceabliss.com

About the Publisher

City Owl Press is a cutting edge indie publishing company, bringing the world of romance and speculative fiction to discerning readers.

Escape Your World. Get Lost in Ours!

www.cityowlpress.com

facebook.com/CityOwlPress
x.com/cityowlpress
instagram.com/cityowlbooks
pinterest.com/cityowlpress
tiktok.com/@cityowlpress